Also by Gene Thompson

Gene Thompson

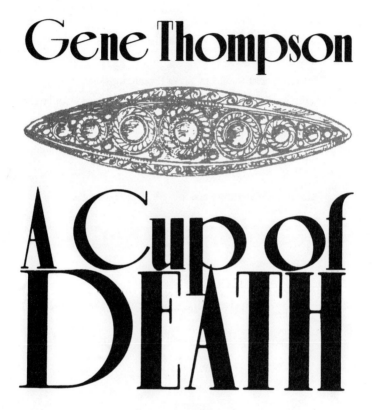

A Cup of DEATH

Random House New York

F

Copyright © 1987 by AVO Productions, Inc.

All rights reserved under International and Pan-American Copyright
Conventions.
Published in the United States by Random House, Inc., New York, and
simultaneously in Canada by Random House of Canada Limited,
Toronto.

Library of Congress Cataloging-in-Publication Data

Thompson, Gene.
A cup of death.

I. Title.
PS3570.H614C87   1988   813'.54   87-9610
ISBN 0-394-56140-6

Manufactured in the United States of America
24689753
First Edition

FOR GLORIA STUART

A Cup of
DEATH

I

As Dade Cooley afterward remarked, the whole thing began with the kind of coincidence that might lead a man to think the universe was being run by somebody with a penchant for bad practical jokes.

That afternoon, the fog had come in early. By five-thirty, when Dade got off the cable car on California Street, the houses were shrouded in mist and even the string of amber lights which marked the low arch of the Golden Gate Bridge from San Francisco to the hills of Marin was scarcely visible. He ran a hand through his thick white hair as he walked down Locust and then went along Jackson to his house, quickening his pace because he knew Ellen was waiting for him. She had arranged for them to go out to dinner. It was his birthday.

Once home, he called out hello to Ellen and then went upstairs to dress. Changing his gray Donegal suit for a dark blue, he knotted the lawyerly Sulka tie Ellen had given him that morning. He looked at himself approvingly in the mirror over the cherry bureau, narrowing his crocodile eyes. Ellen, wearing a blue Cacharel suit that matched the color of her eyes, came in the room. She gave him a hug.

"Ready?" she asked.

He nodded. "Where are we going?"

"Mammy Pleasant's."

"That whorehouse?"

"Not everybody thinks your calling it that is funny."

"Fact."

"That was a hundred years ago! Now, it's a restaurant."

"Downstairs."

"Dade—"

"Damn place costs a fortune."

"If you're in one of your moods—"

"You sound like you're in one of yours."

"It's those cards," she said, annoyed.

"What cards?"

"The ones I sent for from the Met. Gorgeous. All with lovely blue flowers on them. I wanted them for Letty. You know, she sends out a hundred cards to her friends every Christmas, and they're all way up in their eighties, but when the cards arrived, I opened one and inside was a printed greeting which said, 'Soon, thou shalt see angels.' I was just furious. Speaking of cards, here's one that came today." She handed him a postcard Paul Van Damm had sent with "Thinking of you, Paul" written on it. It showed the grave circle at Mycenae where Schliemann claimed to have found Agamemnon's body.

At the restaurant, Ellen ordered veal piccata and Dade decided on veal sweetbreads braised in cream and served with chanterelles. Ellen asked for a salad of limestone lettuce and Dade said he would have the same thing. After examining the wine list, he ordered a Grgich Hills Chardonnay. While they waited, he took Paul's postcard out of his pocket and studied it. "Nice of him," he said.

"Yes."

"Aren't they due back?"

"Any time."

"Let's bring them here the next time they're in town. See if this place rates an A with him." Paul always graded the meals, rarely giving one more than a C plus. He could almost hear Paul's dry laughter, the half whisper in which he spoke, as if from a lifetime's habit of lowering his voice in libraries.

4

"You think he's happy?" Ellen asked.

"With Sophie?"

"Yes."

Dade met her eyes in the candlelight as the sommelier finished pouring out their wine, then lifted his glass in response to her birthday toast. Six months earlier, Paul, a professor of classics, had married Sophie Galanos, a Greek actress half his age. She was quite well known, particularly in Greece, where she often appeared on the stage at Epidauros.

"Is he?"

Setting down his glass, he said, "Why shouldn't he be?"

"Why should he be?"

"What's that supposed to mean?"

Ellen shrugged. "When a man of sixty, a bachelor and a scholar, suddenly ups and marries Sophie Galanos—well, look at the card. Why isn't her name on it? Why just his?"

"Habit, I suppose. I guess he forgot."

"Exactly."

That night, as they were going to bed, Dade turned on the television to hear the eleven o'clock news. He was in the midst of thanking Ellen for his birthday dinner when he looked at the screen and saw a picture of Sophie Galanos hurrying out of the Van Damm house in Los Angeles. The voice of the newscaster identified her. Then a still of Paul Van Damm appeared on the screen. The newscaster's voice identified him and went on to say that he and his wife had just returned home from Greece and that according to the police, Professor Van Damm had apparently surprised a burglar who had shot him to death. Dade continued to look at the television set in disbelief.

"My God," he said. He turned to Ellen.

"Oh, Dade." She looked at him, horrified.

In the morning, he took his usual cable-car ride down California to Montgomery and then walked the short distance to his office. He rode the brass cage elevator up one floor, got out and walked down the hall to a mahogany door with gilt letters reading DADE COOLEY, ATTORNEY-AT-LAW. Entering, he found Rose typing a letter, her green eyeshade askew, her glasses halfway down her nose. Her expression was serious.

Getting to her feet, she said to him, "I'm sorry, Mr. Cooley. About what happened."

"Thank you." He started into his office. "Put in a call to Sophie Galanos in Los Angeles, will you do that, Rose? I don't have to talk to her. I don't want to bother her. If that maid of theirs answers, that Luisa, I'll talk to her."

"I'm not sure she speaks English, Mr. Cooley."

"I know a little Spanish."

She looked at him doubtfully. "Mr. Cooley—" she began.

"I just want to leave my name. I know enough Spanish for that." He went into his office and took off his coat and hat and, hanging them on a tree in the corner, stared out one of the narrow, arched windows that gave onto Montgomery Street. He saw lights blinking on his phone.

Then Rose knocked and entered. "How's your Greek?" she said.

"What?"

"I've got Mrs. Polykleides on the phone. That's the lady's dresser."

Dade picked up the receiver. "I'll talk to her."

"Good luck."

"Mrs. Polykleides?" he said into the phone.

"What your name is?" a woman's voice with a thick accent said loudly. He said his name, repeating it. Then she said, "Madame in bed. No talk."

"I understand."

"Funeral tomorrow ten o'clock. You coming, mister?"

"Well—"

The dresser named a church in Beverly Hills. Dade thought, We have to go.

"Mister? You coming?"

"Yes. Yes, tell the lady we'll be there." He put down the phone. Rose came back into the room, a pencil stuck in her matted yellowish hair. "Rose," he said, "we'll need—"

"Reservations. I heard."

"For tonight. The Bel-Air Hotel, please."

6

"Cost you."

"What's money?"

"What you need to stay alive."

"The Bel-Air, Rose."

"All right. I have Mrs. Cooley on One."

"Thank you." He picked up the phone. "Ellen?" He told her about the funeral. "Want to drive down?"

"Can you spare the time?"

He turned pages of his desk calendar with a pencil eraser. There were no immediate court appearances. He reminded himself they had been planning to take some days off. "Yes," he answered. "Let's leave by noon."

He put down the phone and then seated himself in his leather armchair, tipping back, eyeing the mahogany-paneled walls, the glass-fronted bookcases, trying to collect his thoughts. Lights flashed on his phone. A call had come in. Rose had answered it. After a few moments, the light went out. Then there was another knock and Rose came back into his office, a folder in her hands. She looked at him carefully.

"That call was from Los Angeles, Mr. Cooley."

"Oh?"

"That producer died. Sam Kellerman." She had not liked him. She said as much in the way she pronounced his name.

Dade looked at her, surprised. "Accident?"

She shook her head. "Natural causes."

"Not like him."

She put the folder down on the desk in front of him. He opened it. It contained various legal documents, a copy of Sam Kellerman's will and a tape he had left with them, to be played at the time of his death. Dade said, half to himself, "No funeral. At his request. Inter-Vivos Trust. No need to file for probate. Widow informed?" Rose nodded. "Estranged. Lives in Switzerland. Children live out of state." He thought of short, balding Sam Kellerman. Again he heard the querulous, nasal voice, which had once described Proust as "that guy that went to bed in a fur coat for twenty years and wrote a book." Sam Kellerman had begun in films working on a picture for

Jeanette MacDonald, whom he described as having "er." Asked what that meant, he said, "It's how you look when you say it." After he was fired, he went to work at another studio doing comedy. After a long successful career devoted for the most part to musicals and comedies, he had surprised everybody the year before by announcing an ambitious project: a remake of *The Trojan Women* with Sophie Galanos.

Sam had said to a reporter from *Variety*, "Shoot it in Greece for next to nothing, ask for a percentage of the gross, damn thing'll run forever in every goddam art house in the world. Want to know what I'll end up with?"

"Bucks?"

"Class." He was ready to go when Sophie withdrew without explanation. The money dried up and the production was canceled. Embittered, Sam said disparaging things about her to the press.

Dade put the cassette on the tape deck. He listened to it with Rose. It was a long rambling speech delivered by Sam himself and addressed to nobody in particular. In it, Sam Kellerman discoursed on what he thought about everybody and everything. He said he did not believe in a hereafter and, as far as he was concerned, that was just as well, since he didn't know anybody in whose company he would like to spend eternity. After that, he made mocking remarks about a number of friends, among them, Sophie and Paul, saying that theirs was one of those cases where the couple had had to get married, but not for the usual reason. The tape ended abruptly. Dade pursed his lips. It was a coincidence, he told himself, but a strange one.

Shortly after eleven, Dade put on his coat and hat and started out of the office. He looked at Rose. "What about insurance? For Mrs. Van Damm."

"I looked at our files. He had full life with Travelers with a very substantial paid-up sum. Have a good trip."

He nodded. "Why don't you take some time off while I'm gone? Run down to the Mechanics' Library and raise a little hell with a few of your friends."

"My best to Mrs. Cooley."

He was home in time to pack the car and drive off with Ellen at noon. "We have to go," he said. "You mind?"

She sighed. "You know what I think of funerals."

"This one's not for you."

Ellen looked uncomfortable. "I hope she doesn't—well, *do* anything."

"Such as throw herself on his bier?"

"You know what I mean. And, if the press is there—"

"Be grateful she's not going to burn his body on the beach, as Shelley did Byron's."

"Don't suggest it, she'll do it."

They were on Leavenworth, headed south out of the city. She took out her compact and examined her nose, which she found needed powdering. "What I wonder is, how come someone like her ended up marrying someone like him?"

"De mortuis nihil nisi bonum."

"That would still be cliché, even if you said it in Swahili, and I'm not saying anything against the dead, I'm only talking about odd combinations." She wrinkled her brow. "I remember being someplace or other with them just after they were married, where we all had to sign a book. We were in line behind them and when I went to write down my name, I saw his tiny, tiny scholar's handwriting, all spidery and precise, and above it, her big, extrovert's scrawl, exactly the kind of handwriting every actress in the world always seems to have. I wondered then what she was doing married to him. I thought maybe she was attracted to older men—she was quite taken with you, I suppose you know—but then I happened to catch sight of her eyeing a young waiter when she thought nobody was looking and that opinion went straight into the fire. What I'm saying is, I never could figure out what drew them together."

"Hm." He frowned, pursing his lips.

"What are you thinking?"

He told her about Sam Kellerman and what he had said on the tape about Sophie and Paul. She opened her mouth in surprise.

"Had to get married but not for the usual reason? What an odd thing to say! Don't you think it's odd?"

9

"Maybe Sam was just being nasty."

"Sam was always just being nasty. What has that got to do with anything? He was always right!" She made a face, impatient with herself.

"I'll race you to the next *de mortuis*."

"I shouldn't have said that. Don't quote me."

He held up three fingers. "Scout's honor." His expression changed. Pulling a little notebook and a gold pencil out of his pocket while he steered with one hand, he said, "Scout: to seek, to reject!"

"Not again, Dade."

"A man made me a bet—"

"The same man?"

"He already paid me for the last two times. Now, it's double or nothing for another ten opponyms."

"Do we have reservations?"

"At the Bel-Air. I don't know why. I got to thinking that some of the best places we've ever stayed in, we just happened on. It's like when you're in the service overseas and you go to a bar, as opposed to some fancy party, when you want to meet girls."

"Go on."

"I don't know what made me say a thing like that."

"I do."

She reached behind her. "Hungry? I packed us a picnic lunch."

"I'll find somewhere to stop."

"Not if you want to be there by seven." She unwrapped a sandwich and handed it to him.

"What is it?"

"Black Forest ham."

"No kidding!"

"Now that I think of it, it may remind you of your days overseas. Maybe bring back memories we can share."

"I have none."

"That we can share, you mean."

His mouth full, he said, "Is there some other topic of conversation in which I can interest you?"

"Yes. Why did they have to get married?"

"I have no idea."

"Make up a reason."

He looked at her. "Why?"

"Because I can't. That's what's so fascinating about what Sam Kellerman said." She looked at him, her blue eyes sparkling.

"I know one way to find out."

"What?"

He turned to her. "Ask her. After the funeral, of course."

She set her mouth. "I'm going to get you for that," she said. "Just you see if I don't."

Just before ten the next morning, they arrived at the Episcopal church on Santa Monica Boulevard in Beverly Hills. As they joined others climbing the steps to the door, a gust of wind blew something in Ellen's eye. She took a compact out of her purse and began dabbing at the eye with a scrap of handkerchief. Dade said, "Here. Let me."

"No. It's all right."

They went on into the church, others following them. Dade looked around and caught sight of a black-veiled Sophie Galanos entering the church. A girl who did not look as if she were out of her teens yet accompanied her. Unlike Sophie, whose hair was blond, the girl's hair was dark. Straight, it hung down to her shoulders. Sophie walked slowly, her arm linked with the girl's.

Dade and Ellen sat down in a pew. Touching Dade's arm, she whispered, "Where's Luisa?" He glanced around him, then, not seeing the maid, gave a little shrug by way of answer. An organist improvised. Then a minister, dressed in an academic robe with belled sleeves ribbed with black velvet, came out of an antechamber, palms pressed together, fingers pointed downward. "Dearly beloved—" he began.

Dade remembered hearing Paul speak at Berkeley on the subject of classical archeology. Paul had not liked the campus. "It's that damn Campanile," he had said. "Too many bells. Now, they've even installed some that tinkle. Sounds like a department store at Christmas." He remembered Paul banging his pointer at a schematic map on the wall. "People litter. And then, of course, there was no regular garbage collection in those days. Everything just got thrown out the window or over the walls. Well, after a few centuries, places tend to disappear, so to speak, under heaps of rubbish. It would not be inaccurate to say I do most of my work in garbage dumps."

Dade, lost in his thoughts, looked up to see that the minister had raised his arms and was blessing the congregation. The organist began to play again. Dade got to his feet. "Let's get out of here," he said. They started toward the back of the church. "I wish we didn't have to stop by the house. I just wish she weren't expecting us."

"She wasn't."

"What's that supposed to mean?"

"I got a look at her. In my compact mirror. When she caught sight of us, she stiffened. She wasn't expecting us. Believe me." Then Ellen squeezed Dade's hand, elbowing him. He followed her glance and saw Sophie standing at the end of the aisle, looking in their direction.

Taking Dade's arm, Ellen walked over to her with him. Sophie lifted her widow's veil and looked at them through heavy dark glasses. What always struck him about her face was a well-marked prominence over the eyes, what he had once heard described as "the bar of Michelangelo." Ellen held out her hand. "Please accept our sympathies," she said.

"Ellen. Dade. Thank you for coming." In a soft voice, she introduced her daughter to them. "You remember Irene," she said. Her daughter went to school in the East. They had not seen her for a long time. She took each of their hands in turn, looking into their eyes, not saying anything. Seeing others coming toward her, Sophie started to move away, saying over her shoulder to Ellen and Dade, "I'll see you at the house, then."

"All right," Ellen answered.

They went outside. "You and your 'all right,'" Dade said.

"What would you have liked? 'The hell you will!'"

"Don't mind me."

"I don't."

"The last time I enjoyed a funeral was in Austria."

"Between bars?"

"Little walled town with a cathedral. Mayor died. Well, I want to tell you, they put on the damnedest show I ever saw in all my born days. Whole brass band marching down the street and playing Chopin to beat hell, all of them dressed up with pointy helmets and high black boots, and after that come high-stepping plumed black horses pulling the hearse, which was some kind of black wagon with gilt decorations, and on top of it, a glass-sided coffin with Mister Mayor himself lying on his flower-strewn bier in full regalia, wearing all his medals, men with round black hats over their hearts, women crying and waving farewell with lace handkerchiefs, everybody then following the procession on foot to the churchyard, where there was an open grave, the earth all ready to swallow him up. Now that, my dear, was what I call a funeral. But you got to have you a brass band and black plumes and all the rest of it and a town where everybody's lived and died for hundreds of years for any of that stuff to be worth Jack Shit—I mean, here, dying's hardly worth giving the time of day for."

"Then show 'em. Don't."

Dade drove slowly, as Ellen fished in her purse for directions and then told him how to get to the house. It was in Brentwood on one of the Helenas, a succession of cul-de-sacs opening onto Carmelina, a street that ran from San Vincente to Sunset Boulevard and a few blocks north of it, where the houses were built back in the days when film stars had names like Vilma, Theda and Pola. They found Carmelina. It was lined with clipped umbrellas of coral trees. The small houses were hidden by high hedges and surrounded by lawns and flower-filled gardens. There were a couple of houses at the end of each cul-de-sac.

"Here," said Ellen. Dade parked on Carmelina, where there was a long line of cars, then they walked down the 25th Helena to the Van Damms' house.

The house was stucco with huge dark beams and carved doors. A flagstone path under the spreading branches of a fig tree led to a two-story, tile-roofed building.

The door was open. Through it, they could catch a glimpse of the crowded living room, the Oriental rugs on the quarry tile, the open Steinway, the high, beamed ceiling. A stairway with a wrought-iron railing led up to an open gallery over the hall. They went in and joined the others in the living room. Doors were open to a dining room where a bar had been set up. A bartender mixed drinks. A maid offered a tray of hors d'oeuvres. In the living room, they could see Sophie to the right of the fireplace, receiving guests. Dade and Ellen moved through the crowd toward her. Sophie held out her hand to them. She wore a plain black dress and no jewelry except for her plain gold wedding band. Her thick blond hair was tied up at the back of her head in a gold cord, Greek fashion. She wore no makeup. She stood motionless, looking like one of the statues from the Porch of the Maidens. She took each of their hands in turn, clasping it firmly.

Sophie's daughter said, "Paul's brother is here with his wife. Have you seen them?"

"No."

"Shall I bring them over?"

"Not now."

"But—"

"I've only met her something like once or twice and—" Sophie put her hand on her daughter's arm.

"Mother? You okay?"

"I'm all right," Sophie said to her, patting her hand.

"I really think she ought to sit down," Irene said.

"I'm quite all right," Sophie said. She removed her dark glasses for a moment, wiping at her eyes with a handkerchief. Dade saw that her pupils were the size of pinpoints and wondered whether her doctor had sedated her.

Ellen took Dade's arm. They walked away. Near them, a woman said to someone, "Well, at least that's something. I mean, that they caught him. And after all they'd done for him."

15

Dade and Ellen looked at each other. As they moved toward the dining room, another conversation took up the same thread. A man asked, "Why? Do they know?"

"Drugs, I think," a woman's voice answered. "Things like that are always drugs, aren't they?" Her voice had risen. Someone hushed her. She turned away, embarrassed.

Indicating the piano, Dade said to Ellen in an undertone, "Pat and Mike were due at this wake, the two of them go out and get blind drunk first, then they end up at the wrong house, kneel down in front of an open grand piano and mumble prayers, and after they stagger out into the street, Pat says to Mike, 'Holy God! Did you get a look at the teeth on the guy?' "

He had caught her off-guard. She burst out laughing, then buried her face in her hands. A husky man with sun-bleached hair turned abruptly to look at her and spilled wine on Dade's sleeve. Quickly setting down his glass, the man reached for a paper napkin, apologizing.

Dade said, "It's all right." Excusing himself, Dade went down the hall to the lavatory. There was incense burning in a holder. The scent filled the small room. It made him queasy. He reached over to open the window. It was a small, double-hung window and he could see that the frame had been recently painted. The window was locked and he was afraid the lock would be stuck. But the metal disc turned quite easily. He lifted up the sash, leaning out and taking a deep breath of fresh air. The window gave onto a narrow walk that ran alongside the house. A high, dense hedge of eugenia bordered it. As he pulled in his head, he saw that there were flecks of dried blue paint on the window sill. It occurred to him that someone else must have disliked the smell of incense as much as he did. After he had sponged the wine off his sleeve with a wet hand towel, he closed the window again, relocking it, and left the room.

When he came out into the hall, he heard the sound of a woman crying. He looked around but saw no one. The hall ran back from the living room. A wall separated it from the dining room and kitchen. At the end of the hall was the lavatory, next to which a door opened onto the side of the house. The sound seemed to be coming from the kitchen. It occurred to him that whoever it was must have left the room to avoid upsetting Sophie. Then, abruptly, the woman's crying stopped, a sob choked off with what sounded like a gasp of surprise. He had the feeling someone was watching him. He waited for a moment or two, thinking he might hear his name called. Then, when nothing happened, he went back into the living room and found Ellen.

Later, after the two of them left the house and started down the path to the cul-de-sac, Ellen heard her name called.

"¡Señora Cooley! Señora Cooley, por favor!" It was Luisa, the maid. Red-eyed, she came toward them.

Ellen greeted her, saying, "¿Que hay, Luisa?"

"¡Es mi hijo!" she said. Ellen put an arm around her and the two of them moved away. Dade could hear the soft Spanish of their speech. After a few moments, Ellen hurried up to him, her face full of concern.

"It's her son. They've arrested him. They say he killed Paul. She says he didn't. That he couldn't have."

"Hard for her."

"She wants to know if you'll just talk to him. She says somebody told her that she can get twenty-five thousand dollars on her house to post bail. She doesn't know what to do. The boy has never been in any kind of trouble in his life."

"Where does he live?"

"With his mother."

"What does he do?"

"Works in the neighborhood as a pool boy—and gardener. Nights, he goes to school part time."

Dade looked up. Over Ellen's shoulder, he could see Luisa standing where Ellen had left her. She stood under what looked like a used broom of a tree, a tamarisk, hands clasped. She was a small woman, slender and fine-boned. She wore a maid's uniform. As Dade's eyes rested on her, she lifted her head.

"What's the boy's name?"

"Manuel. Manuel Garcia," Ellen said.

"All right," he said, nodding in the woman's direction. "All right, Luisa."

"*El señor dice que si,*" Ellen said to her.

Luisa lowered her head, murmuring, "*Gracias.*"

Dade said, "I'll take you back to the hotel." He went down to Sunset, turned east, and then drove past the northern boundary of the campus. When they got to a pair of stucco pillars with iron gates, he turned left onto Bellagio Road and drove up to the Bel-Air Hotel.

"Can you do anything for him?"

"Well, if his story rings true, I can see about getting him some bright young lawyer in the Public Defender's Office out to make a name for himself. I'll call Waldo Postel. He'll know somebody." He came to a stop in front of an awning over the walk leading to the hotel entrance. It was a long one-story building set in a garden. Glancing out at the sycamores along the stream running through the rock-walled garden, he said, "Did you know that the man who once owned all of Bel-Air didn't like California? Didn't care at all for what grew out here, so he had the whole of his property planted with trees and shrubbery and flowers from the East. Why he didn't just stay home, I'll never know."

"Now that I think of it," Ellen mused, "why didn't *she?*"

"Who?"

"Sophie."

"What are you talking about?"

"Sophie was out. And when she got home, she found the body."

19

He stared at her. "Who told you that?"

"Professor Slaughter. The man who spilled the wine on your sleeve. A woman asked what had happened and he told her what the papers had said."

He looked at her, not understanding. "People do go out of the house, Ellen."

"After fifteen hours on a plane?" She took a quick breath. "The two of them had just flown in from Athens. After that, the only place I'd go is to bed."

"Unless you had business to attend to. And if I did—"

"You're not a woman. With puffy ankles and bags under my eyes, there's almost nothing I wouldn't postpone—if I could." Picking up his briefcase from the car floor, she slammed it into his chest like a Spartan woman giving her husband his shield, saying, "Here. Return on it or beneath it." A husky red-coated boy with a freckled face and ginger hair came up then and helped Ellen out of the car.

"Mr. and Mrs. Cooley," the boy said. "I hope you had a nice morning."

"We went to a funeral," Dade said.

"I'm sorry."

"So am I." Dade eyed him. "You always remember people's names?"

"I try to, sir."

"What's your name?"

"Watmough, sir."

"Don't tell me your mom sticks her head out the window and calls out Watmough when she wants you home."

"My folks, they call me Harm. For Harmon."

Dade handed him a bill. "You escort Mrs. Cooley to her room for me, Harm." Dade drove down to the Santa Monica freeway, turned east, and headed downtown.

At the Criminal Courts Building, he stopped by the office of a judge he knew slightly, Fielder MacBride. The judge was at lunch. Dade left his card and best wishes, picked up a *duces tecum* from the law clerk and, armed with that, went downstairs to police headquarters. A burly sergeant with a jutting jaw and a shock of dark hair in his eyes came toward him. His nameplate read SGT. R. BURNS. Dade asked him who was in charge of the Van Damm case.

"Lieutenant Persons, sir," the sergeant said.

Dade offered the sergeant his card and said, "Will you tell him I'd like to see him?"

"He's out of the office for a few minutes, sir. If you'll just have a seat—"

Dade took the *duces tecum* out of his pocket. "While I'm waiting, I'd like to see the police report on the Van Damm case." The sergeant searched through a file and then gave Dade a copy of the report. Dade seated himself on a long bench opposite the counter separating the reception area from the row of desks in the office beyond.

He read rapidly through the report. The day of the murder, Paul and Sophie Van Damm had arrived on a TWA flight direct from Athens at 4:00 p.m., on schedule. They had been met by her daughter, Irene. An interview with the customs official who had examined their bags indicated that they had brought nothing into the country but the clothes with which they had left and Sophie's costumes and jewelry. She had taken the precaution of registering her jewelry, as well as Paul's gold watch, so that it would not appear that they were bringing back anything which had been purchased abroad. They had been gone a total of two weeks, during which time they had stayed at the Grande Bretagne in Athens, renting a car and taking drives to such places as Cape Sounion and Delphi. Sophie had appeared twice at Epidauros, both times in *The Trojan Women* playing Helen of Troy. Sophie and Paul had taken the plane at seven o'clock the morning after the second performance.

According to the daughter's statement, she had driven them to the Van Damm house on the 25th Helena in her own car and they had arrived at four-forty. The daughter remembered looking at her watch because she had to get back to campus to the library, to study for an exam in botany. Afterward, she had dinner in the student cafeteria and then went on to her botany class at seven. Sophie's statement indicated that on arriving home, she herself had taken a tub while Paul made them both drinks, after which he showered and then went through the mail and checked for messages on the answering machine. After that, he sat down to watch the news on television shortly after 5:00 p.m., leaving the door open so that she could hear the program. At 5:30 he turned off the television set and turned on the radio instead to listen to music.

In answer to questions by the investigating officers, Sophie Galanos replied that there were no telephone calls made or received between the time they returned home and the time she left the house, except for one the professor made to the local garage about his car. She said he had tried repeatedly to reach them before they left for Greece, but the line was always busy, so he had not been able to arrange to have his car serviced while they were away. He arranged for it now. She left the house alone at five-forty, Professor Van Damm remaining behind. A witness, a boy of nineteen named Korty Beyer, was working on his car on Carmelina at that time. Because he had a date at seven o'clock that evening to pick up some friends and drive them to a rock concert, he remembered looking at his watch just as Sophie Galanos drove out of the 25th Helena. The time was five-forty.

Sophie Galanos said she did not return until three hours later. Asked to account for her whereabouts during that period, she explained that she had visited Mrs. Tinka Kanavarioti, a psychic whom she frequently consulted. Mrs. Kanavarioti lived in San Bernardino, about an hour's drive from the Van Damm house. Questioned, Mrs. Kanavarioti confirmed Sophie's visit to her house on the night of Paul's death, saying that Sophie had called her from a public phone just after five forty-five, had appeared to be in great distress and had asked whether Mrs. Kanavarioti could arrange for a sitting immediately. Mrs. Kanavarioti said she was planning to be in all evening. Sophie told the police she arrived at Mrs. Kanavarioti's house at approximately six-forty and left there an hour later.

Paul had received three visitors between five-forty and six forty-five. Korty Beyer saw all of them arrive and leave but the visitors themselves had come forward of their own accord, to tell their stories. The first of the three visitors was a colleague of Paul's, Professor Harry Slaughter from Paul's own department. He had arrived just after 6:00 and left at six-twenty. He said he had tried to telephone, to tell Paul about a change in the time and date of a faculty meeting, but the phone was busy and since Paul's house was only a couple of streets out of his way on his route home, he had decided to stop by and try to catch him. He said that they had only discussed schedules and that he had left shortly afterward, gone home and had dinner alone. Korty Beyer was beginning to think he ought to go telephone his friends to tell them he might not make it but he was blocks from a pay phone and in a neighborhood like this, people didn't like having you ring their doorbells, asking to use the phone. He remembered looking at his watch when the first visitor arrived and again when the visitor left.

Paul's second visitor was his brother Vincent, who arrived at six-thirty. His address was given. He lived in an apartment on King's Road, above Sunset. Dade made a note of the address. Vincent Van Damm's wife then arrived shortly afterward. She told officers that she had gone there not to see Paul but Sophie. Vincent and his wife Fanny had left together at six forty-five, driving home in separate cars. Korty Beyer was even surer of these times because when Vincent Van Damm drove down the 25th Helena, Korty was tempted to flag him down and ask if the people he was going in to see would let him use the phone. He didn't, though. He got his car fixed and was just starting it when both of these visitors drove out onto Carmelina again.

Paul's brother Vincent and Vincent's wife Fanny were the last people known to have seen Paul alive. Nothing was known about Paul's movements between six forty-five and eight-forty, at which time Sophie returned home. A neighbor who lived in the other house in the cul-de-sac, a Mrs. Ogilvy, reported seeing Sophie Galanos's car drive up and saw her get out of it. She unlocked the front door and entered the house. That established that no one could have left earlier by the front door unless he had a key, since the front door, unlike the back door, could not be locked by simply closing it. Either it had to be locked from the inside or locked from the outside with a key. Only Sophie Galanos and her late husband possessed keys to the front door. She had hers with her. His was discovered in a small change purse in a pocket when the body was found.

Some minutes after Sophie Galanos entered the house, Mrs. Ogilvy heard her screaming. Others heard her as well. They ran to the Van Damm house and up the stairs and all reported seeing Paul Van Damm lying on the floor of Sophie's bedroom, Sophie kneeling beside him, holding his head and calling his name. Someone immediately phoned for the paramedics, who arrived at eight-fifty-two. The victim was taken by ambulance to UCLA Medical Center a few minutes away and was pronounced dead on arrival. Death, according to the statement by the attending physician, had been almost instantaneous. The statement went on to say that the body was still warm when he examined it and there was no sign of pooled blood, which meant that the victim had been dead less than half an hour, which would make the time of death coincide with the time at which Sophie Galanos returned home.

The investigating officer's report noted that some time before Sophie's departure at five-forty, Sophie and Paul had been engaged in a violent argument, overheard by their next-door neighbor, Mrs. Ogilvy. Sophie's voice, the voice of an actress, could be heard clearly. Paul's could not. By the time this had been reported, Sophie Galanos was prostrate and her dresser, Mrs. Polykleides, whom Sophie had sent for, acted as her spokesman. Mrs. Polykleides said that Sophie Galanos told her they had been rehearsing, not arguing, that she had been going over her lines for an upcoming performance of *Medea* in the Greek Theater in Los Angeles. After explaining this to the investigating officer, Mrs. Polykleides said, "Medea, she is very angry woman, you understand it? Is for why the great Galanos is shouting and you tell for me that old lady busybody who leans out the window all times to hear the great Galanos say something, I say to her, 'Shit on your head, you old bat!'" Sergeant Burns dutifully transcribed what she had said to him word for word.

As a matter of routine, the investigating officer had ordered a powder-burn test run on Sophie Galanos' hands, "for her own protection," as he put it. When the reason for this test was explained to her, Sophie submitted to it without objection. It was then discovered that since she had gotten her husband's blood on her hands and her clothes while holding his head, a neighbor had taken her into the bathroom and helped her change her clothes and wash her hands, then attempted to remove traces of blood from her hands with some petroleum-based cleaner that she found in the kitchen. The result of this was that the powder-burn test was rendered invalid.

Sophie Galanos, who until this time had scarcely spoken a word to anyone, now permitted herself to be questioned. She told the investigating officer that, on entering the house, she went into the long hall closet under the staircase and was hanging up her coat when she heard what she was almost sure was a gunshot. She stated that she heard someone's footsteps "clattering down the stairs," as she put it. She stepped out of the closet and through the open double door into the living room just in time to see the person running out of the living room into the rear hall. Asked whether she could identify the person, she said yes unequivocally: Manuel. She was sure that what she had heard was a gun being fired, that she was alarmed, and that her impression was that Manuel was chasing someone. She heard the back door open and then bang shut and she reported that her first thought was to call out to him, "Manuel, don't," afraid that whoever he may have surprised—a burglar, she thought—might fire at him. She then went upstairs, calling out her husband's name, and that was when she found his body.

That same evening, the suspect, Manuel Garcia, was arrested and charged with the murder of Paul Van Damm.

IV

Dade got to his feet, went to a pay phone in the hall and tried to reach Waldo Postel. A secretary told him Mr. Postel was not expected back until late that afternoon. Dade left his name and said he would call back. Going back into the office, Dade went over to the counter. The sergeant told Dade Lieutenant Persons had returned and would see him now.

Dade was shown into the office of a police lieutenant. He eased himself into the chair across the desk from the detective, studying him. He was a ferret-faced man who looked to be in his forties. A nameplate on his breast pocket read Lt. RALPH PERSONS.

Dade said, "I'd be obliged to you if you'd tell me how the boy happened to be charged."

The lieutenant picked up Dade's card from his desk and examined it. Then he looked at Dade, puzzled. "From San Francisco?" he asked. Dade nodded. "You representing?"

"I know the boy's mother. I told her I'd talk to him."

"Nice of you."

"Anybody from the Public Defender's Office talk to him yet?"

Persons shook his head. "He hasn't had any visitors at all. Well, except for the mother."

"Well, maybe I can help him get somebody over at the Public Defender's Office, somebody who'd take an interest."

"Not much time. Arraignment's at nine tomorrow."

"Whose court?"

"MacBride's."

"You were going to tell me how come you charged him."

By way of an answer, the lieutenant opened a manila folder, took out a couple of eight-by-ten glossy photographs and laid them side by side on the desk in front of Dade. The first one showed the victim lying on the floor in a small pool of blood, the face clearly visible, the eyes fixed in death. The second was a close-up of a fragment of a footprint in the blood on the tile floor.

"Our men went to the boy's house afterward. Mother, she said the boy was in bed, had been in his room ever since dinner. Boy's room was searched. Shoes found in closet. They're his, all right. Blood on the edge of one sole." The lieutenant tapped the close-up of the shoe print. "Same blood."

"Boy able to describe person Sophie Galanos thought he was chasing?"

The lieutenant said, "Hell, no. He even denied ever having been at the house that evening until we showed him the blood on his own shoe. No, Mr. Cooley, he wasn't chasing anybody. That was the lady's idea. The lady saw him. But we didn't tell him that. We wanted to give him a chance to dig his own grave. Which he sure as hell did."

Dade said, "I see."

"Open and shut."

"Motive?" Dade asked.

"Robbery." The lieutenant read aloud: "Defendant is charged with first-degree burglary, that is, entering an occupied building with the interest to commit a felony; after so doing, defendant shot and killed the deceased and then seized a piece of jewelry and ran off. Witnesses report there was no car except the one belonging to Sophie Galanos parked there—that is, in the cul-de-sac or on Carmelina. You know, once she started screaming, there were people all over the place and nobody saw any car take off. Must have hidden it somewhere."

"What was stolen?"

"Dresser—that's the woman who helps Sophie Galanos backstage"—he glanced down at his notes—"woman named Zoë Polykleides, reported theft of some piece of costume jewelry."

"Insured?"

"No."

"I see."

"Wife confirms that it's missing. Wife says it's of no particular value but kid must have thought it was."

"You find it?"

Lieutenant Persons shook his head. "No. Search of kid's place turned up nothing."

"Nothing at all?" Then, when the lieutenant shook his head again, Dade said, "What does this piece of costume jewelry look like?"

"I don't know."

"You didn't get a description of it?"

Exasperated, the lieutenant said, "The lady—that is, Sophie Galanos—she said it was just cheap costume jewelry and the dresser shouldn't have bothered us about it in the first place and to forget it. As I say, we searched the kid's place for costume jewelry—"

"That must have been extraordinarily difficult, not knowing what it was you were searching for."

The lieutenant stared hard at Dade. Pointing a finger at him, he started to say something. Then, as if thinking better of it, he clasped his hands on the desk before him and said quietly, "We got a description of it, Mr. Cooley. Our people turned the mother's house inside out. Nothing like that there. What we figure is, the kid showed up there with a gun, killed Van Damm for it—this piece of costume jewelry I'm talking about—and then stashed it someplace and he's not about to tell us where. Well, we don't need it as evidence. All we have to show is that the kid was there and that some junk jewelry is missing. We tend to believe the kid grabbed it, thinking it was real, killed Van Damm and ran out of there."

"You talk with the dresser yourself?"

The lieutenant consulted the papers on the desk in front of him. "Mrs. Polykleides? No."

"Anybody here talk to her?"

"Some attempt was made to interview her that night when she showed up there to do what she could for Mrs. Van Damm. Incidentally, she was in south central L.A. visiting some Greek relatives when all this happened and she doesn't even know how to drive a car. We had no questions for her. From what I hear, she can barely speak English. She didn't know what the hell was going on. Somebody where she was visiting had to bring her when Sophie Galanos started asking for her."

"She asked for her, you say?"

"As I understand it, the Galanos woman—Mrs. Van Damm, that is—was terribly distraught and the neighbors felt she needed someone with her."

"What about the daughter?"

"Takes an evening course at UCLA. They couldn't reach her until a lot later."

"I overheard some mention of drugs. Anything in that?"

The lieutenant glanced at the sheet in front of him. "Urinalysis says clean."

Dade narrowed his eyes, sitting back in his chair. "Funny, isn't it?"

"What?"

"Well, those folks, they've got a lot of nice things around that place, but according to you, there's nothing else missing, at least you didn't mention anything else."

"The lady, she just reporting missing the one thing, like her dresser said."

"What did he say, the boy? I suppose he denied taking anything?"

"Pretended he didn't know what we were talking about."

"Pretended." Dade studied him.

"All right, said." The lieutenant picked at a thumbnail. "Hid it somewhere is my guess. Figured we might show up."

"But he didn't hide the shoes."

"Well, he most likely didn't realize there was blood on one of them."

Dade sighed, lacing his fingers. "I still say it's a funny kind of a story."

"How do you mean?"

"Two people get off the plane from Europe and go home. The wife she goes out and while she's gone, this boy shows up, steals a piece of costume jewelry, shoots the husband—now, why was that? I must have missed that part."

"Well, I suppose the victim tried to stop him."

"And a boy who works outside all the time doing manual labor couldn't handle a man in his sixties?"

"It's not up to me to make out the case against him, Mr. Cooley. The DA will do that. All right, maybe he didn't try to stop him. But the decedent could have identified him. The boy knew that much."

"Which is why the boy showed up there with a gun, is that the thought here?" Then, when the lieutenant slammed shut a drawer in his desk and looked away, Dade said, "You find the gun?"

"Not yet."

"Must have hidden it along with the costume jewelry, is that the idea?"

"I don't know what he did with it, Mr. Cooley."

"What kind of a gun was it, may I ask?"

The lieutenant hesitated, moistening his lips. Then he said, "Ballistics says a thirty-eight. Somebody down there says cartridge reminded him of something. Looked English. Like from a Webley. Just a guess on his part."

Dade raised his eyebrows. "Is that so? Not exactly your run-of-the-mill Saturday night special, is it, Lieutenant?"

The lieutenant said, "Any other questions I can answer for you, Mr. Cooley?"

"Your men search the Van Damm house and the grounds for the gun?"

The lieutenant met Dade's eyes, his mouth still open as if he had forgotten to close it. Then, leafing quickly through his papers, he said, "Well, once it was determined that the suspect was not in pursuit of anybody—" The lieutenant trailed off.

"You searched it later, is that what you're telling me?"

"As I say, after it was determined—"

"Later. I see." Dade half-closed his eyes in thought. "The pool boy in the neighborhood, that right? Does odd jobs, gardening, that sort of thing?"

"Yes. He worked for the Van Damms as well."

"Damn fool not to break in while they were away and steal whatever this thing was then, instead of waiting till they both get home from Europe, then having to shoot somebody in order to get it."

The lieutenant's lips were compressed in a thin line of anger. "You're quite a comedian, aren't you, Mr. Cooley?"

"It just struck me as an odd thing to do, is all I meant."

"Well, it so happens that it didn't happen quite that way."

"Oh?"

"What was stolen, they had just brought back with them."

Dade looked at him sharply. "Oh? Something they bought there, was it?"

"No, sir. Something she took with her and brought back with her. Customs vouched for that. Costume jewelry is all." Lieutenant Persons put the sheet from which he had been reading back into its manila folder. Leaning on his folded arms, the lieutenant said, "Anything else I can do for you, Mr. Cooley?"

Dade rubbed a thoughtful forefinger along the side of his nose, not answering for a moment or two. Then he said, "Now we've really got ourselves a case here, haven't we? Two people come back from Europe with a piece of costume jewelry they took with them. That night, when the wife, she goes out to visit some seeress an hour away, the pool boy, after waiting about three hours to make sure the coast is clear, sneaks onto the premises with a kind of fancy gun and then shoots the husband dead, presumably so that the man won't be able to identify him, after which the boy goes home and goes to bed. That is a strange story, isn't it?"

"And, along with his mother, lies to the police about his whereabouts earlier that night, let's not leave that part out."

"Oh, he was there, Lieutenant. You've just proved that to me. I wouldn't doubt it for a moment. Of course he'd lie if he went there and found the body. Wouldn't you, if you were a scared kid, say?"

"And what was he doing there at that hour?"

"That's just what I mean to ask him, Lieutenant." Dade shifted his weight and leaned back in his chair, meanwhile making a pyramid of his hands and studying the lieutenant through half-closed eyes.

"Is that all?" the lieutenant asked.

"I'd like you to tell me about the earlier visitors. Let's see now—" Dade glanced down at his copy of the police report. "Professor Harry Slaughter paid a call on Paul Van Damm and, after that, the brother, Vincent Van Damm, and then, I take it by coincidence, since they showed up in separate cars, the brother's wife, Fanny Van Damm. You run a check on the visitors?"

"The visitors came and left hours before the crime. One was a fellow faculty member, the others, the victim's brother and his wife. What can I tell you?"

Dade sat forward abruptly, an elbow on the lieutenant's desk. "You're not telling me you didn't run a check on these people? You don't want to tell me a thing like that."

"As I've already stated—" Spots of red appeared in the lieutenant's cheeks.

Dade said mildly, "Any one of the three of them could have gone into the downstairs bathroom and unlocked the window there during his or her visit—as a matter of fact, somebody forced that window open because it was recently painted and there are flakes of dried paint on the sill—and then returned under cover of darkness and climbed back in from the alley, thus gaining access to the victim's house unobserved, and killed him then, which makes information about those earlier visitors vital." Dade fixed his eyes on the lieutenant's face. "Does the report you were given mention those flakes?"

The lieutenant gave Dade a quick, defensive look, then rapidly thumbed through the papers in the folder in front of him. Finding something, he stabbed at the page with a triumphant forefinger. "The detective conducting the investigation, Sergeant Burns, that is, reports that the window was found locked. Satisfied?"

Dade sat back, folding his arms and studying the lieutenant in silence. Finally he said, "The murderer could have locked the window after gaining entrance, and would have, if he had ten cents' worth of brains."

The lieutenant slammed his pencil down on his desk, turning away. Then he said, "All right, what is it you want to know?"

"Any of these people got alibis for the time of the murder?"

"By 'these people' I suppose you mean Slaughter and the brother and his wife?"

"Yes. Slaughter on the faculty there?"

"As a visiting professor."

"I see."

The lieutenant shuffled through the papers in his folder. Then he said, "Not that it matters but for the record, Professor Slaughter was home alone for the evening reading a book. Vincent Van Damm and his wife returned to their place of residence after leaving his brother's house and, according to them, stayed home for the whole evening."

"And what else did you find out about those three visitors?"

The lieutenant looked at him with hostility, gripping the sides of his chair. "It'll come up at disclosure."

"Disclose it now."

There was a silence. Dade watched the lieutenant struggle to control himself. Then Persons said, "Mr. Cooley, with all due respect—"

"I know, I know. You think you've got yourself an airtight case and you don't want me shooting holes in it. Here's the first hole: those flakes of paint I mentioned were on the outside of the sill. My guess is, they're not in your report. They're not there because your man didn't open the window to look out, so he didn't see them. That's too bad, isn't it? A mistake like that can follow a man around for twenty years." The lieutenant dropped his eyes.

Dade said, "Maybe the omission won't come out. Nobody has to know. Now, one more time: what did you learn about his visitors?"

Lieutenant Persons put his elbows on his face and rubbed his eyes with the heels of his hands. Then, he said, "Okay. Okay. Slaughter had a romp with an under-age girl. Not a kid. Thirteen, maybe fourteen. Charges were dropped. From what I learned, parents didn't want the kid in court. Some counterclaim that it wasn't the first time for the little miss, that she could have given him lessons and probably did and that she was as much to blame as he was, and that the defense might have chewed her up and spit her out if they ever got Goldilocks up on the stand. That's all I know. There was talk about him but that seems to be the only time the guy was ever caught. A man like that might be happier in some place like New Mexico where the age of consent is fourteen."

"You tell him that?"

"I did not."

"I see. Go on."

"The brother's a flake. A gambler."

"How much does he owe?"

Persons looked at him sharply. "What makes you think he owes anything?"

"Story of his life."

The lieutenant nodded. "Word on the street is, he's on the hook to Vegas for thirty-five grand."

"Well well well."

"No way we can show any connection."

"Worth trying."

"The footprint belongs to the kid."

Dade nodded, lips pursed, eyes half-closed. There was a knock. Sergeant Burns entered with a copy of a supplemental police report. He pointed at something in it, calling Persons' attention to it. Persons and Burns exchanged a glance.

Persons said, "Turns out the gun probably belonged to Professor Van Damm himself. Maid told us. Says he kept it in a drawer in the desk in his study. We checked. There's a Webley .38 registered to him. And it's missing."

Persons handed the supplementary report to Dade, who thanked him for it. The sergeant hitched up his trousers and left the room. Dade said, "And the wife? The brother's wife?"

"Nothing."

"So far." Dade pulled at the tip of his nose. Then, getting to his feet, he said, "Have someone take me up to see the boy, will you do that, please?" The lieutenant sent for an officer, then escorted Dade to the door of the office. Dade said, narrowing his eyes in thought,

"About that junk jewelry. When a man is killed, there's a lot of confusion. People think they remember and they don't. Maybe that stuff was just mislaid. Maybe it'll turn up. Then your motive goes right out the window."

The lieutenant shook his head. "Burns," he pointed toward the desk, "he thought of that, and with the lady's permission, that house was searched top to bottom, along with the garden and both cars, the lady's and the one in the garage, the professor's. At first, the lady, she told us not to bother, that it wasn't worth anything, but when we explained why it was important to make sure it had been taken, she cooperated. She says it was in an open blue-and-white leather case standing on her bureau. She says it looks like a cosmetics case. She'd left the case for the dresser to put away in the theatrical trunk full of the lady's costumes, which she keeps in the basement. Case was gone. No sign of the thing in the trunk downstairs. It's missing, all right. Stolen."

"When Sophie Galanos reported seeing the boy running out of there, did she say he was carrying anything?"

"You mean, the leather case?"

"I mean anything."

"She didn't mention anything. When we asked her about it, she said all she saw was his back as he ran out of the living room into the back hall."

"Did the lady in fact say he was carrying anything?"

The lieutenant hesitated. Then he said, "She couldn't say. One way or the other."

"What did she say was in the leather case?"

"Something she wore on her head, from the way she described it. She was pretty shook up when we questioned her. She went like this." He pantomimed something like a coronet.

"Made of what?"

"Gold. Only not real gold."

"Fake."

"You've got it."

"Hm."

"Open and shut. Like I say."

The officer escorted Dade down an empty corridor. He was lantern-jawed with deep-set eyes and walked with the keys at his waist making a jangling sound. He chewed gum slowly. Dade could smell it on his breath. Their footsteps echoed. Dade scanned the supplemental report. There was nothing in it he didn't already know. The officer stopped at a door and unlocked it, showing Dade into a small room with an oak table and several matching armchairs. At one end of the room were two windows covered with heavy mesh screening. The officer looked around the room briefly, as if inspecting it, then indicated a button next to the door with a sign below it reading RING FOR GUARD. Nodding at Dade, the officer went out, pulling the door shut with a locking click behind him.

Dade put his briefcase down on the table, eyes on a second door across the room. A few moments later, the second door was opened by another guard and a prisoner shuffled in. He wore prison denims and sneakers with no laces. His wrists were manacled to a chain fastened to a leather belt around his waist. He kept his eyes on the floor. The guard who escorted him was youngish, with a thick mustache and a scar on one cheek. He opened his mouth slightly, drawing in breath and showing irregular, chipped teeth.

"You'll be okay, sir?" he asked. Dade nodded. The second guard went out the way he had come in, closing the door carefully behind him. The boy remained standing where he was, not looking at Dade.

Dade took a card out of his case and proffered it. "My name is Cooley," he said. "I'm an attorney. Your mother asked me to have a talk with you." The boy looked at him for the first time. He had a shock of black hair and dark eyes with long, straight lashes. When he made no move to take the card, Dade put it down on the table and slid it across to him. "You want to talk to me?" he asked. Manuel continued to look at him in hostile silence. Dade took out his hunting watch and opened it, glancing at the time.

The boy's dark eyes traveled quickly up and down, taking in Dade's well-tailored suit and the heavy gold hunting watch on its gold chain. "My mom," he said finally, "she don't have your kind of money."

"I'm just here to talk. As a favor to your mother. And to see if I can arrange bail for you. That's all I'm here for." The dark eyes were watchful, opaque. The boy said nothing. "Sit down," Dade said. The boy remained standing. "Sit down," Dade said a second time. His tone was sharp. The boy stiffened. Then, slowly, he did as Dade had told him. A chain ran from his waist to his ankles, hobbling him. The chain made a clanking sound as he eased himself into a chair. "I want you to tell me what happened that night," Dade said.

The boy's eyes moved. "If it's all the same to you, I'd just as soon talk after—man, you know something? It's hard for me to talk in a place like this. You get to feeling that every word cuts both ways. If you don't mind, I'd like for them first to spring me. I mean, for you just to get me out of here, like you said. Then, I'll tell you whatever you want to hear."

"I'm sure you will."

"Sir?"

"Never mind. We'll talk now."

Manuel got to his feet and pressed his hands against the edge of the table as if pushing it away. "I didn't know what to say to anybody. Jeez, they had me in there, questioning me on and on and me asking for a lawyer and them telling me, 'Later.' I said, 'I got rights.' They said, 'You're not booked.'" He raised his right hand in an elo-

37

quent gesture of explanation, the manacles lifting his left hand at the same time. "'We just brought you in here to ask you some questions.' I said, 'Okay.' I thought, Maybe that's all it is. I answered their questions. Then, when I thought I was through, other guys came in and they asked me the same questions all over again and I would say, 'Look, I already told them'—you know, this or that—and they'd say, 'No, kid, that's not what you said, that's not the way it went'—and this went on, Jeez, it went on forever, and when I saw that they just didn't believe me, I mean, no matter what I told them—"

"No matter what you told them."

"Pardon me?"

"And then?"

"They booked me."

"You asked for a lawyer then?"

"Yes, sir."

"And what did they say?"

"Well, by then it was way past midnight and they said they couldn't get anybody out there from the Public Defender's Office at that time of night."

"You tell them you didn't want to talk without having a lawyer present?"

"Yes, sir."

"What did they say?"

"They said, 'Look, you already talked to us. If what you already told us is the truth, why should you worry?' So I figured, all right, and I went along with that."

"In other words, you waived your rights to having a lawyer present?"

"I guess I did."

"Let's hear about what happened that night. Before you were arrested."

Manuel took a quick, involuntary breath, at the same time raising his manacled hands to rake his fingers through his long, dark hair. Then he said, speaking rapidly in an undertone, "I knew what time they were supposed to get back and because I drive him and run errands for him—I mean, I used to—I called up to see if he wanted me for anything."

"When?"

"I'm not sure. Like around seven."

"Who answered the phone?"

"Professor Van Damm, he answered it himself."

"And you said?"

"I said, 'This is Manuel, sir. I'm calling to find out if you want me for anything this evening,' and he said he wanted me to drive him somewhere—you know, the professor, he didn't drive. It's a funny thing in this day and age, and for all I know, maybe he could but just didn't like to, so I drove him, and he said he wanted me to come for him at eight-thirty, so I said I would."

"Drive him where?"

"To Mr. Clinton's house."

"Who's Mr. Clinton?"

"That's Mr. James Clinton. He's like a writer. On the *Times*. The *Los Angeles Times*, the newspaper. That was a friend of his. He said—this is the professor I'm talking about—that Mr. James Clinton wouldn't be home till then."

"I see. And then what did you do?"

"After I hung up, I thought, I should have said, 'Welcome home,' or something like that, but I didn't think of it. I thought maybe I should call him back but that would be kind of stupid, so I thought, I'll just say that to him when I see him." He wet his lips, looking up at Dade.

"Then what happened?"

"At eight-thirty, I showed up at his place—"

"How did you get there?"

"I got this car."

"What kind of car?"

"It's—you know, old. Maybe fifteen years or so. It's a Dodge. It's a two-tone job, brown. It's kind of banged up but it runs okay and—"

"Where did you park?"

"Where I always park."

"Where is that?"

"On the street."

"I've got witnesses who say there were no cars parked on the street."

"Whenever I drove him, we took his car. It's an old house with just a single garage and his car is kept in there. The lady, she always parks in front of the house. Since there's not much parking room in that little turnaround they've got there, and my heap being—well, beat-up looking, you know, I always park on the next street over, that one that runs along the edge of that creek, where it's all over-grown and you have to cross them little bridges-like they each have to get over to the houses. I park there and then take this sort of path through the garden gate and by the pool to the professor's back door. I always come in that way. I knew he was home because I could see lights on in his study even with the drapes closed. And the ones in her bedroom."

"The what?"

Manuel looked at him, puzzled. "I could see the light on upstairs in Mrs. Van Damm's bedroom—see, her bedroom is on the side facing over the path and the front of the house. It's a big room, what they call the master bedroom, but the professor, he slept in a room by himself, which when I first went there, I mean, to work for them, made me think they was having trouble because where I come from, the reason you get married, I mean, a big reason, is to sleep with your wife, but here he was, sleeping in a room all to himself, the small bedroom next to it."

Dade closed his eyes and pinched the bridge of his nose. "Let's go over what you told the police. You saw those lights because you came in the back way. Is that right?"

"Yes, sir."

"Then what happened?"

"I went to the back door."

"The back door?"

"Yes, sir. It's that door on the side of the house."

"The south side?"

"Sir?"

"The front door is on the west side. The back door opens onto a path on the south side. Is that the door to which you are making reference?"

"Yes, sir."

"Go on."

"I let myself in."

"How?"

"I got a key. It was his idea. I would go there when nobody was home, to work, you know, sometimes doing the floors, whatever, and they trusted me to handle things on my own, so he give me a key."

"You let yourself in and then what happened?"

"I said, 'Hi, it's me, Manuel.'"

"With the door open?"

Manuel thought for a moment. Then he said, "No, I closed it first."

"Why?"

"Well, you know—"

"No, I don't know. Why did you close the door? You were walking into somebody's house at night unannounced. For all you knew, they could have been in bed together."

"He was like expecting me!"

"You worked there. They paid you well. You damn well didn't want to embarrass them. Now, why did you close that door?"

The boy looked up at him, the whites of his eyes showing. "Honest to God—" he began.

"You let yourself in with your own key. You stepped inside. You announced yourself. Do you mean you called out to them?"

"No, I just said, 'Hi.' Like that."

"Why not any louder?"

"The professor, he played music all the time. I could hear it playing upstairs. He wouldn't have heard me. So I just said, 'Hi, it's me' in case he was downstairs."

"After closing the door?"

"Yes."

"You're sure of that?"

"Positive." He looked around, as if feeling he had made a mistake in his answer.

"Why?"

Suddenly, the boy broke into a grin. Looking at Dade, he said, "I remember now! Funny, with all the questions they asked me, they never asked me that. Sure, I remember. She was always afraid, like for her throat, you understand me? Because of her being an actress and all. And it was a foggy night and all I had to do was let in a good dose of that cold, damp air and she'd of been after me, yelling at me and the works, you know what I mean? So I quick went inside and shut the door." He stopped, looking at Dade, as if waiting to find out whether he had answered correctly.

"And then?"

"I went upstairs to the professor's study."

"Just a minute. You were in the back hall. Was the light on or off?"

Manuel frowned, thinking. Then he said, "It was on. They always kept it on."

"You're standing in the hall facing the door leading into the sitting room. Was that door open or closed?"

Manuel blinked. Then he said, "It was closed."

"What did you do then?"

"I went and opened the door and—"

"Did you knock?"

"No, sir."

"Why not?"

"Well, I—"

"The Van Damms might very well have been in the sitting room. Why did you go into that room without knocking?"

"I—I don't know." He looked away.

"Look at me, please." Dade's tone had sharpened. The boy's eyes looked at Dade again. "Why didn't you knock on the door to the sitting room?"

"I don't know, sir."

"Close your eyes." Manuel did. "You're standing in the back hall-way, as you were that night. Ahead of you is the door leading into

42

the sitting room. You're looking for Professor Van Damm. Why don't you go over to that door and knock on it, to see if he's in that room?"

The eyes opened suddenly. "He couldn't have been in there."

"How do you know that?"

"The lights were out!"

"But if, as you say, the door was closed—"

"You could tell. Mrs. Van Damm, she used to complain about it. See, over the years, the wood had shrunk and there was this big gap under the doors and it made for a draft and that's something that always bothered her. Because of that, you could always see light under the door when somebody was in there."

"All right, go on."

"I went in the room and then over to the door that leads into the front hall and opened it."

"Did you say anything then?"

"No, sir. The lights were on over the stairs, the chandelier, that is. And the lights were on in his study, I remember I saw that when I got there, so I figured he must be upstairs 'cause I could hear the stereo playing, so I ran up there. I figured I'd just go up and knock on the door. Like I say, he was expecting me. His study is that little room at the top of the stairs, at the back. It's just a little room, nothing in it but his desk and all books except for that little fireplace he's got. Well, I went up there and—" He broke off.

"Go on."

"Well, you know the place, don't you, sir?"

"Tell me what you did next."

"Well, his study door was open a little and I knocked. When he didn't answer, I opened the door wider and went in there. When I saw he wasn't there, I went down the hall toward her room, where the lights were on. I was going to knock on the door and call out that I was there. Well, the door was open and I didn't take but more than one step and then I saw him. He was lying there on the floor, I mean, right there next to the doorway, so I almost stepped on him— pardon me for putting it that way—and it was—"

"I'm listening."

"You know how it is. You see something like that and you look at it and you know what you're looking at but at first, you can't react, you just stand there, because you think, It's not what I'm seeing—it's something else—and your mind tries to figure out what it is you're looking at, the way it does when somebody, he plays a practical joke on you—and then it hit me. I could see the bullet hole in his head. There was this blood trickling down the side of his head, like here—" He drew a line with a forefinger along his temple to his ear.

"How do you mean, trickling?"

"He was bleeding."

"You say he was bleeding?"

"Yes, sir."

"Go on."

"His eyes were open and his mouth, too, a little, and it was as if he was saying something to me, like, 'Call a doctor'—anything—and I knelt down next to him and started to say his name, and then I saw that he wasn't saying nothing, that he was dead."

"How did you know he was dead?"

"I—I—he wasn't breathing. He was dead."

"You thought."

"Yes, sir."

"But you couldn't have been sure. Why didn't you call the paramedics?"

"I just got out of there fast. I was scared to death. And I just ran down the stairs and out the door."

"Which door?"

"The one I come in by. The back door."

"When you ran down those stairs, did you hear anything?"

"Sir?"

"Did you hear anybody speak, call out something, anything like that?"

Manuel shook his head. "No, sir."

"Positive? Now, think. Take your time."

Manuel's eyes moved. He said nothing for a long time. Then he started to say something. "Well—" he began. He fell silent.

" 'Well' what?"

"I didn't hear anything. No way."

"I see." Dade walked slowly up and down alongside the table, his hands clasped behind his back. Manuel's eyes followed him. Neither of them said anything for a little while. Then Dade turned to Manuel and asked, "Who else was in the house?"

"Nobody."

"You went through the house, did you?"

"No, sir."

"Then how did you know nobody else was in the house at the time you found the professor's body?"

"Well—" Manuel thought. "I didn't see anybody else and I didn't hear anybody—" He licked his lips, his eyes moving, watchful.

"I'm going to ask you again. Who else was in the house?"

Manuel lifted his head. Lank strands of black hair had fallen over his face. He threw his head back to get the hair out of his face. He looked at Dade. The dark eyes with the long, straight lashes were hard and challenging. "I didn't see nobody. That's how it is. I don't care what anybody says."

Slamming his briefcase down hard on the table, Dade leaned on its polished surface with the flat of his hands and said, "You listen to me. For your own good, you listen to what I've got to say. The district attorney, he's going to say that you went there and took the professor's gun from his desk and that you killed the professor with it, killed him for gain, and that you ran away with what you stole. He's going to say you ran out the back door through the dark shrubbery to wherever it was you'd hidden your car so no one would see it and know you were there, jumped into it and hightailed it out of there, and that if it hadn't been for that tell-tale blood on your shoe—they couldn't do it with fingerprints—hell, you worked there, your fingerprints were all over the place—you'd be free and clear, with nobody suspecting you because nobody knew what you'd killed him for. See, they say that stuff that was stolen is junk. It was only by accident that anybody mentioned it. Later, Sophie Galanos would just figure she'd mislaid it. That's the case against you, sonny. It's ironclad, it sounds

45

good to the police and to the DA, and it's going to sound good to a jury."

Manuel sat back down and stared at his shoes. "You don't think I've got a chance, is that it?"

"Not for me to say." Dade turned and started toward the door by which he had entered, at the same time stretching out a hand to ring the buzzer for the guard.

"Sir?" the boy said. Dade turned, looking blankly at him. The boy said, struggling to his feet and gesturing awkwardly with his manacled hands, "Don't we have to talk? I mean, about the bail. I don't know what I'm supposed to do."

"Ask the Public Defender."

"I thought—"

"I'm not going to help you."

"Oh." The boy was taken aback. "Oh. Okay." He forced a brief smile and lifted two fingers in a half-salute. "Anyway, thanks."

"You lied to me. That's my reason." He kept his eyes fixed on Manuel's face. Manuel looked down, expressionless. His throat worked. He looked up at Dade.

Their eyes met across the table, Dade's unflinching, the boy's moving quickly back and forth. Then Manuel slumped, leaning on the table and slowly shaking his head. "I told you the truth," he said.

Dade pointed a thick forefinger at him and said, "You tell the police what you told me?"

"Yes, sir."

"Then you're not only a liar, you're a damn fool to boot." Dade shoved his face close to the boy's. "Want to know why I say that?" The boy met Dade's eyes defiantly. "Dead men don't bleed! Coroner's report says death was practically instantaneous. You know what makes a man bleed? The action of the heart. When you're dead, your heart stops. Bleeding stops. You told me you saw him bleeding! There can be a trickle of blood from such a wound but only for a few moments. If you saw blood trickling out of that wound, that means either you killed him or found him moments after he was killed, which would mean the murderer had to pass you as you came

46

in. Nobody can have gone out by the front door. It was locked and nobody had a key but the two people who lived there. Understand me? You killed him or you saw who did. It's that simple. You lied to me."

"What I told you was true!"

"What didn't you tell me?"

"I don't have any more to say."

"There was someone else in the house, wasn't there?" Manuel looked away, not saying anything. "Did you see that someone else? Answer me."

"No way. No way I'll say anything." He blinked rapidly. "And if they ask me in court, did I see anybody? I'll say no, and that's all there is to it. And I didn't go there to kill him to steal something. That's the way it is. And thanks. Thanks for wanting to help me. To help my family." He offered a manacled hand. Ignoring it, Dade began walking up and down again, hands once more clasped behind his back, talking to himself, the thick eyebrows going up and down, the lips moving silently. Then, the crocodile eyes turned in Manuel's direction.

"Because you're afraid you'll be next, is that it?"

When Manuel said nothing, Dade nodded to himself and then he said softly, "Tell me. Did you see the murderer?"

Manuel shook his head, lips pressed together. He blinked rapidly. "No," he said.

"What are you holding back?"

Manuel swallowed. There was a long silence. Dade waited patiently, arms folded. Then, finally, Manuel said, "After I heard—"

"Then you did hear something! Was this after you ran down the stairs?"

"No, before! I heard him! I heard him yell out, 'No, don't!' Then I heard this shot and the sound of him falling to the floor. I had just gone into his study and seen he wasn't there when I heard what I heard. I was scared. I didn't move. Then I could hear footsteps coming down the hall. My back was to the door and it was still open. The footsteps stopped. I knew that whoever it was was standing there, looking at me, with that crazy stereo still playing the whole time. I thought, Now they're going to shoot me. I couldn't move. I couldn't do anything. I just stood there, waiting for it to happen. Then, all of a sudden, I heard somebody running down the stairs. I know they saw me. I just know it. At the time, I couldn't figure out how come I didn't get it, too. After whoever it was ran out of there, I sneaked a look."

"You see anybody?"

"Nobody."

"Was the front door open or closed?"

"It was closed."

"And what about the door from the entryway into the sitting room?"

"That one was open."

"What did you do then?"

"I thought, Jeez, I've got to get him help. I thought, I should call. There's a phone in his study. That's when I went down the hall and pushed open the bedroom door."

"Her bedroom door?"

"Yes, sir. It was open a little and I could see him just lying there. When I saw he was dead—well, I told you what happened then. I ran like hell. That's why I didn't call the paramedics or anything." Manuel looked at him, eyes wide, mouth hanging open. "You understand what I'm saying to you, mister? I thought, Whoever it was saw me said to themselves, Wait a minute. Let him take the fall. That's how it is. They saw me but I didn't see them. They don't think I did. But if they get the idea maybe I did, they'll come after me next."

"Could you tell whether this person was a man or a woman?"

"No, sir."

"You smell any perfume?"

"No, sir."

"You said you heard footsteps."

"Running. Could have been anybody's."

"You hear a door slam?"

"No I didn't, sir."

"You hear any screaming?"

"Sir?"

"Did you hear a woman start screaming?"

"No, sir, I did not."

The two of them looked at each other for a long time in silence. Then, nodding to himself once again, Dade said, "You know why he was killed?"

"No, sir."

"What did the police say?"

"They kept asking me about some costume jewelry thing. I don't know what it is. I told them I didn't know what they were talking about but the cops, they don't believe me. They keep saying I killed him. I wouldn't have done that. The professor, he was like a friend to me. He would give me things. Help me out. I go to night school. He helped with my homework, sometimes. Once, when my mom was sick, he tried to give me money, so's I wouldn't have to take her to County General and sit there all day, waiting for somebody to see her. It just rubbed me the wrong way and I said—I don't know what ever made me say such a thing, him being so kind and all—I said, we don't take charity. And then he told me that a man once said that if somebody's poor, sometimes you have to ask him to forgive you for helping him."

"Saint Vincent de Paul."

"Pardon me?"

"He built hospitals for poor people. He said it."

"I never should have left him the way I did. I was just scared to death and I guess I just lost my head and ran out of the house."

"Out through the sitting room and then out the back way, the way you came in?"

"Yes, sir."

"I know it was the back door because a witness saw you."

"A witness?"

"Sophie Galanos."

Manuel looked at Dade as if he thought Dade was trying to trick him. "You're kidding!"

49

"No, I'm not."

"She said that? She told them that?" Dade nodded. Manuel turned away. "Jesus," he said under his breath.

Dade looked at him, eyes narrowed. "Arraignment's at nine in the morning," he said.

"Sir? You got any idea who's going to be my lawyer?"

"Me."

"Holy shit."

"If that's all right with you." Not waiting for an answer, Dade rang for the guard.

VI

Dade went back downstairs to Fielder MacBride's office, a judge he had come to know through Waldo Postel. Through the opaque glass pane, he saw lights on and went inside. The law clerk was gone. The door to the judge's chambers was ajar. A voice called out, "Dade? That you?"

"It is."

"I figured."

Dade went into Fielder MacBride's office. MacBride was a string-bean of a man with a long face, a cold smile and a habit of letting his eyes slide away from your face when you were talking to him, whether out of impatience or simple shyness, Dade had never been able to decide. They shook hands. MacBride did not like shaking hands and his grip was not firm, nor for that matter, slack, he simply clasped hands briefly, as if performing some ritual in which he did not altogether believe. He waved at a chair and then sat back down behind his desk.

"I got your card. Later, I ran into Persons at the candy counter and he told me what you were here for. Who's representing?"

"I am."

MacBride looked at him, surprised. "You?"

Dade nodded. "As for bail, I'd appreciate it if you'd keep it to twenty-five thousand, will you do that for me, Scotty? That's all his mother can raise on that house of theirs and since he's not a boy who's going to run off and leave his mother to be put out on the street—"

Now, MacBride looked at him. "You have read the police report?"

"Look, we're going to respond that defendant did not go to the Van Damm house on the night in question to rob the decedent and—"

"You're not going to try a negative pregnant on me, are you, Dade?"

"Scotty, you're not going to get any argument from me about whether the boy was at the house that night. The defense will stipulate that he was. But we are pleading Not Guilty. Now, twenty-five grand—"

"I can't do it."

"What are you talking about? The kid hasn't yet been tried, much less convicted."

"As far as the general public is concerned, he's perceived as guilty. And if I let him out—"

Dade raised his eyebrows, a surprised look on his face. "You're talking like a man who doesn't have both oars in the water."

"If he's let out and kills again—"

Dade rose. "Habeas corpus. I'll go down the hall right now and file timely notice and then take all necessary steps to perfect that appeal."

"Suit yourself."

"I'll state my case now. I'll appeal on the grounds that it is manifest abuse of discretion. *People* vs. *Norman*, 1967."

"Go ahead."

"Not to mention *McDermott* vs. *Superior Court*, 1972, unconstitutional penalty assessment. You sure you want me to do a thing like that, Scotty? Make a lot of waves."

MacBride said, brushing lint from his dark trouser legs, "Take it easy. I didn't say I was going to refuse bail."

"Oh?"

"I'm just going to set it at a hundred thousand."

"Knowing he can't make it."

"Not my concern."

Dade put his hands behind his back and walked up and down. Then, turning back to MacBride, he said, "There are two reasons I think you'll change your mind. You want to hear them?"

"Say your say."

"There's never in the history of this country been one millionaire as sat on death row—"

"We all know that."

"I'm going to remind folks of it tomorrow when I talk to the press and explain why I'm making bail for him myself."

MacBride looked up, meeting Dade's eyes, a dull flush reddening his face. "The hell you are."

"The hell I'm not."

"And when the damn kid ups and kills somebody else—and that's what's going to happen, that's what always happens. This is a capital case. Boy could go to the gas chamber, if convicted, and you want me to—?" Beads of perspiration popped out on his forehead.

" 'Boy' is right. Incidentally, the first juvenile executed in this country was back in 1642 when a seventeen year old named Thomas Granger was hanged in Massachusetts for sodomy. You trying to bring back those days?"

" 'Boy' is wrong, you bastard! Kid is twenty-two."

"Oh, hell, I didn't know that. Then, let him hang."

"For Christ's sake, Dade—" MacBride waved Dade back to his chair. Pulling out a handkerchief, he began blotting at his face. "Don't tell me you really think the kid's innocent."

"Twenty-five."

"Go to hell."

"Twenty-five or I'll bail him out myself and folks'll start saying, 'He must know something. If he puts up his own dough, he must really know something. Maybe the kid didn't do it.' "

"It's open and shut."

"That's what's the matter with it, Scotty. It's just too damn open and shut. Twenty-five and I throw in drinks at Clancy's."

MacBride heaved himself to his feet, put his hands flat on his desk and, leaning in Dade's direction, said, "Okay." He shook a warning finger at Dade. "But when they find whatever the hell it is that kid killed him for—"

"Junk jewelry, from what I hear tell. Not that I won't have a few questions to put to that Mrs. Polykleides, when the time comes."

"You mean the dresser?"

"I do."

"You're too late. She's on her way back home to Greece."

"Who told you that?"

"Persons. He's the one who just gave her permission."

"Son of a bitch!" Dade turned on his heel and strode out the open door.

VII

Persons said, looking up at Dade defensively, "You don't know what the score is. The dresser, she came back with Sophie Galanos to help with the new play but since she's not going ahead with it, the woman's job's ended. Since she's in the country on a work permit, no job means no visa. She could only stay here if we wanted her to and then we'd have to pick up the tab and what with budget cuts, I couldn't justify anything like that, so when she said she had to leave, we said, Go ahead."

"When was this?"

"A few minutes ago. Around one, say."

"When she left here, where did she go, can you tell me that?"

"To the airport. To LAX."

"How do you know that?"

"Sophie Galanos, she's the one who brought her in here, and then she drove off with the lady herself."

"You don't know what airline?"

"I just know her flight was at two o'clock. Listen, it's the kid," Persons said.

Dade reached across the desk for the lieutenant's phone. "With your permission," Dade said.

Less than an hour later, Dade left his car in the parking structure opposite the Pan Am Building and was hurrying toward the terminal. Inside, a clerk directed him to Gate 54. The plane was due to board any minute. Since it was to make another stop in New York, the passengers would not go through customs here. Dade strode down the long corridor, then stepped onto the escalator, hiking up the slow-moving staircase and murmuring excuses as he brushed by people. On the upper level, he broke into a half-run, hurrying past fast food places and a newsstand to the waiting area in front of Gate 54. At a desk, he saw a uniformed attendant checking over a list. Behind the desk, a door opened and a crew member of a plane emerged, a youngish man with a gold stripe on the dark sleeve of his uniform. The passengers got to their feet, picking up the luggage they were carrying on with them.

Dade stepped over the velvet rope separating the waiting area from the rest of the satellite, went rapidly up to the attendant behind the desk, a clean-cut young man with horn-rimmed glasses, and said to him, "I want you to page Mrs. Polykleides for me, will you do that, please?"

"If you'll step to a white telephone over there—"

"This is urgent and I want you to help me."

"If you'll just wait till we board these passengers, sir—"

"She's here but I don't know what the hell she looks like, so I want you to page her for me."

"Sir, if you'll just let me call my superior—"

"The police lieutenant downtown told me I'd find her here. Now, if you want me to get him on the line for you—" Dade reached for the telephone on the desk.

The young man reacted to the word "police." Picking up a pencil, he said to Dade, "Mrs. who?" Dade spelled the name for him and the young man wrote it down. Then, looking up, he said into a microphone on his desk, "Will Mrs. Polykleides step to the desk, please?" An older woman with a shapeless felt hat on her white hair looked up, surprised, then, carrying a string bag and a battered purse, came slowly toward them. The crew member said something into the ear of the young man behind the desk and the young man said to Dade, "Any reason we should delay boarding the other passengers, sir?"

"None whatever."

"Flight 115 from Los Angeles to Athens, making a stopover at Kennedy in New York, is now boarding," he said, as the door behind him banged open and he began checking tickets and passengers pushed past him and started down the carpeted ramp to the plane. The older woman came up to the desk.

"Here it is, my ticket, and here is my passport," she said, offering both to the young man.

"Are you Mrs. Polykleides?" he asked.

By way of answer, she pointed at the Greek passport. He opened it, revealing her picture and her name written in Greek letters. Indicating Dade, the young man said, "This gentleman wants to speak with you, ma'am. He's from the police."

"Police? You from police?" She gave Dade an alarmed look.

Taking the string bag from her and leading her gently by the elbow, Dade escorted her to a chair away from the press of the crowd. Several of them had heard the mention of the word "police." Heads turned. Dade seated the woman. "The police told me where to find you," he said.

"Is for what reason they send you? I do nothing."

"They didn't send me in the sense you mean," he said. He looked at her. She watched his lips carefully as he spoke. He saw that, under her wispy white hair, a hearing aid was fastened to one ear. She was having trouble hearing him. He was not sure how much English she understood. "I'll only keep you a minute," he said. "*Eiste bebaios,*" he added in Greek, trying to reassure her.

"*Mileite hellaynika?*" she asked, a surprised look on her face. He did not speak Greek. He remembered only a few tourist phrases and he saw that what he had said to reassure her was now making her afraid. He shook his head, at the same time patting her hand. She looked over his shoulder at the last of the crowd now going through the doorway. She turned back to him, alarmed. He patted her hand again and then turned, holding up a hand and catching the attention of the young man at the desk, signaling him to wait. The young man nodded, understanding. Reaching behind him, he fastened a short length of chain to the door leading to the ramp, to hold the door open. He gestured at it, smiling at her. Now, she was reassured.

"The jewelry," Dade said to her. "The costume jewelry belonging to Mrs. Van Damm. Can you describe it for me?"

"Mrs. Van Damm?" She looked at him blankly.

"Sophie Galanos," he explained.

"Ah!" Now, she understood.

One of the flight officers had emerged from the ramp tunnel and was speaking to the young man behind the desk, gesturing toward Mrs. Polykleides. They both looked in her direction. Dade racked his brains for a Greek word that would make clear what he meant. Then it came to him. To the ancient Greeks, the universe itself was one vast ornament, a jeweled arrangement they called the Cosmos. Now, he remembered. "*Kosminos!*" he said.

"Aha!" Her face lit up.

"The *kosminos* of Sophie Galanos, *katalabeinete?*"

She understood. She shook her head vehemently, in the Greek way of saying yes. "*Neh! Neh!* Yes! Yes, I understand, *kyrie!*"

"Describe it to me."

"Was the *kraydemnon,* you understand?" The word, as she pronounced it, rhymed with Agamemnon. Seeing Dade look puzzled, she gestured at her head, then frowned, trying to think of the word in English. Dade was sure he had heard the word before but couldn't remember what it meant. Now, they both heard a voice on a loudspeaker, announcing the imminent departure of her flight.

Dade took her string bag and, helping her out of her chair, escorted her to the boarding ramp. "Valuable?" he asked.

"*Axia?*" she asked him, translating the word into Greek to make sure she understood what he was asking. He nodded vehemently. She looked at him and laughed soundlessly, lifting her chin in the Greek way of saying no. "*Ohi!*" she said. "Junk!"

"Junk?"

"Is for no good! Nothing!" A stewardess hurried up to them and, taking the string bag Dade held out to her, took the arm of Mrs.

Polykleides and helped her hurry down the ramp to board the plane. Turning, she waved at him, smiling. *"Kraydemnon!"* she called out. *"Kraydemnon,* you understand it?"

Then she was gone. A door slammed behind her. Dade turned away, at a loss.

VIII

Dade thought, I have to talk to Sophie. Stopping at a pay phone in the lobby of the satellite, he dialed her number. She answered the phone herself.

"Sophie, this here's Dade Cooley."

"Dade! I have to thank you again for coming down here."

"Sophie, I only wish we could have done more."

"Where are you now, back in San Francisco?"

"No, honey, we're still in town."

"Oh, are you?"

It occurred to him she must have thought they had taken a plane down, then flown back. "And I've just got to see you." He checked his watch. It was two-twenty. "Can I come by after three, half-past, say?"

"Will Ellen be coming with you?"

"I'm sure she'd like to."

"Three-thirty is fine. We'll see each other then." There was a click.

When he got back to the Bel-Air, he found their room was empty. He heard the sound of running water coming from the bathroom. He called out to Ellen, then opened the door. She was sitting in the tub, a phone in one hand, and watching an old Bette Davis film on the screen of a television set suspended from the wall. She blew him a kiss, meanwhile nodding and making "um" sounds into the French telephone by way of answer. Going back into their room, he went over to the built-in bar next to the room's artificial fireplace and took out a bottle of Perrier, poured it into a couple of glasses, added rounds of lemon, carried the glasses into the bathroom and handed one to her, then sitting down on a little chair, raised his glass in her direction and sipped from his drink as he looked at the television screen. Ellen had turned off the sound (he could see the wet foot-prints on the marble floor made when she had gotten out of the tub, presumably after the phone rang) and he watched Bette Davis smile bravely at George Brent and knew that, in a little while, she would look at him the way she always looked when she was angry (Popeye the Magnificent, they used to call her) and say in her clipped New England speech, "What does 'prognosis negative' mean?"

Then, Ellen reached over and hung up the phone on the wall. He turned to her. She said, "Now, don't worry. I asked. I actually called the telephone company and asked. You can't get a shock unless it falls into the tub while ringing and, the box being fastened to the wall—"

"Is 'shock' a euphemism for 'electrocuted'?"

She slid down for a moment under the foam of the bubblebath, then, surfacing, reached for the hand shower at the side of the tub and, gesturing at the luxuriously appointed bathroom, she said plaintively, "All this and I can't enjoy it."

"You seem to be making every effort."

"I don't approve. I feel like Aunt Ida."

"We can't have that." Getting to his feet, Dade crossed to the tele-vision set and turned it off. "Excuse me a minute," he said. Going into the other room, he picked up the phone and gave the operator a San Francisco number. Through the open door, he heard Ellen singing:

> "We never mention Aunt Ida,
> Her picture is turned to the wall;
> She lives on the French Riviera,
> But Mum says she's dead to us all."

"Motke," Dade heard a voice say on an answering machine, followed by a beep.

"This here's Dade, Arnie. Talk on the street is, the late Paul Van Damm's brother Vincent owes thirty-five grand to the boys in Vegas. What's the story?" Dade left the number of the hotel, then went back into the bathroom.

"What was all that about?" she asked.

"Tell you in a minute. Who was on the phone?"

"Sophie."

"Oh. You call her?"

"No. She called me."

"How come?"

"To apologize. She said she should have asked to speak to you but she's just so—well, distrait is the word she used."

"I want to talk to her. She said we could both come over this afternoon," Dade said.

"That's the reason she called. To tell us that she won't be in after all."

"Figures."

She looked at him with surprise. "Dade?"

"I have a hunch she's avoiding me."

"Tell all."

"Don't know anything. Much."

"What happened with the boy?"

"I know you don't approve of this place," he said abruptly. "Mencken didn't approve of Los Angeles in general. Went home and said the whole place stank of orange blossoms."

"Not any more. The groves are gone."

"What would he say today? Money? No, you can't say that. Money has no smell."

"*I* don't disapprove of Los Angeles."

"Then would you mind staying on just a bit?"

"How long?"

"Hard to say. But if I could find us some fleabag—it seems to me I passed a motel with broken window screens and Astroturf out front for a lawn, and if that's the kind of place where you'd feel more at home, my little dove—"

She turned on the hand shower and aimed it at him. He let out a yell and ducked out of the way. "All right, Dade, what's going on?"

"I'm going to represent him."

"What made you decide to do that?"

"Again, hunch."

"And why is it you have to see Sophie?"

"Honey, I've got a client jailed for murder, the motive turns out to be some kind of junk jewelry she had and what I want from her is a description of it."

She sponged her arms in the soft, scented water. "Does his mother know yet that you plan on representing him?"

"I thought we'd just stop by in a little while and tell her."

"I'd like that. Too bad Sophie won't be there."

"That occurred to me."

She gave him a blue stare. "Dade? What are you up to?" He shrugged. "Dade?"

"You get a look at her eyes?"

"Sophie's?"

"Yes. Pinpoint pupils."

"Maybe she takes drugs, like Helen."

"Helen who?"

"Helen of Troy. The role she's playing in *The Trojan Women*. Helen of Troy took drugs."

"Who says?"

"Homer. Take another look at the *Odyssey*. She took something she was supposed to have gotten from an Egyptian woman. What was it called? Nepenthe, that was it. She used to put it in wine, 'a drug to bring forgetfulness for every sorrow.'" Ellen closed her eyes, crossed her arms on her breast and slid out of sight under the bubbles. Surfacing, she said, "So what happened today? What did you find out?"

He told her. She listened intently, interrupting once to ask, "What's a negative pregnant?"

"It's a little trick in which you deny an allegation in the exact words of the allegation itself. Example: The accused went to the house of the decedent on the night stated and entered by stealth with the avowed purpose of robbing him. Answer: the accused did not go to the house of the decedent on the night stated and enter by stealth with the avowed purpose of robbing him. Courts hold that such language is filled with concealed admissions. Common law says that anybody who permits himself the use of a negative pregnant is only denying some immaterial part of the allegation, such as 'entered by stealth.'"

"I see. And MacBride thought you were trying that on him?"

"Or that Manuel was trying it on me and maybe getting away with it, only Scotty was too politic to put it that way."

She lifted her brows. "Oh. Well, go on. Tell the rest."

When he was finished, she echoed the word *kraydemnon* under her breath.

"Know what it means?" he asked.

"I can't remember." She frowned in thought, at the same time handing him a sponge and leaning forward so he could scrub her back. Then, after she had rinsed away the soap and wrapped herself in the hotel's terry-cloth robe, she sipped her Perrier and followed Dade into the bedroom. He sat down and stared off into space while she dressed.

"In or out?" she said.

"Out."

"*Taramosalata, tsatziki, spanakopita*—and I will dance for you. *Bouzoukia.*"

"You know a place?" She gave him a veiled look, nodding. "How did you find out about it?"

"I asked Sophie, stupid."

"Oh."

"The best defense would be finding out who really did it."

"That is very cunning of you, my dear."

She lifted her chin and looked at him, her blue eyes darkening. "Just for that, I won't tell you what I found out."

"Serves me right."

"And you're dying to know."

"Tell me."

"I don't want to be accused of poaching."

Pouncing on the word, he said "poach" under his breath and, taking out his notebook and his gold pencil, he wrote down the word.

"Poach?"

"To pocket, to dig out."

"It no longer means to dig out."

"Well, once upon a time—"

" 'Once upon a time' is for fairy tales."

"You don't think—?"

"No, I don't. Cheaters never prosper. Cross it out or I won't tell you what I heard."

He drew a reluctant line through the word. Then he said, "All right, what?"

"They took statements from everybody, you know, the way they always do, and Irene told them she was on campus. She's taking some awful botany course, which she hates, a make-up course she could only get at night, one of those lecture things with hundreds of students, where they never take roll and sometimes, people fall asleep on your shoulder—well, anyway, she said that's where she was and then today, who should come by Sophie's but a detective looking for Irene, who said the lecture that night happened to have been canceled and they sort of want her to talk to her. What do you think?"

"Seven," he said. "Seven, by golly."

"Seven what?"

"People without any alibi, who should have one. But that's not what's bothering me."

"What is?"

"Button, button."

"What?"

"What's really missing," he said, "is the motive."

IX

Ellen said, "It really isn't necessary to go by Sophie's. I can tell Luisa on the phone that you're representing him. And since Sophie isn't going to be there—"

"—I'll have a free hand."

"What's that supposed to mean?"

"I just want to look around."

She stared at him. "With Luisa watching you?"

"That's where you come in."

"What is?"

"Take her out shopping. A breath of air does a body good."

"Take her out why?"

"I think I'll have me a little look around."

"Look around for what?"

"That junk jewelry."

"You told me the police had already searched the place and it wasn't there."

"It wasn't then."

"But you don't even know what it looks like."

"I'll soon find out."

"How?"

"With a little help from Paul's Greek-English dictionary."

"Isn't searching someone's house without a warrant against the law?"

"So is murder. And while you're at it, find out whether Paul and Sophie fought often."

"Dade! I don't know how I can ask something like that!"

"You'll find a way."

When Dade rang the doorbell of the Van Damm bungalow, Luisa opened the door. Seeing them, her hand flew to her mouth. She ushered them in. Ellen spoke reassuringly to her in the soft cadences of Luisa's language. Then, turning to Dade, Luisa snatched up his right hand in both of hers and kissed it. He patted her shoulder. "It's all right," he said. "It's going to be fine."

Ellen spoke to Luisa, who nodded and hurried off to get her coat. Alone, Ellen and Dade looked around the sitting room.

The room smelled of furniture polish. Everything had been dusted and the floor had been waxed. On either side of the fireplace were glass-fronted bookcases filled with books with fine bindings, many of them in languages other than English. Over the mantel was a portrait of Sophie dressed in a white Greek dress. He looked at the thick gold hair and wondered how many people knew that the ancient Greeks were blond. Of course, Homer had said so but who remembered? Against one wall was a glass-topped display table filled with curios Sophie had collected from her travels: jade boxes, a silver mirror, a jeweled lorgnette, a necklace made of pieces of painted enamel decorated with tiny rubies and emeralds. Dade frowned. Anyone intent on theft would have smashed the glass, filled his pockets with these small objets d'art and run out of the bungalow.

Pointing at something in the glass-topped table, Ellen said, "Look! Oh, what a shame!"

"What?"

"*Athena Glaucopis.*" Delicately lifting the hinged glass lid of the case, she pointed at a small figure of the goddess, indicating fissures in the painted ceramic work of art. "Look," she said.

"Gray-eyed Athena," he said, frowning as he saw what she was pointing at. "Too damn bad." He picked it up, examining it.

"Careful," she said. "It looks old."

"Smashed," he said. "Then put back together."

Moments later, Luisa knocked, then came into the room. Dade put the painted figurine of the goddess back in the case and reclosed the lid.

"Smash," Luisa said, illustrating the word with a gesture, as if hurling the little figure to the floor. "I find like that."

"Today?" Ellen asked.

Luisa shook her head. *"Hace poco tiempo. Seis meses, mas o menos."*

"About six months ago," Ellen said.

"What happened?" Dade asked.

Understanding him, Luisa shrugged, shaking her head.

"No se, señor," she answered.

"You couldn't break it like that if you dropped it, I don't think," Dade said. Looking at Ellen, he said, "Ask her if she found other things around here broken."

Ellen murmured the question in Spanish. Luisa replied with a vehement denial, shaking her head. Then Ellen said, "Excuse us, won't you?" and went out of the house with Luisa, leaving Dade alone.

When he heard them drive away, he made his way swiftly up to Paul's study at the top of the stairs. In front of the door was a small Tabriz rug. The door was closed. Dade reached out a hand, opening it. Inside, everything was in order. The walls were lined with more books, ceiling to floor, and opposite the west-facing desk was a tiny fireplace. The window behind the desk was covered with a red velvet drape. From outside, one would be able to see chinks of light but nothing more when the drape was closed. Paul kept it closed. Dade remembered that Paul liked working in cavelike surroundings.

Dade went quickly through the desk drawers. Paul was orderly. The drawers contained only paper and pencils, paper clips and artgum erasers. He ran a thumb along the inside edge of the top drawer. There was no trace of dust. Whatever had been in the desk had been removed. There was nothing left of any consequence. Catching sight of a Greek-English dictionary, he looked up the word Mrs. Polykleides had used. The dictionary defined *kraydemnon* as "a large veil or mantilla, such, for instance, as the sea-goddess Ino gives

Ulysses, to buoy him up on the water (Od. v. 346)." A second meaning told him that, used as a metaphor in the plural, it meant the battlements on a wall. A third meaning was the lid of a vessel. These definitions made no sense to him. A large veil could not be described by any stretch of the imagination as a piece of costume jewelry. Had he misunderstood her? No, he was sure he hadn't. *Kraydemnon* was what she had said, she had said it quite distinctly, she was a dresser, Sophie's dresser, she ought to know the vocabulary of her craft, and *kraydemnon* was what he had heard. He remembered now that she had put her hands to her head as she had said the word and that made him think that perhaps "veil" was exactly what she had meant, and that not knowing English, she had said "costume jewelry" to the police investigator, using it as a collective term because she could not think of the word "wardrobe." But then he remembered that Sophie herself had been quoted in the report as describing the missing ornament as "nothing more than a piece of junk jewelry" and had pantomimed something like a coronet. It seemed to him it could not be a veil. He would ask Sophie to describe it for him.

Then he looked again at the telephone on the desk and, on impulse, picked it up and examined it. Like everything of Paul's, it was the plainest offered for sale, an ordinary black instrument with push buttons in the receiver. But Dade saw that one of them was labeled REDIAL and remembered that Paul had shown it to him and played with it like a toy.

"Busy!" he remembered Paul saying. "Everybody I want to talk to is always busy, even the bank, especially the damn bank! Well, now I've got *this!*" He used it constantly, with great satisfaction. On a hunch, Dade pushed the button and was rewarded first with a rapid series of tones of different pitch and then the clicking sound of a number being dialed. He pressed REDIAL again, this time letting the number ring. There was no answer. Taking out his notebook and pencil, he pushed the REDIAL button once more, then listened to the clicks, counted them and jotted down the number. The number was local, for no area code had been dialed. The number was 555-6127. He put down the phone. Dade said to himself, Must be the garage. The one he kept trying to reach before they left. He pressed REDIAL again. It rang for a long time but there was no answer. He would try the number again back at the hotel.

He went along the gallery parallel to the open staircase. Paul's bedroom was the first room. It overlooked the path on the side of the house. Then came the bathroom and then Sophie's room. He went into her bedroom first. It was dominated by a large canopied bed. Facing it were French windows looking out at the cul-de-sac. Another window gave onto the path on the south side of the house. The room was in order. Her bedside tables had drawers containing odds and ends, packets of Kleenex, a coin purse, a copy of *TV Guide* several weeks old, the channel changer for the television set which stood in one corner, a notepad and a pencil. There was an envelope of photographs and negatives, pictures taken on an earlier trip to Greece, pictures of Sophie and Paul standing in front of ruined temples and views of the sea. One of them had been taken in front of a Greek grave stele. It was a bas-relief showing the seated figure of the deceased, an older man. Beside him, the carved figure of a robed woman, her hands stretched out to him. Dade remembered the convention: the bereaved try to call the dead back to life but they are unmoved. On impulse, he picked up a photograph of Paul and Sophie laughing together and put it in his pocket.

He went through her closets. They were filled with expensive clothes, most of them in zippered plastic clothes bags. Her jewelry, which was obviously for everyday wear, was in a couple of flat cases and consisted mostly of earrings and necklaces. There were a few bracelets and pins. Her taste ran to imitations of the ancient style, gold set with a few large, irregular stones. None of it looked valuable. Her rings were on a porcelain ring stand, a Victorian piece done in the style of an uplifted hand. Shoe-bags contained a large number of shoes. Sophie was orderly. Everything was hung neatly in place.

He went through the bureau. It smelled of sandalwood and contained carefully folded lingerie and a collection of sweaters in zippered plastic bags. He had opened all the drawers. Now, he closed them again, beginning with the large one at the bottom. When he got to the small center drawer at the top, where she kept her hand-kerchiefs, he was about to push it back in when something attracted his attention: a small bottle from a pharmacy. He took it out of the drawer and read the label. It said: "Isopto-carpine," and the words "Use as directed." It was from a pharmacy in Tarzana and had been prescribed by a Dr. Blinder. The date on the bottle was a month earlier, with an expiration date almost a year away. The name on the bottle was "Mrs. Hester Benson." Dade frowned, examining the bottle. It was a plastic squeeze bottle and it was half-empty. Nothing occurred to him. Taking out his notebook and pencil, he made a note of the doctor's name and address. Then, putting the bottle back where he had found it, he closed the drawer, left her bedroom and went into the bathroom. She had a large supply of cosmetics and unguents, perfumes and bath oils. Apart from Paul's shaving gear, the medicine cabinet contained only the usual over-the-counter cold remedies, coated aspirin and mouthwash, as well as a bottle of ant-acid.

He went from the bathroom into Paul's bedroom. It was a small room with a single bed. There was a pine end table with a lamp on it. He glanced around the room. It was bare. The bed was against the south wall, where a window looked out over the narrow pathway and the high hedge below.

The end table held a reading lamp and a tablet with a pencil beside it. Dade picked up the tablet and looked at it. The top sheet was blank but there was an impression on the sheet underneath it. Faintly visible, it read: "Il xvii.53." There was no indication that anything else had been written on the sheet. Dade studied the page, then put the tablet back where he had found it.

There was a bureau opposite the window and a Greek Floka rug on the floor. Dade opened the bureau drawers in succession. They contained only clothes, all neatly folded. A black leather change-scoop on the top of the bureau held a big bunch of keys. His wallet and the contents of his pockets at the time of his death would have been impounded as evidence and would still be in the hands of the police. Dade picked up the large key ring with its collection of la-beled keys, weighing it in his hand and trying to imagine why Paul had taken only this out of his pocket, while leaving everything else. Then it struck him and, under his breath, he called himself a damn fool for not seeing at once that no reasonable man would carry a half-a-pound of keys around in his pockets all over Greece. He was about to deposit it in the change-scoop on the bureau where he had found it, but first, on impulse, removed the keys labeled OFFICE and DESK and put them instead into his own pocket.

Closing the door firmly behind him, he went into Paul's study, found a shelf where there were half a dozen different editions of Homer and, choosing Pope's translation of *The Iliad,* opened it to the passage Paul had made note of, glanced at it, took out his notebook and pencil and copied down a quatrain:

> The shining circlets of his golden hair,
> Which even the Graces might be proud to wear,
> Instarr'd with gems and gold, bestrow the shore,
> With dust dishonour'd, and deform'd with gore.

A footnote gave a reference to Helbig's *Epos* for "the Homeric custom of tying plaits or locks of hair with gold."

Frowning, he copied that down as well and then put the book back on the shelf. "I said they were blond," he said under his breath. "Didn't I say they were blond?"

As he came down the stairs, Dade heard the doorbell ring. Opening the front door, he saw a stout, middle-aged man with a florid face and thinning strands of reddish hair brushed across his skull. The man looked at him with surprise. "Mr. Cooley!" said the man.

"That's right. I don't believe I—"

"We haven't met. I'm from the *Times*. I recognized your picture from a layout for a story we're running on the boy tomorrow."

"I can't discuss the case, if that's what you had in mind."

"I'm not a reporter, Mr. Cooley." The man took a card out of his wallet and handed it to Dade. "I'm a science editor. I was a friend of Paul's. I couldn't get to the services this morning, so I came by to offer Sophie my condolences."

Dade looked at the card. It was a business card and it bore only the man's name and then, in the lower left-hand corner, the logo and the address of the *Los Angeles Times*. The name on the card was James Clinton. Dade looked at him with renewed interest. "Sophie, she's out just at present."

"Well, if you'll tell her I stopped by—"

"I was a friend of Paul's, too," Dade said. He extended a hand. "Dade Cooley." Motioning for him to come in, Dade said, "Listen, can I have a word with you?"

The eyes blinked and then James Clinton nodded and let himself be escorted into the sitting room. He was a scholarly-looking man. Despite the warm September weather, he wore a rumpled dark scarf which he now removed and draped from his left wrist, as if in response to some memory from another lifetime of a maniple he once carried. Dade crossed the sitting room with him and gestured at a pair of high-backed carved Spanish chairs placed on the tile floor on either side of the stone fireplace. They seated themselves.

Dade said, "Paul, he had an appointment with you, am I right?"

"How did you know that?" Clinton opened his eyes with surprise. When Dade only opened his hands, not answering, Clinton stuck out his lower lip in thought and then, as if he could see no harm in replying, said, "Yes, he did. He called me just after he got back."

"Personal matter? I hope you don't mind my asking, but since we were both friends of his and given the circumstances of his death—"

"Professional."

"Mind giving me some idea what it was about?"

Clinton hesitated. Finally, he said, "It was confidential."

"Paul, he's gone now."

"Still—"

Dade shifted his weight. "Anybody you can think of would be harmed by your talking about it?"

Clinton sat back in his chair. "I don't want him made to look foolish."

"I think we're both reading off the same page."

Clinton responded with a brief nod of assent. Then he said, "Paul had an announcement to make. It was the kind of thing the press gets hold of and sensationalizes. He didn't want it handled that way. He had written an article on it for a scholarly journal and he wanted me to go over it with him. He was going to let me do a feature on it for our Sunday edition. You see, if a scholar makes a sensational find, he sometimes does that to preempt the field, so to speak."

"What was the subject of his article?"

Clinton went over to the bookcase, took a volume from a shelf and opened it. It was *Schliemann's Discoveries of the Ancient World*.

He opened it to the account of the discovery of the shaft graves at Mycenae. "He talks about how three male bodies lay in the tomb, inlaid weapons beside them, 'golden masks covering their faces and golden breastplates on their chests.' Two of the corpses crumbled away as soon as they were exposed to the air. But—here. Read this paragraph." Clinton handed the book to Dade. Dade read:

> But of the third body, the round face, with all its flesh, had been wonderfully preserved under its ponderous golden mask; there was no vestige of hair but both eyes were perfectly visible, also the mouth, which, owing to the enormous weight that had pressed upon it, was wide open, and showed thirty-two beautiful teeth. From these, all the physicians who came to see the body were led to believe that the man must have died at the early age of thirty-five. The news that the well-preserved body of a man of the heroic age had been found, covered with golden ornaments, spread like wildfire through the Argolid, and people came by thousands from Argos.

Dade closed the book. Taking it back from him, Clinton said, "After that, Schliemann is supposed to have lifted up the gold mask and kissed it. Then, according to popular belief, he wrote out a telegram to the King of Greece, saying, 'I have gazed on the face of Agamemnon.' Of course, Schliemann's dates were off by a couple hundred years or more, as everyone said. The Trojan War was fought in about 1250 B.C. Those graves date from the fifteenth or sixteenth century B.C. The reason we know is that the shaft tombs contain artifacts showing strong Cretan influence from that period. Agamemnon lived in the *thirteenth* century B.C., two or three hundred years *later*."

"You spoke of Paul's having planned on saying something sensational."

"Paul told me he thought the body really was Agamemnon's."

Dade stared at him. "Paul said that to you? He give you a reason that made him think such a thing?"

"It all started out with a remarkable guess—one of those guesses that somehow ring absolutely true—like Martin Buber's astonishing guess that the Ark of the Covenant was originally the mummy of Joseph."

"That takes the rag off'n the bush," Dade whistled under his breath.

Clinton said, "Now here was Paul's. Just before the time of the Trojan War, the place of the ancient royal tombs in Mycenae was rebuilt and made into the center of a public cult, say around 1250 B.C. Well, Paul said when Agamemnon came home victorious from the Trojan War, he was one of the greatest heroes in Greek history. Paul said that the Greeks would have insisted on opening up the royal grave circle and burying him with his ancestors. It sounds absolutely right, doesn't it? I mean, the minute you hear it, you can't think that they would have done anything else."

"Pretty hard to publish a guess."

"But he had proof."

"He had what?" Dade was astonished. "Some tablet he found, say?"

"That's what I first thought. Something he'd come across written in Linear B, say, from Pylos. A letter from one king to another, for example. That's what you'd expect. But that's not what it was at all. Here's the story: In the basement of the National Museum at Athens, he found a crate of shards which Schliemann had found in the fifth tomb—the one he called Agamemnon's. One of them was an unbroken Grey Minyan cup, the type most commonly found in Troy. Painted on it is the portrait of a woman wearing some kind of headdress, done in a style without analogy anywhere."

"Was that the proof that he was bringing back?"

"I don't know. He was very close-mouthed about the whole thing. All I can tell you is, he wanted to get together the next morning early—"

"The next morning?"

"Yes. He wanted us to meet at his office so that he could show me the draft of the article he'd been working on before he'd gone away, and I was to go over it with him and agree with him on what I could use for the piece, which I promised to let him approve before publication. It had to be early Tuesday because he had to catch a flight to Tucson. Well in the morning, of course, he was dead. I had been out for the evening and I didn't learn about it until I turned on the news the next morning, when I was expecting him to call me, and I tell you—"

"Out for the evening? Weren't you expecting him to come by?"

"Pardon me?"

"At eight-thirty that night. Weren't you expecting to see him?"

"No, I wasn't."

Dade reacted with surprise. "I heard you were."

"From whom?"

"Manuel."

"The boy? He said that?"

Dade nodded. "Funny kind of a thing for him to make up, wouldn't you say?"

Clinton said, "What happened is this. Paul called me just before six. I said I was going out and thought I'd be home by half-past eight. Well, as it happens, I was delayed and didn't return home until just before ten."

Dade kept his eyes fixed on Clinton's for some moments. Then Dade said abruptly, "Possibly Paul changed his mind and wanted to see you that night. Maybe he wanted you to come over here."

"No, he couldn't have expected that. He knew I was expecting a call from my son, who's in Japan. When he plans to call, it's generally around nine at night here, around his lunch break in Japan, so Paul knew I couldn't go out."

Dade's eyes remained on his face. "I see, I see. You say there was a draft of the article in his office?"

"Yes. A draft of what he planned to publish later in *Antiquities*."

"You ever get a look at it?"

"No." Clinton shook his head slowly. "That's all I can tell you. I don't know whether it would be of help to you. I mean, it's hardly a motive for murder, now, is it? I mean, whether the body was Agamemnon's or whatever proof it was Paul brought back with him."

"But it ought to be easy to find," Dade said. "The proof, that is."

Clinton glanced toward the stairs. "Must be up in his study."

"Nothing there. Desk has been cleaned out."

"The proof could be in his office. On campus. Along with the article."

"Since he didn't drive and was apparently alone here, except for a few visitors, from the time he returned from Greece till the time he was killed, there's no reason to think he ever set foot in his office."

"I don't understand."

"It's very simple," Dade said. "The proof, whatever it was, seems to be missing."

"Are you saying somebody made off with it? Why on earth would anybody do that?"

"You familiar with something called the *kraydemnon?*"

"No. What is it?"

"Greek-English dictionary upstairs in Paul's study says it was a veil that the sea-goddess Ino gave to Odysseus to bear him up in the sea." They looked at each other. Clinton shook his head. Dade said, "Well, that's about the only thing around here I can find that's turned up missing." Clinton got to his feet. Dade walked him to the door. Dade half-closed his eyes, his lips pursed. Then he said, "I've seen that gold mask of Agamemnon. You seen it?"

"Yes. In the Athens Museum."

"Quite a piece of work, as death masks go." Dade showed him to the door. "Your son get through to you?"

"Pardon me?"

Dade took out his notebook and pencil. "I just asked whether—"

"No, he didn't, as a matter of fact." Clinton looked somewhat taken aback at Dade's question. Then he left abruptly, banging the door closed behind him.

After Clinton had gone, Luisa came into the hall to tell Dade that the *señora* had gone out the back door and was in the garden next door, talking with a neighbor. Thanking her, Dade left the house.

Outside, he saw Ellen in conversation with an old woman in a bonnet and a long dress, who stood in front of the house next door to the Van Damms' at the end of the cul-de-sac. Dade nodded to both of them. After turning and saying something to the old woman, Ellen came across the lawn to Dade.

"Come on," he said.

"Where?" He took out Paul's keys, jingling them and telling her he was going over to Paul's office on campus for a few minutes. She said, "Let me finish talking with her. You come back for me."

He glanced over her shoulder at the waiting figure of the elderly, bonneted woman standing in her doorway. Nodding and smiling in her direction, he said under his breath, "Who's Barbara Fritchie?"

"A Mrs. Ogilvy."

The name rang a bell. "You onto something?"

"Oh, boy!"

"Good?"

"As gold!" she whispered. "Tell you later." She turned and made her way back toward the old woman. Dade went down the path to his car and drove away. He thought again of the gold death mask of Agamemnon. Someone had described the expression on the face as horror-struck.

XI

Arriving on campus, Dade made his way on past the Research Library to the adjacent building in front of the Sculpture Garden, Bunche Hall. It was a thin glass oblong which the students called "the waffle building" because of the extruded squares of its symmetrically placed windows. He had to admit that he liked the Los Angeles campus. Paul had liked it, too, at the same time disparaging the mother campus of the university at Berkeley, once remarking that the new buildings there didn't have to be cheap, they only had to look cheap. He had gestured at a building which housed Mechanical Engineering. Four stories high and with a shed roof, the whole thing appeared to be made out of sheet metal. Paul had said, with a malicious gleam in his eye, "Of course, this is not a proper view of it—if, indeed, anything is!"

A posted guide in the lobby of Bunche Hall listed the names of those who had offices there and gave their room numbers. Paul's was 1602. Dade took the elevator up to the sixteenth floor, walked down the corridor to Paul's office and tried the door. It was locked. Scanning the hall to make sure it was empty and at the same time listening for the slow tread of a janitor, Dade took out Paul's keys, then stooped down and squinted at the lock. It was a Schlage. Finding the Schlage in his pocket, he opened the door easily. Stepping into the small, crowded office, he closed the door behind him.

The walls were lined with books and there were cartons filled with more books and with publications and papers on the floor. Paul's room contained a desk and two chairs.

The other of Paul's keys which he had taken fitted into a keyhole in the top drawer of the desk and, when that was unlocked, all the drawers were unlocked as well. Dade opened the top drawer of the desk. In it were personal things, ungraded bluebooks, clips, pencils, pads of paper, and a handful of letters. He searched everywhere for a draft of Paul's article on Schliemann. He could not find it. Rapidly, he went through all the drawers in the desk a second time. Everything was in perfect order, labeled, tagged and filed in manila folders. The only envelopes he found contained personal letters written by others to Paul. The postmarks were fairly recent. The contents of the letters was social, innocuous. Dade surmised that the letters had been kept there because they had not yet been answered. There was also an address book. Dade leafed through it, glancing at telephone numbers. When he found 555-6127, he looked to see the name of the garage. But the number did not belong to a garage. The name opposite that number was Professor Harry Slaughter. Dade picked up a pencil and tapped it against his teeth. All the other drawers were filled with files on Paul's research, together with tabs on each folder indicating the date and place in which articles on given subjects had been published.

He sighed, sitting back in Paul's chair. Had the police found it? No. It would have been mentioned in the report and the supplement he had been given said nothing about anything of the sort. Who had taken it? In the back of his mind, he began to imagine a dialogue: Is the department secretary in? My name is James Clinton. Professor Van Damm was to leave the draft of an article in his desk for me. Would you see if it's there? Oh, thank you! Thank you very much! But then why mention it? Because someone else was bound to mention his having asked. He could then later say, Oh yes, I asked! Didn't I tell you? And it wasn't there! But there were other dialogues

Dade could invent. Sighing again, he raked his fingers through his thick white hair.

Paul's chair had its back to the window, which gave onto the sculpture garden below. He could see the thickset nude by Rodin. On the other side of Paul's desk was the visitor's chair. The appointments were modest. He remembered once asking Paul to compare the budget for Classics with that of Physics. Paul had thought for a moment and then answered, "About twenty to one." Classics was a poor relative, almost an almsman. As Dade said the word under his breath, his face lit up, and, taking out his little notebook and pencil, he wrote down the word, chortling as he whispered to himself, "Giver; receiver! Hah!" Putting his notebook and pencil back in his pocket, he glanced at a corkboard next to the window. It had scraps of paper thumbtacked to it. They were for the most part notices about lectures to be given and plays to be performed. There was also a wall calendar pinned to it with detailed penciled notes for appointments in the squares of the dates. Paul had noted the date of their departure for Athens. Dade looked at the dates following their return. There was no reference to any faculty meeting. On the square for Tuesday, the day after Paul's return, Dade read, "Delta: 11:30." Picking up a telephone, he called Delta Airlines and was told that they did indeed have a flight at 11:30 a.m. from LAX to Tucson. Dade put down the phone, muttering, "Thank you."

He continued searching. Nothing he found suggested anything out of the ordinary. In one drawer, he found a journal which Paul had been keeping. The last entry, made just the day before Paul and Sophie had left on their trip to Greece, read: "Nimbus or halo. Reported everywhere. Seems to require some sort of mysterious collaboration between one who has it and one who sees it. The mark of a god or goddess or perhaps the gift of one. Could that be what it represented? Ask Dónal when I see him."

Dade had been reading by the light of the westering sun, but now that it had dipped behind the high buildings of the campus dormitories, he reached out a hand to switch on the desk lamp. Before he could touch it, he heard the sound of a key in the lock of the door. Then the door opened and the man he remembered spilling wine on him at the gathering at Sophie's started to enter the office. The man stopped in his tracks, surprised by the sight of Dade.

"I'm sorry," the man said. "I didn't know that anyone—" He broke off, looking around the small office. He was a man in his forties, deeply tanned. He wore dark blue running shorts and a T-shirt. He had the physique of a man who worked out all the time. His thick hair was sun-bleached and his greenish eyes peered out at Dade from deep sockets set in an angular face. His expression changed. Pointing a finger at Dade, he said, "I know you." He looked at Dade challengingly, as if waiting for some explanation as to what he was doing there.

Not answering, Dade crossed the room to the door, closed it and, turning around, said, "We haven't met. We saw one another today. My name's Cooley. Dade Cooley." They shook hands. "What's yours?"

The man seemed to hesitate for a fraction of a second. Then he said, "Aren't you—? I mean, didn't I just hear that—?"

"I'm representing the boy. Is that what you're asking me?"

The man nodded. "I thought it was you. I heard your name on the news." Dade remembered Ellen referring to him by name. The man held out his hand. He said, "I'm Harry Slaughter."

"You know the boy?"

"I've never met him."

Dade looked at him steadily for a moment, not saying anything. Then, crossing back to the other side of the desk, he inquired, "Well, now that you're here, what can I do for you?"

Slaughter raised a hand. "Don't let me disturb you."

"I'm finished."

"Oh. Good enough. Well, it was nice meeting you." Slaughter stood aside, waiting for Dade to leave the room. Instead, Dade seated himself behind Paul's desk.

"I've just been through all his things. If you'll tell me what you're looking for, maybe I can help you."

"It's all right."

"See, I got to lock the desk up the way I found it, before I go, but if you want to look for something first—"

"I said, it's all right."

"You mean you have a key to the desk as well as one to the office?"

Spots of anger reddened Harry Slaughter's cheeks. "I don't know where the hell you get off, making a remark like that!"

"Didn't mean to fire you up like that," Dade said innocently.

"For your information, I came in here because I'm missing a box of slides from the Santorini dig."

"Ah, the lost Atlantis."

"Well, if you go in for popular fiction—"

"Plato believed in it. Hard to argue with Plato. Sorry. Didn't mean to interrupt you. You say you're missing some slides?"

"I had brought them in here to show Paul just before he took off for Greece and when I couldn't find them, I thought I might have left them on his desk."

"And you didn't miss them until two and a half weeks later, is that what you're saying?"

"I've been away myself! I don't know why I owe you any explanation but just to set the record straight, I was in Santorini myself and I just got back the day before Paul or else I—"

"There are no slides here."

"Oh. Well, all right, then. Thanks anyway."

Dade turned, squinting out the window at the long shadows in the garden below. He could see boys and girls in shorts coming out of the Research Library and walking hand in hand, books under their arms. Slaughter was turning away to leave the office when Dade stopped him with a question. "How come you didn't ask Paul about your slides when he got back? When you went to see him, I mean?"

"I hadn't realized they were missing then." It was a perfectly reasonable answer, marred only by the dead air of the pause before he replied.

"You mind telling me what you went to see him for when he got back?"

"Just what business is that of yours?"

"A moment's reflection will give you the answer to that." Dade narrowed his eyes. "Listen here. My client is accused of murdering a man you went to see shortly before his death. You may know something you don't know you know, something of help. I'd like you to answer a few questions for me."

Slaughter hesitated, then picked up a chair in front of him, swung it around and sat astride it, resting his crossed forearms on the backrest.

"What do you want to know?"

"Why you went to see him."

"To tell him about a change in a faculty meeting."

"What faculty meeting?"

"It was something scheduled for the next day and I found out it had been postponed."

"You could have telephoned."

"The line was busy."

"Is that so?"

"Yes."

"Well, you could have left a note on the office door here."

"It was easier to stop by the place. It was right on my way. And I wanted to see him. Welcome him back. You know."

"Tell me about the faculty meeting."

"A faculty meeting! What difference does it make?"

Pointing at the calendar on the corkboard, Dade said, "No mention of any such meeting up there. He didn't seem to know about it, Paul didn't. The police didn't pick up on that. But they will, with a little prodding. Now, tell me again why you went to see him."

The greenish eyes were open a fraction too wide and Slaughter was breathing harder, trying at the same time not to show it by keeping his jaw clenched, but the nostrils flared and the chest heaved.

"How would I know what he did and didn't know! I went to tell him in case he *was* going!"

Dade said very softly, "If you can't produce a faculty meeting called for that date and then postponed, one to which both of you were invited, you'll as good as nail yourself as a man who lied to the police, can't you see that?" Then, when Slaughter turned his head away and stared at the wall, not answering, Dade said, "You didn't call *him*."

"I've already told you—"

"You told me a flat-out lie. He called *you*." Dade's eyes bored into him, waiting for some response.

Finally, Slaughter turned, facing him again, and said, "Who says?"

"I happen to know he did and I can prove it. He called *you*—called you repeatedly until he reached you—and you went there because he wanted to see you, isn't that the case? And it is a little surprising to me to find you coming in with a key I'm not at all sure you have any business having in your possession." Slaughter was looking at him with his mouth open slightly, his eyes fixed on Dade as if trying to read in his face how much he really did know. Slaughter looked away. On his left hand, he wore a gold signet ring. It was badly scratched and bent out of shape and Dade guessed it was something he had unearthed in his excavating. Slowly, using the thumb and forefinger of his right hand, he began to rotate the ring. It crossed Dade's mind that he was wearing it on his fourth finger, where a man wears a wedding ring and, at the same time, he remembered that the address book had listed his name as Professor Harry Slaughter, with no mention of a wife.

Finally, Slaughter nodded and said, "Paul gave me a set of keys because he has some rare books out on semester loan that I want to consult from time to time. It's as simple as that." Harry Slaughter gave him a sudden, disarming smile. He looked at Dade confidently, a gleam in his eyes now, the smile even wider. He scratched the blond hairs on his muscular forearm with a calloused, sunburned hand. It was as if whatever had come between them was now dissipated and they were free to be friends, to share jokes. "No, I didn't go to see him about a meeting. I just said that because I had to give some reason and I never thought anybody would question something like that. In this place, you spend half your time going to meetings or trying to get out of them. What I'm about to tell you has nothing whatever to do with any of this, as I'm sure you'll see, and I'd appreciate it if you just kept it to yourself, is that okay?"

When Dade said nothing but only continued to look at him steadily, Slaughter held off saying anything more for a moment or two and then went on: "There's a student works here, cataloguing and the like, for minimum wages. Paul had a falling-out with her on the day before he went away and was going to see about having her fired—he couldn't fire her himself because she doesn't work for him, she works for the department—but there wasn't time before he went away, so he was going to take care of it as soon as he got back. I knew he meant it, he was really ticked off, and what did he do as soon as he got back but ring me up to ask me if I'd gotten rid of her and I went over to ask him to back off. I'd have let it go at that except that he'd already rung up the department secretary to find out whether she'd been let go."

"She needs the work, that the idea?"

"Well—yes, that, and the fact that nobody likes to have something like that on her record."

"Um." Dade sat back in Paul's swivel chair, puckering up his lips as if he were about to whistle, at the same time opening his eyes wide and continuing to stare at Harry Slaughter. Then, looking suddenly serious, Dade leaned abruptly forward in his chair and said to him, "Tell me something frankly: do I look like a horse's ass to you?"

"I don't understand."

"I was just wondering what put it in your head to treat me like one." Slaughter blinked, taken aback. Dade rubbed the tip of his nose with a reflective forefinger, then leaned across the desk and said to Slaughter, "How old is she?"

"I don't know how old she is. All I know is, she has a job here!"

"Undergraduate, is she?"

"She's—I believe she's taking a course here, extension, I think. She's a very bright young lady."

"In school?"

"Look—"

"High school?"

"Yes, as a matter of fact." His voice was calm but his face had lost some of its color.

Dade said, "And how did you come to know about Paul's intentions?"

"What are you talking about?"

"He just walked up to you on the day he was leaving and said, 'I don't like that girl. Get rid of her.' Is that what happened?"

"Something like that."

Dade leaned on his elbows and put the tips of his fingers together. "I'm going to make me a little guess. He told you to get rid of her because he caught the two of you together."

"Go to hell." The eyes hardened.

Dade said quietly, "You have the key to this place. My guess is, you brought her here. You sure as hell couldn't have risked bringing her to your own office and locking that door. But nobody would come knocking on *this* door because Paul was away. Let's see, now. He must have walked in on you—most likely because he'd come back for something he'd forgotten—and he would have put an end to her services there and then, except that he had a plane to catch— so he asked you to do it. Ordered you to, isn't that right?"

Slaughter jumped to his feet, his face darkening with anger. "You God damn well better be able to back up accusations like that before going on record with them, or I'm warning you—!"

Dade rose and walked around the desk, then stood in front of him. "Paul could have made trouble for you. Let's see now. What would he have said?" Dade squinted. "He would have said, 'I'll give you one last chance. Have her turn in her resignation.' But she didn't, did she? Why not?"

Slaughter slammed his fist down hard on the desk, turning away in frustration. "That's enough!"

"Answer me or I'll have her to answer me in court, right there in front of God and everybody. Why not?"

Slaughter exhaled noisily through his nose. "Okay," he said. "Okay."

"Why not?"

"The usual reason."

"You mean she's in love with you, that it?"

"Well, it's happened before."

"Yes, but any girl who's taking extension courses and working for the Classics Department while she's still a kid in high school is no dummy. She knows damn well the trouble Paul could have made for you. Now, just why wouldn't a thing like that worry her?"

Slaughter made a helpless, shrugging gesture. "If I knew the answer to that—"

"Maybe I do." Dade eyed the ring on Slaughter's left hand. "She wouldn't worry if she thought you were going to get married." Dade studied him. "Is that what you told her? Is that what she thinks?"

Slaughter sat back down on his chair and put his elbows on the backrest, digging his fingers into his thick, sun-bleached hair. Finally, he nodded. Then he looked up at Dade, his face suddenly haggard. "I tried to stop but I couldn't. She was the one who always initiated it. Nobody would believe me but it's true. She's not what you'd call a kid."

"How old is she?"

"She's—quite mature."

"How old?"

"Sixteen."

"I didn't hear you."

"Fourteen," he said finally. He put a hand to his forehead, as if shading his eyes.

"That's why you went to see him."

"I had to go."

"What did he say?"

Harry Slaughter took his hand away and looked up at Dade. He opened his mouth to speak and then, as if he had thought better of what he was going to say, he got to his feet and, turning away, walked up and down the small office, hands thrust into the shallow pockets of his running shorts. Then, looking up, Slaughter said, "He was understanding."

"Was he?"

"Yes."

"Didn't he want to know why you hadn't gotten rid of her?"

Slaughter turned toward him, hands outspread. "I told him I was trying to get rid of her but that it wasn't easy, that I needed time. I said to him, 'Christ, you know what the press will do with a thing like this.' We get money for a lot of our expeditions from religious institutions, places full of nuts who'll ante up if you'll just tell them you've got a line on the whereabouts of the Ark on Ararat or some such shit, but something like this would cut me off at the knees. I said to him, 'Paul, *please*—' "

"You just told me he understood."

"Yeah. Yeah, sure I did. But that was at the beginning, when I was first explaining my situation to him—"

"So that was that? You saw him, told him what your situation was and he agreed to back off, that what you're saying? Then why wouldn't he have called the department secretary back, saying he'd changed his mind? Obvious to me he damn well didn't or you wouldn't have told me one word of all this."

"All *right!* He wasn't understanding." Slaughter put his head in his hands.

Dade said, "Awhile back, you told me you'd appreciate it if I'd keep all this to myself. You remember that?"

"Yes." Slaughter looked at him, nodding.

"You also remember that I didn't answer you."

"What are you getting at?"

"If what you just told me is true, it's grounds for murder."

"Do you know what you're saying? Do you know what the Christ you're saying?"

"A man threatens to ruin another man's whole life. The other man goes to him and pleads for mercy. When the first man refuses—"

"He didn't refuse!"

"That's your story. One of many, I might add."

"You bastard."

"To resume: when the first man refuses, the other man shoots him."

"You've got it all wrong! I left hours before he was killed! There are witnesses!"

" 'Course you did! Which is exactly what you'd have done if you meant to come back, after dark, say—"

Slaughter was staring at him, incredulous, his eyes wide, his breathing hard. "You're crazy."

Dade looked at him in silence, nodding to himself. Then Dade said, his eyes going to the office keys in Slaughter's hand, "I have me a little guess as to what you came here for. That draft article Paul was planning to publish on Schliemann." Slaughter continued to meet Dade's eyes with no change in his expression but Dade watched all the color run out of his face. Dade said softly, "But you're too late. Somebody else has already beaten you to it."

Slaughter stood there motionless, the eyes open a fraction too wide, a muscle twitching in his cheek. Dade said, "Then again, maybe you're the somebody else. Maybe you already came by and collected it and now plan to publish it, thinking that what would have made Paul world-famous will do the same for you. Of course, that won't work without the proof. The proof he brought back. You show up with the proof and you've as good as signed your death warrant." Out of the corner of his eye, Dade saw Slaughter's hands tighten into fists. Dade's eyes bored into him. Then, turning suddenly, Slaughter wrenched open the door and slammed out of the office.

Dade locked up the desk and the office and, going back downstairs, walked through the twilight, past the outdoor tables of the student cafeteria, all of them crowded with students oblivious of his presence, books open before them as they hurried through dinner. At the ramp, he turned and took a last look at Paul's sixteenth-floor window.

"We'll find out," he said. "Son of a gun." Then he hurried up to the parking structure, got in his car and went back to the Helenas to collect Ellen.

When he got back to the 25th Helena, Dade drove down into the
cul-de-sac and saw Sophie's car parked in front of her house. On
impulse, he rang her doorbell. After a few moments, Luisa opened
the door. Her eyes looked out at him from her delicate, haggard face.

"*Señor Cooley,*" she said.

"*¿Está en casa, la señora?*"

Nodding, she opened the door wider, then showed him into the
sitting room. He went over and stood at the windows to the left of
the fireplace. Behind him, he heard the sound of Luisa's footsteps
echoing as she climbed the tile stairs. He stood looking out at the
garden for a long time.

Then a voice said, "Dade." He turned. Sophie was standing in the
doorway. She wore beige lounging pajamas of raw silk. The sleeves
were very full, cut like big triangles with the wide end at the wrist.
Her right arm hung at her side and her left arm was extended, the
hand flat against the jamb, the long sleeve hanging straight down,
motionless. She still wore her dark glasses. "Dade," she said, "let me
fix you a drink." She moved to a table with a tray of bottles. "Bourbon, isn't it?"

He nodded. "How come you remember?"

She shrugged. "I guess it's the theater. You learn to remember

things. Even when you don't want to remember, you can't help yourself. Somebody told me that once about Dylan Thomas. That he couldn't stop thinking about words, that he kept hearing them, even in his sleep, like a dripping faucet, and that that was the real reason that he drank, to make it stop. I remember too much. There are lots of things I wish I didn't remember." She had poured herself an ouzo and water and now came toward him, holding out his glass. She spilled a few drops and then said, as if she had done it deliberately, "For the gods."

"Sorry for barging in. See, I've got this question I wanted to ask you earlier, and when I saw your car—"

Interrupting him, she said softly, "I wasn't here earlier because I was out seeing your client." She looked at him without expression. "Yes, I heard. My husband is killed by a boy who works for us and you suddenly appear to defend him. Why?"

Not replying, he drank some of his bourbon, then set down his glass. "How come?" he asked. "That you went to see him?"

"I had to know why. Paul was good to him. And I thought, for some crazy reason, that—well, that Manuel would talk to me. Would tell me what happened."

"What did he say?"

"Nothing." She shook her head slowly, as if at a loss. "He didn't even want to see me."

"They told you that?"

"Yes."

"I don't understand. If he didn't want to see you, he didn't have to. A prisoner has a right to refuse to see visitors. How did you get to talk to him?" He stared at her. She turned away. When he continued to look at her steadily, she made a little gesture of surrender.

"I said to the policeman, 'He killed my husband and I want to see him. I want to look at him. And I want him to look at me. If he has anything to say to me, I want him to have the chance to say it now.'" She lifted her head slowly, meeting Dade's. "He knew what I was feeling, the policeman did. And so he sent for a woman to search me and then they took my purse away and after that, I was shown into a little room with heavy screens on the windows and nothing

but a table and chairs and after a little while, they brought him in through a rear door. I looked at him. He did not meet my eyes. I went over to him. He still did not look at me. I said, 'What happened? Isn't there anything you can tell me?' And when he wouldn't look at me, wouldn't even speak to me, I began to cry, not out of grief but just out of frustration." She put her head in her hands for a moment. Then she lifted her head again. "I begged him to tell me why he had killed Paul and he wouldn't even look at me! He wouldn't speak to me! Finally, I gave up. I went to the door and rang the buzzer. A guard came and took Manuel away and someone else opened the door and let me out." She shrugged. "Maybe he will talk to you. He won't talk to me."

"I see."

"I was good to him. I didn't say anything cruel. I just wanted to give him a chance to explain. After all, he killed my husband."

"Did he?"

Suddenly, she raised her voice. "He didn't deny it!" She took a step toward him and said, "If he didn't kill him isn't that the first thing he'd say to me? But *he didn't say anything!* Dade, he wouldn't even look at me!"

"About that question I came here to ask you."

"What is it?"

"I'd like a description of that costume jewelry."

"Of what?"

"The *kraydemnon*."

"Oh, that!" Her face cleared. "For goodness' sake, it's nothing. Just something I wear to keep my hair down. It does the same thing as a hairnet." He thought, "veil," "hairnet." Comes to the same thing, he told himself. That must be the connection, the reason the dresser had used that word. Nothing. "You know," Sophie went on, "we perform out of doors and if there's a sudden gust of wind and your hair goes flying, well, for some reason that's terribly distracting for an audience and so I wear something to keep that from happening."

"What?"

"A sort of heavy mesh veil."

"Gold?"

"Fake."

"Has Manuel ever seen it? I mean, could he have?"

"I don't know."

"Let's say, for the moment, that the police could be right. That Manuel did see it and then killed Paul for it. Tell me this much: what was there about it that would make Manuel think it was valuable? What would have made him grab it and run with it?"

"I can't imagine."

"Nothing a young man would kill his benefactor for, is that what you're saying?"

"I don't know why he killed him." She put out a hand, leaning on a chair back. Her shoulders sagged. "I don't know anything any more."

He said goodnight, letting himself out. He heard the oiled click of a dead bolt sliding into place.

XIII

Ellen waved to him from the car. He hurried to it, getting in beside her. "Why wait out here?" he said. "I mean, why didn't you come in?"

"When I saw Sophie drive up, I was about to come over and then I saw you arrive and I thought I'd better leave you alone with her. I just stayed at Mrs. Ogilvy's."

"You were over there a long time."

"I found what she had to say so engrossing, I decided to accept her kind invitation to visit even longer."

"Mrs. Ogilvy?" The woman's name was familiar. As he turned down Carmelina, he said, "Where's the Greek place?"

"Downtown."

He drove back down to Sunset and headed east. Then, he remembered where he had heard the name. She was the woman who had said Sophie and Paul were having a fight. "You find out from Luisa about those quarrels?"

She nodded. "I just said it was a pity that a neighbor who overheard the *señora* and her husband going over the lines for her next play should have misunderstood and told the police they were quarreling."

"And she said?"

"Luisa told me, they never quarreled. She said she tried to tell that to the police but they reminded her that she wasn't there that night."

"Where was she?"

"At home. She wasn't due in until the next morning."

"And then after they came and arrested her son, she still reported for work?"

"Yes. She says Sophie couldn't have been kinder to her. Sophie even insisted Luisa stay there with her—at least for now."

"Sounds like she's watching her."

"Sounds like who's watching whom?"

"Take your choice."

"I think you are awful!"

" 'Awful!' Impressive, ugly."

"Oh, is slang allowed?"

"Spoilsport!"

"Incidentally, that's what Charles II said about St. Paul's. I was going to tell you once but you never let me finish. He described it as 'awful, appalling and terrible.' "

"Okay, no awful. Speaking of words, let's get back to 'engrossing.' "

"What?"

He turned onto the San Diego Freeway and headed south. "You told me that lady's conversation was engrossing. You question her?"

"I did no such thing. People like Mrs. Ogilvy are very quick about that sort of thing and don't like it. I wouldn't dream of questioning Mrs. Ogilvy. What happened is this. After Luisa and I returned, I looked out and saw the lady putting out snail-bait in her front garden, so I took my leave of Luisa and when I went outside, I stopped to admire her Lady apple. It's espaliered on her brick wall and I told her how much I liked it. We introduced ourselves. We then spoke of apples, of the Seed Savers Exchange, of which she also happens to be a member and of how we both long to grow that thousand-year-old Hopi blue corn. She invited me in, hopping on upstairs ahead of me, leaning on her crutch, most agile, despite her handicap."

"Handicap! Hold the wheel!" Taking out his notebook and pencil, Dade said, "Handicap: advantage, disadvantage!"

"Bully."

"Pray continue." He took back the wheel.

"Well, afterward, when I alluded to what had happened to Professor Van Damm, saying how frightful it all was, she agreed."

"She mention the argument she claims to have overheard?"

"She told me she'd read that Sophie was supposed to be going over her lines for *Medea*. Then she said, 'Must be some new translation that's come out, unfamiliar to me.'"

"Then she heard what they said?"

"Only the swearwords, which she said she had no recollection of hearing Judith Anderson use when she played the role."

"Judas Priest! So they were having a fight!" Dade let out a shout of laughter.

"She said that she knew a thing or two. She looked at me and said, 'I see what goes on. Now, we'll say no more about it.' So we didn't. For at least half an hour. I did learn that she watches everything that goes on around her. Mrs. Ogilvy is what, in my youth, we called a curtain-peeper. When I looked up at her house, I saw that in her second-story bedroom, she had her television set placed next to a window, with an armchair in front of it, thus enabling her to watch two shows at once, so to speak."

He made the loop at the interchange, now going east on the Santa Monica Freeway. He headed toward the center of downtown Los Angeles, its tall buildings visible in the haze of a late autumn afternoon. "Well, what did she tell you, finally?"

"First, she said it was a pity that we had come there to pay a call when Mrs. Van Damm was out and was my husband just going to wait over there for her to return or would he like to join the two of us in a glass of Madeira?"

"Translation: what's he up to?"

"I said we were friends and that you were an attorney who had gone over there to be of help."

"Liar, liar, pants on fire—"

"I didn't say to whom. Well, then after you left, we sat in the bedroom. I think she was enjoying holding out on me, what with hints and thin smiles and subjects changed as often as little babies, so finally, when she happened to bring up the subject of 'the present generation,' I asked her straight out whether she found them as bad as they were painted and she answered, 'Not that their elders haven't given them a worse example,' then saying out of a clear blue sky that it wouldn't surprise her to find out that Mrs. Van Damm knew more than she was letting on about her husband's death, concupiscible woman that she was, and that's a word I've never heard anyone use."

"She said *what?*" Dade said.

"She told me that on nights when the professor would have Manuel drive him off to Wednesday faculty meetings—"

"How did she know where he was going?"

"The front door would open and there would be the professor and Mrs. Van Damm, he would say he would try not to be too late and ask her not to wait up for him and then she would kiss him goodnight and go back inside. Then after a while, she'd see the figure of a man coming up that narrow path at the side between the house and the hedge. I stole a look myself, when she was out getting more Madeira, and I will say, with considerable effort, Mrs. Ogilvy could lean out her bedroom window and catch a glimpse of Sophie's back door."

"Damn lucky the old beldam didn't fall out the window and break her neck."

"Lucky for you. Because otherwise I wouldn't be able to report that this man would then knock and be let in through the back door, the lights being turned off first."

"And Mrs. Ogilvy could see all that in the pitch dark?"

"That's what she told me."

"Old lady must have eyes like a buzzard. Never found out who the gentleman caller was, I take it?"

"Oh yes."

"Who?"

"I saved best for last."

"All right."

"One night—perhaps in her haste, Mrs. Ogilvy surmised in an

arch aside—Sophie neglected to turn out the light before opening the door and that's when Mrs. Ogilvy caught sight of the visitor's face."

"Who was it?"

"Manuel."

"Son of a bitch!" He changed lanes abruptly, aiming at an off-ramp.

"Where are you going? This isn't the way."

"It is now. We're going down to the jail. This puts a whole new light on things. That little sneak held out on me and if I don't get me a damn good reason why, he gets a new lawyer."

At the Criminal Courts Building, he went toward the elevator, saying, "I'm going to kick me some butt. Then we'll have us our dinner."

Shown into the same room as before, Dade waited, hands plunged into his pockets, eyes half-closed. The fluorescent lights in the ceiling were harsh. The air conditioning was not working properly and the room was hot.

"Any visitors since his mother was here to see him earlier?" Dade asked the guard. Seeing the man hesitate, Dade said, "I know about the lady. I won't mention it. Anybody else?"

The guard shook his head. "Nobody," he said, scarcely moving his lips.

"Any phone calls?"

"Nope."

When Manuel was shown in, Dade eyed him in silence. After the guard had left them alone, banging the door shut behind him, Dade still said nothing, only letting the silence stretch out until finally, Manuel said, "What do you want from me, Mr. Cooley?"

"The truth."

"Everything I told you was the truth. No way I can make you believe it, if you don't want to."

Indicating that Manuel was to sit down, Dade seated himself and, after a few moments of hesitation, Manuel did the same.

"You told me you called the house around seven."

"Yes, sir."

Dade measured his words, his voice hard. "I'm going to suggest that you rang up the house to talk to Mrs. Van Damm. You hoped she'd answer the phone herself and when Professor Van Damm answered instead, you pretended you were calling up to see if he wanted anything. When he said he wanted to see you at eight-thirty that night, you knew from his tone that something was damn well wrong, and you didn't want to go see him but had to."

"That's not true, sir." Manuel had half-risen to his feet in protest. His face was pale.

"Sit down." Dade waited until Manuel was seated again and then said sharply, his voice cracking the air like a whip, "I put it to you that when you showed up at the house, Professor Van Damm threatened you. That he had a gun in his hand."

"Man, what are you talking about?"

"I know! He wasn't that kind of man! That's what you were going to say, isn't it? But anybody turns into that kind of man when he's pushed too far. You want me to tell you a secret about the world? Little scaredy-cat animals, they run for their lives when a predator's chasing them—but that predator can only get so close before something real surprising happens: when pursued, there is a precise and measurable distance at which any animal will turn and fight. I put it to you that he was in a fury, having found out what kind of games you were playing behind his back. What he was planning to do was shoot you right then and there and then call the police and say he thought that you were an intruder who had broken in!"

"No!"

"You expect me to believe you just sort of dropped in at almost exactly the same moment he was killed?"

"I didn't drop in, he sent for me!"

"But you can't prove that, can you?" Dade countered softly.

"No, sir."

"You bet you can't, because James Clinton, he didn't have any appointment with him that night at all!"

"But the professor, he told me—!"

"You went there, he met you with a gun, he was going to kill you,

you tried to run away from him, he was blocking the way to the stairs so you ran the opposite way, toward his wife's bedroom—you told me you'd seen lights on in there—for all I know, you thought she was home—and when he ran after you, brandishing that gun, you struggled with him, you got the gun away from him and then you shot him yourself, and after that you grabbed that jewelry you saw, so it would look like he'd been killed by some burglar he'd surprised, and then you ran downstairs and out of the house just as you heard Mrs. Van Damm coming in the front door. That's what happened, isn't it?"

"Sir, I swear to God—"

Jumping to his feet, Dade went around to the boy and stood in front of him. "Listen to me," Dade said. "If he threatened you with a gun—his own gun, the police have established that—and the gun went off when you were struggling with it, or if you took the gun away from him, and, when he still came after you, you were afraid and shot him in what seemed to you self-defense, the time to tell me is now! Because, you tell me a thing like that, I damn well think I can get you off! At least get the charge reduced to involuntary man-slaughter, if not self-defense!"

Breathing hard, Manuel backed away from him. "I didn't do it! I didn't and ain't no way anybody's going to make me say I did! That's all these people here want, is for me to make up some story more like what it is they want to believe and never mind what I say happened with the professor, who was like a friend to me, and not trying to kill me. If they think that, they're crazy. I told you the truth. Take it or leave it, Mr. Cooley, it's all I got." The dark eyes were riveted on him, the boy's mouth was open slightly and his breathing was shallow and rapid.

"What is it, you trying to pretend you don't know why he'd do such a thing? The district attorney will give the jury the answer to that one: he found out you were sleeping with his wife! You were, weren't you?"

Manuel turned slowly toward him, his face expressionless. Finally, Manuel spoke. "The lady, she tell you that?"

"I asked *you*." Manuel said nothing. At length Dade said, "Are you going to answer me or not?" The boy shook his head, eyes on the floor. Dade took a step forward and said to Manuel with a note of urgency in his voice, "Look, son, the police, they don't know about it yet but they'll sure as hell find it out, just the same way I did, and when they do, they're going to come to roughly the same conclusion as I did—excepting that they're going to argue that you went there because he had threatened to make trouble for you and you knew he could, you saw your chance, and killed him not in self-defense but in cold blood and then grabbed something and ran off with it to make them think the motive was robbery."

"It's not true!"

"It's a good line of attack. And one I think they'll use. Then, when I try to argue self-defense, they'll turn around and say, If that's true, why didn't he come forward at the time? Or why didn't he break down and admit it before the arraignment? I'm trying to tell you that if that's what happened, the time to plead self-defense is now. Otherwise—"

Manuel stared back at him, immobile. There was a kind of Indian dignity in his bearing. The face had the look of something carved from mahogany. It had a sheen, as if it had been polished afterward. "There's no otherwise, mister," he said. "I told you the truth."

"With certain omissions. Anything else you're holding out on me?" He waited. Manuel made no answer but only looked down at the floor, his jaw tightening. "I'll see you in court tomorrow morning," Dade said.

Ellen was waiting in the marble lobby, sitting on a bench next to the newsstand and reading the *Los Angeles Times*. Seeing Dade get out of the elevator, she rose and went toward him. He offered her his arm and they walked out of the building together. The heat had lessened a little. They went at an angle down the long flight of steps.

Dade said, hands in his pockets, "You know something that bothers me about Sophie's story? Most people are unfamiliar with the sound of a firearm being discharged and don't recognize it. Case in point: a man and his wife were asleep in bed when an intruder entered and she was raped at gunpoint. She submitted, in fear of her life and to save her husband's as well, unaware that he wasn't lying there asleep, he was lying there dead, a bullet in his brain. She said later when she found out what had happened, 'All I heard was a popping sound! I didn't know he'd been shot!'

"I'd like to know why Sophie was so damn sure of what she was hearing, especially from downstairs in the back of that long closet under the stairs. Manuel, he says he heard Paul cry out, 'Oh, no! Don't!' and then heard the gunshot and after that, the sound of a body falling. I have less trouble with that. Manuel's story has detail to support it. All Sophie tells us is, she walked in just in time to hear a shot and see Manuel run out of the house. Walked in from where?

From going off to the boonies on a drive that's a two-hour round trip after getting off a fifteen-hour flight, so she could consult the Sibyl of San Bernardino? Well, I'm going to have me a little chat with Mrs. Tinka Kanavarioti and if that story is phony, Sophie, she's as good as perjured herself, and me, I'm going to find out why."

They came to a public phone. Calling San Bernardino Information, he got the telephone number of Tinka Kanavarioti. He punched it out and the number of his telephone credit card as well, and then waited.

A woman answered the phone. Learning that she was Tinka Kanavarioti, he told her his name. Then, informing her that he was representing Manuel, he said, "I'd like to have a little chat with you before the arraignment tomorrow morning." He consulted his watch. "It's just after five. I can be there in an hour. Is that convenient?"

"You want come now?" she asked, surprised. She spoke with an accent that sounded Russian to him.

"As I indicated, I can be there by six. Will that be all right?"

"Well—" He heard the yielding note in her voice. Then she said, "You tell me please what this is all about?"

"The minute I get there." Dade put the receiver back on the hook, then turned away, hands behind his back, and squinted at the late light bouncing off the washboard of parked cars in an adjacent lot. "Rain check on that Greek dinner?"

"We'll have something sent in when you get back," Ellen said. "I'll take a cab to the hotel."

"Good girl." He escorted her to the stand in front of the city hall.

"What do you hope to find out?"

"Don't you see? It's all backwards. They're lovers, right? First thing you'd expect her to do is get hold of him and say, 'Tell me what happened!' "

"She did!"

"*Afterward.*" He squinted at her, shielding his eyes from the westering sun. "The first thing she did was tell the police about him."

"What choice did she have?"

"In her place, I would have sent for my doctor, had them tell the police I was prostrate and then stalled until I could talk to him. Hell, he was her lover! But she didn't do that, honey. She told them about him right off the bat. Why?" Ellen frowned, turning away from the glare of the yellow sun. Dade said, "Only one answer. She wanted to make sure they locked him up right away. Now, just why was that so important to her?"

XVI

Swinging east onto the Santa Monica Freeway, the sun reddening the windows of the tall buildings downtown, he settled back and turned on the radio for company. After a while, he heard the opening strains of a piano concerto. It's the Saint-Saëns, he told himself. The G-minor. He could not be sure. Now, with a vested interest in the outcome, he went on listening to it. Or was it Liszt? Huneker had written that, for Liszt, the keyboard was "spangled with scales," and, yes, this could be Liszt but it wasn't Liszt, it was Saint-Saëns, he was sure of it and they would just see. He drove, conducting the orchestra with one hand, following the soloist and helping the pianist out under his breath: puh-puh-puh-PUM . . . puh-puh-puh-PUM . . . puh-puh-puh-PUM . . . PUM . . . PUM . . .

Just before six, he came to the sign reading SAN BERNARDINO. Taking the first off-ramp, he pulled over onto a side street, parked and examined his map. Looking out through the windshield, he saw nothing familiar. Years before, it had been a pretty town. From here, the highway climbed up into the mountains to Arrowhead and Big Bear. At the turn of the century, private railroad cars had been brought here and put on sidings and then the opulent visitors had been taken on rides on narrow-gauge open-sided trains up into the mountains to play in the snow, in a day when skiing was something one thought of as being done by Lapps, if, indeed, one thought of it at all.

Arriving at Orange Show Road in San Bernardino, he followed the street up to Lapeer. The concerto ended with a brilliant cadenza. The announcer told him in a muted voice that it was the Saint-Saëns. "Son of a bitch," Dade said. It was a good omen and he liked that.

On the northwest corner was a 7-Eleven. He saw two pay phones outside on the wall and made a mental note to call Ellen from there, on his way back. The neighborhood was going downhill. Across from the 7-Eleven was a bleak laundromat with a vacant apartment above it with grimy windows.

No. 3158 Lapeer was in the middle of the block. A large plum tree grew in front of the house, its branches heavy with fruit. Dade got out of his car and started toward the stairs. A drape in the front room of the house moved.

He pressed the doorbell. After a moment or two, a small grill in the front door opened and a woman's face looked out at him. The eyes were dark, surmounted by bristling eyebrows beginning to turn gray. She looked out at him, not speaking. Greeting her, Dade took a card out of his pocket and held it up to the grill for her to see. "I represent Manuel Garcia," he said formally. "The boy accused of the murder of Professor Van Damm."

The door was yanked open. She gestured for him to enter. She was a stout woman and she wore a man's dark wool coat sweater and stockings rolled below the knee. Her feet were thrust into scuffs.

"Mrs. Kanavarioti?" he said.

"You come this way," she said. She led him from the small entrance alcove into a small sitting room where the curtains were drawn and no lights burned. Against one wall was a high brass daybed. Beside it was a small table holding a half-filled teacup and a plate of cookies. Books were stacked on the floor. They had Russian titles. Her accent and her books made him think she spoke Russian oftener than English. A fireplace had a pair of chairs placed stiffly on either side of it. In the center of the room was a high round table with a paisley cover that hung to the floor, which was in turn covered by a stained linen tablecloth. Drawn up to the table were a pair of carved Chinese armchairs. A cat mewed. It was a black-and-white cat and it lay curled on a pile of cushions on one of the armchairs. She motioned at the cat and said, "Go, go!" and then impatiently picked it up and set it down on a worn Oriental rug. She seated herself in the chair where the cat had been lying and indicated that Dade should make himself comfortable in the other chair. "You want some light?" she said. She reached out and pushed a button on the frayed cord of a lamp which hung over the table. The light went on. On a television set was a photograph in a silver frame of a handsome young man in his twenties. He wore the uniform of an American soldier. There was a boyish grin on his face.

Dade walked over, hands behind his back, and studied it. Then, crossing toward her, he sat down in the other armchair. "Is that your son?" he asked. She looked at him, not answering. "He favors you," Dade said. "That's what made me ask." She said nothing.

The cat jumped up into her lap. Stroking it, she crossed her ankles. The chair, with its many cushions, was too high for her and her feet did not touch the floor. "Excuse it, my appearance," she said finally, gesturing at herself. "A man calls up and says to me, 'If it's convenient' that he comes here in an hour and am I to be like a little doll for this whoever-he-is?" She made a moue and put her hands on either side of her face, thumbs outspread under her chin, her head a little on one side. Then, setting her mouth, she looked into Dade's face. "What is it you want, Mister Important Attorney?"

Dade leaned back in his chair, putting the tips of his fingers together, looking back at her. "Been in a fight," he said.

"Who has been in fight?"

"That cat," he said, pointing.

"Ah." She lifted her fat chin. "With a coyote, I think." She nodded. "We take their land. They are bolder now. I hear them. Early in the morning." She put a finger to her lips. "Sh. I look out. I see them. They are close to the house. Like the deer. The deer are close now. They eat up all the garden. But the coyotes, they eat the pets."

"Sounds like you knew this place back in the old days."

"Yes."

"You lived here a long time?"

She looked at him sharply. "What do you want from me?"

"Have the police been to see you yet?"

"Yes."

"Sophie Galanos told them she came to see you the night her husband was killed. Did you confirm her story?" The dark eyes looked up at him from under the beetling brows. "Was she here Monday evening between approximately six-thirty and seven-thirty?" She nodded slowly. "I'd like to know why."

"Is personal."

"You are a seeress, is that right?"

She gave him an elaborate shrug. "What is it, a seeress? They come to me, saying, 'What should I do?' I listen. I say this or that. Sometimes, I feel things." Resting an elbow on the arm of her chair, she lifted her small hand and pointed a finger at him. "That's what they come for. Because they think I sense what they don't sense. Who knows?"

"All I was getting at is, you're not a doctor or a lawyer or a priest. If you're asked that question in court, the answer, 'It's personal,' won't do. You have to answer!"

"Have to answer."

"Or a judge can hold you in contempt."

Her expression changed. Her eyes glinted as she flashed a look at him. "You think I don't know that? I know it. I'm telling *you* it was personal. I'm telling you as Paul's friend. I know you were friends. He told me about you."

"You knew him?"

"Sure, I know him a long time ago in Europe. Here, I don't see him so much. He don't drive and I don't go out much."

"You were friends?"

She smiled at him. "Yes," she said. She lifted the lid of a cloisonné box and offered him a cigarette. When he declined, she helped herself to one. There was a matching cloisonné box of matches on the table. He picked it up and pushed at the matchbox inside to open it. The matchbox together with its cover began to slide out and he could see the words "*spirti Helleniki*" printed on it in Greek letters. He lit her cigarette for her.

Putting the box back down on the table, he said, "If you were friends, you'll want to help me see that his murderer is brought to justice."

She leaned back in her chair, exhaling a great cloud of smoke, and answered, "Police know who kill Paul. The boy, he killed him."

"Do you know why they think so?"

She shrugged. "He steal something. A piece of junk but he think it worth something. Boys like that, what do they know?"

"Did you ever see the piece of costume jewelry they say he stole?"

She shook her head slowly, saying, "I don't go to it much in this country, to theater."

"Is the name *kraydemnon* at all familiar to you?"

"Is Greek."

"Yes."

She shook her head again. "I don't know anybody by such a name."

He nodded his thanks for her answer, then asked, "You acquainted with him, the boy?"

"No. I have seen him, is all."

"How do you mean?"

She lifted her shoulders. "He cleans the pool. He is gardener. He runs errands."

"And Sophie Galanos? What would you say her relationship with him is?"

"He works for her."

"Did you know they were having an affair?"

She made a face and put her cigarette down in a matching cloisonné ashtray. "So?"

"I mean, he wasn't just someone who worked for her, and I just wondered whether you knew that."

She said impatiently, "Here is not like in Europe. There, two people, they are having an affair. Sometimes, the people, they come from two different worlds." She put her hands apart on the surface of the table. "They make love." She clapped her small, plump hands together. "And when is over"—she put her hands back on the table, apart, as before—"each one goes back to where he come from. When a duchess is making love with the stable boy, he don't think he's a duke. When is over, he goes back to the stable, where he belong. Sophie, she know that. But I don't think your Manuel Garcia know it. And when he find out, is going to make him very angry, I think. Or maybe he is angry already, is that what you say?" Lifting her chin, she gave him a knowing look.

Dade said, "You think Paul knew?" She shrugged, turning down the corners of her mouth. "By the way, when did you meet my old friend Paul?"

She made a gesture, as if pushing something away. "Was long time ago."

Nodding at the picture of her son, Dade said, "When you looked like that?"

She shot him a surprised glance. Then she let out a single laugh, then a succession of laughs, now with a broad smile, showing the gap between her short front teeth. "You want me to tell it to you, my life story? I tell it and you will cry your eyes out! Listen! A long life and comes time to talk about it, you are telling all of it in few words!" She rocked back and forth on her mound of cushions, swinging her small feet, crossing and uncrossing them and toying with the scuffs. "Listen. The end of the war was coming. Everywhere are people running away. But where is away? Nobody knows any more. I get to Frankfurt, in Germany. The sky is black with smoke. Bombs everywhere. A girlfriend is with me. We are running for our lives across a bridge. It is day but it is like night because there is black smoke everywhere. Once, we look back and I see the whole city is burning and we are thinking, This is end of the world. Then, somehow, after the war ends, we get to Heidelberg."

She put the backs of her hands together and parted the air, like someone doing the breast stroke. "It was not bombed, you know, Heidelberg. You know what we saw? Windows. Everywhere windows." A plump hand described a curve in the air. "Blown glass windows from old times. None broken. We couldn't believe it. The Americans are there. They have jobs for people. All Russians know a few languages. I, too. I am only eighteen but I have been already at the Gymnasium and my father was teaching there. I think maybe they will give me some work. And they did." She laughed bitterly. "I was a scrubwoman. That's what I was good for. I clean for the officers, washing the floors in the BOQ where they live. I meet Paul. He is kind to me. It is Paul who introduces me to a man, a translator who is working for Americans, a Greek, a poet, a beautiful man, with hands like glass." She held up her hands to illustrate, in the fashion of a surgeon who has just come out of the scrub room. "I love him and when he ask me to marry, I say yes. We are very happy. I do not know how sick he is, that he is dying. Early one morning, I wake up and he is not in the bed. I look for him. I find him on the toilet. He is dead. I think, I can't let nobody see him like this. I try to move him. I can't do it. Excuse me, please." Struggling to get out of her chair, she went quickly out of the room, closing a door behind her. Dade got to his feet. After a few moments, the door opened and she came back into the room. Clasping her hands, she said, "Enough talk."

Dade took her hands in his. "Sit down," he said. "Please." He led her back to her chair. When she was settled in it again, she looked at him, red-eyed, and he pulled his own chair closer and, sitting on the edge of it, he took hold of her hands again and said, "Listen to me. I want to help you."

Stubbing out her cigarette, she took another and lit it, exhaling slowly. "What is it you come to me for?"

"To find out if Sophie Galanos is telling the truth."

"Listen to me something. Paul, he was good friend to me and friend after I lose Andreas. If his Sophie say she was here, she was here, you understand it?"

"If she wasn't here, you could be putting yourself in jeopardy. Do you understand that?"

She faced him, getting out of her chair and looking up at him defiantly. "I don't care!"

He pointed at the framed picture. "And that son of yours? If you get yourself into trouble, what's young Andreas over there or whatever his name is to think?"

"His name is Paul," she said. He met her eyes. She did not look away.

"Paul?" Dade turned, looking at the soldier's picture again.

He thought, What woman protects her successor?

"You go now. Please." Tinka Kanavarioti went to the front door and opened it for him. He took her hand and held it for a moment, then he went out the door and down the steps to his car. The sky was a dull orange. He could taste the smog in the air like grit between his teeth. He knew that when the sun set, no stars would come out. To see stars now, you had to go out in the country, down to Baja, say. He sighed, wishing he were going to Baja with Ellen. He drove slowly back to the freeway, saying under his breath, "What I want is a drink."

XVII

It was just after eight. He went to the bar and made martinis. Ellen said, "Will you please tell me what's been going on?"

"First, order dinner."

Picking up the telephone, she asked to be connected to Room Service and ordered them each half a dozen fresh oysters and then filets mignons and potatoes Anna, with a dish of petits pois and coleslaw salad and a Cabernet.

"I don't fancy cabbage."

"You need a brassica."

"I ever tell you the Romans brewed a cure-all sort of bathwater, so to speak—"

"Dade!"

"—with the help of them as had recently partaken of cabbage—"

"Are you quite finished?"

He opened his eyes very wide. "Cato's wife, they say, died of it."

"I will substitute broccoli for the petits pois—"

"What you choose to refer to as a brassica makes me flatulent."

"All right, *all right.*"

"Which reminds me, St. Augustine speaks of a man he knew who could break wind in tune."

Ignoring him, she glanced at the wine list. "Here's a Martha's Vineyard Cabernet from Heitz—no, we can't afford it."

"Get it."

"No!"

Dade reached out for the phone. "I'll get it."

"You'll also get to explain the bill to Rose." She found another wine and, ordering it, said, "You're going to be surprised." She put down the phone and over drinks, he told her what he had found at Sophie's and then what Clinton had told him about Paul's theory. When he finished, she said, bewildered, "What on earth kind of proof could Paul have had?"

"I thought I'd find the answer in Paul's office but I didn't. I did find this. At his house." He showed her the piece of paper he had taken from Paul's tablet.

"There's a Gideon in this room but not a Homer. I don't know what xvi:53 says."

"I do. I looked it up in Paul's study. Here." He showed her the quatrain he had copied out, together with the footnote. "It's where Menelaus is protecting the body of Patroclus and kills a Trojan. What do you think?"

"Agamemnon to Menelaus," she said, thinking aloud.

"Well, they were brothers."

"And kings."

"Not such a much. In those days, there was a king every couple of miles."

"And the two of them married sisters."

"So?"

She made an impatient gesture. "I don't know!"

"I'll tell you what I think. A man like Paul doesn't go into his bedroom between, say, five-forty and eight-thirty, to make a note to himself on a pad on his bedside table. He would have gone into his study. Which means he made that note before leaving for Greece."

"And someone destroyed it."

"He could have been that someone."

She mused. "Tying plaits or locks of hair with gold . . ." She spread her arms helplessly, then slapped her thighs and got to her feet. "Go on," she said, "what happened with Tinka Kanavarioti?" He told her about his visit with Tinka. Then he mentioned the box of Greek matches. "Well doesn't that pretty much tell you Sophie was there? You said Mrs. Kanavarioti was using them. And a box of matches doesn't last long. That means she hadn't been keeping them as a souvenir. Anything else?" He told her about Tinka's son. Ellen looked at him, astonished. "You think she named her son after Paul?"

"I'd put it differently. My hunch is, she named the baby after its father." Her blue eyes widened. "It's just a guess. But one I think she wanted me to make. There's a little more to it. The boy was in an American uniform with decorations from the Vietnam War. Born in, say, 1946, that would make him just the right age."

"I frankly don't see how—"

"Honey, the boy was born to a Russian mother and, presumably, a Greek father. The baby would have been issued a Greek passport. Tinka herself would have been a displaced person with no passport at all. Given our quota system, about which I am going to refrain from saying anything at this time, he would have had to wait years just to get a visa—unless, of course, the baby was brought here by his mother as an American."

"How could he have been?"

"If Paul had put his own name on the boy's birth certificate—and perhaps with good reason. That would explain not only how mother and son got to this country but the coincidence of their proximity to Paul. It's easy enough to check up on. If it seems relevant, I can find out from Immigration and Army records."

"They never married, of course. Well, that's understandable. They came of two different worlds."

"So did Sophie and Paul."

"Which brings us right back to square one. They got married, according to Sam Kellerman, because they had to. Why?"

"Can't tell you, honey. All Sam's name brings to mind is someone renowned for having once described the head of his own studio as a man who shits gold, for which everyone was sure he would get the sack, except that the studio head took it as a compliment." He shook his head. "Sam Kellerman's secret died with him."

"There are such things as exhumations. Didn't anything she say help?"

"Tinka?"

"Yes."

"No. She knows the boy is supposed to have killed Paul for some junk jewelry but she doesn't seem to know any more about it than anyone else." He got to his feet and, walking over to the beige draperies, lifted up a corner and peered out at the lighted gardens of the hotel grounds. Then he said, "I just wish we could get us a look-see at that missing jewelry, that's what I wish."

She said impatiently, "But if it's nothing but junk—"

"Is it?"

"It has to have been! You know perfectly well that Sophie had beautiful jewelry. It seems to me I read she used to own some fabulous pieces. Any woman who owns jewelry like that has it insured. She has a floater and the pieces are scheduled. The moment she gets a new piece, she has it listed. If she didn't list it, that proves it's junk."

"This piece wasn't insured."

She shrugged. "The only women I know who own valuable jewelry and don't carry insurance are women who have had the pieces copied, keep the originals in a safe deposit box and wear only paste. But if, as you say, this is something she took with her to Europe and then brought back with her again—"

He looked at her from under his thick brows. "Honey, it wasn't insured. 'Hold 'er, Deacon! She's a-headin' for the barn!' "

"You must someday confide in me the secret location of this well of aphorisms from which you draw such astonishing rejoinders."

"My great-granddaddy, born in Muskingum County, Ohio, en route there just after the great earthquake of 1811 that not only altered the course of the mighty Mississippi but had it to running backwards for two days, and that's the God's truth."

"All right, all *right!*"

"Wonderful old man. Used to sing his head off, I'm told." Dade burst into song.

'Six for the six proud walkers,

Five for the symbols at your door . . .'

How I wish we knew what it was, that piece of junk jewelry, so-called."

"I thought you did know."

"The dresser, she called it the *kraydemnon*."

"Yes, you told me that." She stared off into space.

"You know the word?"

"It's familiar."

"Dictionary says it's some kind of a veil such as the sea-goddess Ino gave to Ulysses to buoy him up in the water."

"A woman wouldn't use a veil to tie up locks of her hair. And the only man in history I can think of who wore a veil was Joseph, in Egypt. No, it can't be a veil."

"Well, since that's what the *kraydemnon* is—"

She shook her head, frowning. "That's not what it is."

"Honey, I'm telling you what the dictionary says."

"Well, the dictionary's wrong."

He drew back. "You watch yourself."

"Oh, I don't mean *wrong*. I just mean wrong in the sense that it's—well, not *right*."

"Sophie told me it's some kind of hairnet."

"She's also wrong."

"Sophie and the dictionary both?"

She said heatedly, "Dade, I know what I'm talking about! I can feel it!" She struck the table with the flat of her hand.

"Listen, honey, if you're getting ready to prophesy, I'll send down for a tripod." There was a knock at the door. "There it is now."

She crossed to the door, saying over her shoulder, "You'll be sorry!"

"If you know something, tell me."

"That's just it. I don't know what I know. I just know I know it!" She opened the door and saw Harm Watmough standing there.

Holding up Dade's car keys, he said, "Gas is low. Want me to get it tanked up?"

Nodding, Dade took out a twenty-dollar bill and handed it to

him. Harm came toward him and took the bill, Dade thanked him and then said, "You like hotel work?" Harm made a face. "You going to college?"

"I'm not much for school. Once I got out of high school, that was it for me. Right now, I'm job hunting."

"For what kind of work?"

The big boy grinned at him. "Whatever pays."

"Got a line on anything?" Harm shook his head.

After Harm left the room, two waiters wheeled in a cloth-covered trolley set for two. Ellen indicated the space in front of the sofa and the older waiter, who had wispy gray hair and a mournful expression, clapped his hands and pointed at the younger waiter, who was moon-faced. The younger lifted covered dishes from a hot box under the table, handing them to the older waiter, who served them with a warning that the plates were heated then opened the wine and poured a bit of it, waiting for approval.

Dade's mouth puckered. Looking at Ellen, he said, " 'Surprised' is a masterpiece of understatement." He turned to the waiter. "It needs to breathe," he said. "For about two days."

The older waiter handed Dade the bill, who signed it and handed it back. After the two waiters left the room, Dade lifted his glass. "At any rate—" He broke off, his eyes glowing. "*Rate:* 'To value, to hold cheap!' Bingo!" He took his notebook and his little gold pencil out of his pocket and wrote down the word.

Helping herself to an oyster, Ellen said, "I'm so happy for you, seeing the joy you take in your simple pleasures. Other women's husbands watch football on television or cheat or go out with the boys, which I happen to think is a terribly sexist way for us to put it, but you, my dear—"

" 'Sticks and stones . . .' as my friend Merda Chaffee was wont to say."

"You never knew anyone named Merda Chaffee."

"Not only that, she came from a town called Intercourse, Alabama, and you can look it up in the atlas if you don't believe me."

"You never knew any such person!"

"Did so. Came to San Francisco when young and lived in a Gothic

sort of house in St. Francis Wood, with a huge stone fireplace. Used to smoke at the age of fourteen, she did, but to hide it from her mother, she stood in the fireplace and blew the smoke up the chimney. It looked awful peculiar to see little Merda in her bobby socks and her pleated skirt standing in the fireplace, her head up out of sight. Well, one day I heard a sound and turned to see Mrs. Chaffee in the doorway, purse in hand, and I got the hell out of there fast."

The phone rang. Dade answered it.

"Papa?" a voice said. "This is Jonah."

"I'd know your voice anywhere, son. Everything all right?"

"Yes, Papa. I tried to reach you earlier but couldn't and then there was this meeting I had to go to about condo conversions—I won't go into all of that now—but this is the first chance I've had to call you. Motke called."

"He did, now?"

"He said he was off to go fishing in some town up in Canada, the name of which he made up, and—"

"Farting Horse Creek?"

"How did you know?"

"You sound just like your mother. There is such a town and that is where Arnie goes fishing when he takes his vacations. What did he want?"

"He sent a message."

"Which is?"

" 'All paid up as of yesterday.' "

"That's the message?"

"That's it, Papa."

"Son of a gun."

"Mean anything?"

"Plenty."

"What's up?"

"I'm going to be representing the boy. The accused."

"Son of a bitch."

"Don't talk like that. Just because I do."

"You take care, Papa. Okay?"

"You want to go up to Volcano when we get back? Up to the gold

country, you and that pretty Penny of a bride of yours, and go here and there?"

"I'd love that, Papa."

"And your brother and your sisters, they still in the land of the living?"

"They were this afternoon, when I talked to them."

"Give them all our love. Listen. Paul Van Damm had a policy with Travelers. Just make a call when you can and find out, for his sake, because he'd want me to be concerned whether the policy is in order and current."

"I'll let you know, Papa."

After they had said goodbye, Dade put down the phone and said, "Remember when he was little, can't have been more than two but talking already, and I had him in my arms and we were walking in Buena Vista Park, that pocket handkerchief of a place way up at the top of Duboce, and there was this huge big harvest moon just peeking up over the top of the hill in the park and he stretched his hands out to it and said to me, 'Oh, take me up to it, Papa! Take me up to it!' and I started running up those broad, shallow stairs set in the lawn, must be a few hundred stairs they got in that place, or so it seems, and he kept stretching out his hands and crying out, 'Take me up to it, Papa!' and I was all out of breath and like to die when we got to the top, just in time to see the moon sail up above us over the trees, and I said to him, 'We're too late!' and he was that disappointed. He thought I could get him the moon!"

"He still thinks so."

"Well."

"Why did he call?"

"Message from Motke."

"Which was?"

"Two days before Paul was killed, word in the street was, brother Vince was on the hook for thirty-five grand. But as of today—"

"What?"

"Nothing."

Picking up the phone, he opened his notebook, looked up Vincent's number and then called it. After several rings, a man's voice answered the phone. Identifying himself and telling Vincent he was representing Manuel, Dade said, "The boy's arraignment is tomorrow morning. I know it's after business hours, but is there any chance I can see you for a few minutes tonight?"

"Something wrong?"

"Got a question I want to ask you. For Paul's sake, I'd just as soon ask it in private. Then, if we both end up satisfied, we'll just leave it at that."

"Oh?"

"I know it's inconvenient, but—"

"Come on over."

"I'll be there by nine-thirty."

Ellen said, "Why not tomorrow?"

"What makes you think he'll still be around then?" He pulled on his coat. Ellen lifted her eyes, meeting his.

"Button, button," she said.

XVIII

Shortly before nine-thirty that night, Dade reached King's Road, a steep street to his left off Sunset, above the Strip. He looked for the address. It had to be somewhere on the right side of the street. Ahead, the road narrowed and the trees and oleander bushes were thick, with dirt alleys intersecting the road as the town ran out of streets and the hills began.

He had met Paul's brother Vincent only once, years before. He had met him by accident, having arrived early at Paul's for an appointment. Luisa had shown him into the house on the Helenas where Paul had lived even then, years before he married Sophie, and he remembered now the surprised look on Paul's face as he caught sight of Dade over a man's shoulder. Paul was in the act of giving his brother some money and, for a moment, Dade felt as if he had caught Paul in the act of placing a bet. That was foolish, of course. Paul didn't gamble. He never gambled. He didn't approve of gambling and made a particular point of telling you so, as if to separate himself from his brother, to whom gambling was, as Maugham once said about money, a sixth sense without which he could not enjoy the other five.

"Dade," Paul had said, "this is my brother, Vincent." It had sounded less like an introduction than an admission. Certainly, in all the years they had known one another, Paul had never made any move to bring the two of them together. Turning to his brother, Paul had said to him, "Mr. Dade Cooley," as if he could avoid introducing them by turning the whole thing into an announcement and letting it go at that. Vincent turned away from his brother at that moment, smiled a weatherbeaten smile in in Dade's direction and held out a strong hand. Dade went over to him, shaking hands with him.

"My brother's just leaving," Paul said.

"No hurry." Vincent smiled again, as if letting Dade in on a joke. His eyes were a watery blue. His face was a sailor's face, browned and creased. His graying hair was short and unruly. There was nothing handsome about him at all but when he looked at you and grinned, you couldn't look away from him. It was as if something extraordinary were about to happen and you didn't want to miss it.

"Mr. Cooley! Mr. Cooley!" he had said, in the tone of someone who has just guessed a riddle.

"Mr. Van Damm."

"Excuse us," Paul had said, taking his brother's elbow and steering him to the door. Afterward, when Paul had come back into the Spanish-style sitting room, he had said to Dade, throwing a glance in the direction of the front door, "Sorry."

"It's all right."

"I have to."

"It's all right, Paul."

Paul sighed. "He has a way of finding out whenever there is money around, as if he can smell it. And if I don't give him some, he'll go to our mother. She hasn't got it but she'll get it somehow." Paul sighed again. "It's only when he's into them for a lot. The guy does have rules. I mean to say, he wouldn't if he didn't have to."

"I understand."

But that had been several years earlier. Paul and Vincent's mother had since passed on to what Paul had referred to as her reward, parenthetically adding that escaping from Vincent could not be better described. Paul had taken pleasure in telling Dade that he had not seen Vincent since, but kept in touch with friends in common only because if some misfortune were to befall his brother, he did not want to be the last to know.

Dade found the address. The sidewalk was overgrown, with weeds cracking the pavement and springing up along the foundation line of the stucco building. He climbed cracked tile stairs and went under an archway with broken wrought-iron gates sagging on their hinges and then into a courtyard with a silted-up fountain overgrown with weeds. The doors to the apartments opened onto the courtyard and a good many of them, as well as the apartment windows, were barred.

Dade went up to Vincent's apartment. A light burned behind a drawn shade. He rang the doorbell. From inside, he could hear what sounded like voices on a television program. Then it struck him that it was an argument. Somewhere, a door banged shut. He rang the doorbell again. After a few moments, a scratchy voice on an intercom said something unintelligible. Dade put his mouth close to the speaker and pronounced his own name. Whether it was understood, he wasn't sure. Nothing happened. After a few moments, he rang the bell again. Then, without warning, the door was yanked open and Vincent Van Damm stood leaning on it, smiling the way Dade had remembered him smiling the one time they had met. His face was bruised, as if from a fall.

"Well, come on in," said Vincent. He led Dade through a small, arched foyer into a tiny sitting room. A couple of needlepoint chairs were drawn up in front of a small fireplace in which an electric heater burned. On a little coffee table with a brass gallery was a covered glass candy dish and an Art Deco ashtray surmounted by a metal figure of Mercury. There were double-hung windows covered with net curtains and the shades were drawn. From somewhere in the apartment, Dade heard the sound of a door opening softly.

Seeing Dade looking at the furnishings, Vincent gestured at the room and said, "My wife fancies herself as a decorator." There was a crash from the other room, as if something had been flung down. Not appearing to notice it, Vincent said, "Of course, when one must employ one's talents on so limited a budget as that to which we are at present restricted—" Another crash, this one accompanied by the splintering of glass, attracted Vincent's attention. "Excuse me," he said with a slight bow. He left the room. Dade heard no words spoken but, after a moment, there was the sound of a hard slap, followed by whimpering, and after that, Vincent returned to the room, closing the door carefully behind him and gently rubbing his hands. Vincent said, "How about a little drink?" He took a pint of whisky out of his coat pocket and offered it to Dade.

"Thanks just the same."

"Well, all right." Vincent started to put the bottle back in his pocket, then changed his mind and set it down on the table. He was, as Dade was later to tell Ellen, "shit-faced drunk," but still able to hold his liquor, in the manner of someone who has long been an alcoholic. He had what Dade had years before heard described as smoker's face, a grayish pallor. As if in confirmation, Vincent took a package from his pocket, shook out a cigarette and lit it with yellowed fingers. Exhaling, he turned away, coughing.

Dade remembered that Vincent had been a Rhodes Scholar and had later dropped out of Oxford to paint. For years, he had done nothing but paint and was well thought of, but then he had stopped painting. Paul had never said why. Dade glanced around the tiny apartment again. There were none of Vincent's paintings in evidence. As if reading his mind, Vincent said, "I got rid of them. I don't paint any more."

"I see."

"You know something? The bottom can drop out of an art form. It did for me. Once, I was at the Prado with a friend and we were looking at Goyas—not the God damned court paintings but the real thing—and he looked at me and said, 'It's all a trick!' "

He gestured at one of the two chairs. "Why don't we sit down?" he said.

They both sat down slowly. Dade said, "My condolences."

"Thank you." Another smile, brief, like a match guttering.

"I tried to say a word to you at the house but when I looked around, you were leaving."

"I don't care much for those affairs," he said in the tone of a man commenting on Sunday dinners with one's family. "I put in an appearance," he went on. "I felt it was the least I could do. And, of course, the least I could do was exactly what I had in mind." He flashed a look at Dade, the eyes glittering. "For Sophie, I mean. After all, I had to do something!" He touched Dade's knee with his little finger and started to laugh, then caught himself.

"You don't care for her?"

"And I don't intend to!" He gestured at the room, with its worn furniture. "Nor am I in any position to, for that matter. Well, what is money? *Outoi ta draymat idea kektaytai brotoi.* 'Man's wealth is but a loan from heaven,' as the poet says." Another flashing glance cut the air like a sword. "Now, how can I help you? You're defending that boy they think killed my brother. How did they happen to fasten on him?"

"They think he killed your brother while making off with a piece of Sophie's jewelry. Junk jewelry, according to her."

"That is not much of a description."

"I do agree."

"I mean to say, all Sophie's jewelry is worthless, which is only fitting, considering her taste, of which your client is a splendid example." The eyes glinted in Dade's direction, to see whether the remark elicited surprise. Vincent then nodded to himself, satisfied. "I am glad to see your young client is honest with you—or is he the source of this revelation?" Taking the pint from the table, he unscrewed the lid with delicate fingers and, turning away, murmured, "Excuse me," and took a sip from it. Then, turning back to Dade, he returned the bottle to his pocket, saying, "His equally youthful predecessor was a garbage collector, which argues a certain *nostalgie de la boue,* and, apart from the noise he made and the hours he kept—" He broke off, laughing soundlessly.

Dade kept to the subject of Sophie's jewels. "All worthless? Thought she had some good stuff."

"Gone. Sold to make ends meet. When they didn't, as so often happens, she married Paul. Anything more I can tell you?" A fit of coughing seized him. When he had recovered himself, he went on. "When I first caught sight of her at a crowded reception, it was like catching sight of the Statue of Liberty indoors. Myself, I am not fond of that statue. I suppose you know that its sculptor used as models the face of his mother and the body of his mistress, which makes him, to my mind, the archetypal—but don't mind me. I just mean to say anybody who can advertise such a proclivity in the middle of New York Harbor—No, I don't care for Sophie Galanos."

"But your brother did."

"As did Odysseus for Circe."

"You trying to tell me Sophie didn't care for Paul?"

"Circe turned men into swine. Well, men like that appeal to a certain class of women, which may be why they do it." He looked up at Dade. "But we both know that that is not what drew this Hero and Leander together." He smiled slowly, as if it hurt him. "A lovely tale. I think what appealed to the Greeks was not so much that he swam the Hellespont every night to screw hell out of Hero but was up to swimming back again afterward."

Dade remembered that Leander set out every night from the Trojan shore and wondered whether an unconscious connection had suggested such an example to Vincent. Dade veiled his eyes and said in an offhand voice, "What drew them together, Paul and Sophie?"

Vincent shrugged as if he did not know. But his lips folded themselves into a hard line, as if trying to keep him from telling the truth.

Dade sat back, rapping his knuckles lightly against his strong, white teeth. Then he said, "Did Paul happen to mention Manuel when you went to see him? I mean, say he was expecting him or anything like that?"

"No, he did not."

"Was he expecting visitors, do you know?"

Vincent shook his head. "Not to my knowledge."

"Then he must have been surprised to see you." Vincent turned and looked at Dade as if the light hurt his eyes. "Since he wasn't expecting anybody, I mean. Why did you go to see him, you mind my asking?"

"To welcome him home!" Vincent saluted Dade with his bottle and then took another drink out of it.

There was a sound on the other side of the door which led from the small sitting room into the rest of the apartment, a kind of scraping, as if whoever was in there had brushed against something. They both heard it. Vincent was on his feet, quick as a cat, moving over to the door and seizing hold of the glass handle, pulling it toward him. "Excuse us," he said to whoever was on the other side of the door. "Excuse us, please." The knob rattled in his hand. He half-turned, giving Dade a grimace of a smile, as if trying to pretend all this was a joke and he was inviting Dade to laugh with him. At the same time, there was a pounding on the door and the sound of a woman's voice raised in anger, calling him by name.

"Vince! Vince, you lousy bum! You open this door!"

"I said, Would you excuse us?" he said to the door. He tried to brace himself, slipped on a scatter rug and then lost his balance, almost sliding to the floor as the door was yanked open and a small woman with blazing eyes and a mop of brown curls stood before them, arms akimbo, swaying in the doorway. Her eyes were bloodshot. She looked at Vincent.

"Shut up," she said.

Vincent clambered to his feet, saying, "My dear, may I present—?"

"Shut up!" she shouted, ignoring Dade. "I told you to shut up and I mean, shut up!" Jabbing a pointing forefinger in Dade's direction, she said, without looking at him, "Do you know what kind of trouble he can make for you? I've been listening—"

"I applaud the way you improve each shining hour."

"—I mean, once the two of you get together, him and your big mouth—"

"My dear," Vince began again, with an exaggerated bow, staggering to regain his balance, "let me present—"

His attempts at introduction were lost in the struggle between the two of them as she tried to pull him out of the room, meanwhile saying to Dade over his shoulder, "He's not himself. You must have seen that he's simply not himself."

"This is my self, my dear," Vincent said to her, swaying on his feet and giving them each a jocular smile in turn. "I know it may come as something of a surprise to you, Fanny, but this really is me!" The notion struck him as funny. He shook with silent laughter. She let go of him then.

"Would you excuse us?" she said to Dade. "Please?"

Dade studied her. Then, as if he had not heard what she had asked him, he said to her, "Statement I saw says you happened to arrive at Paul's house just after your husband did. That right?"

She looked at him quickly. Then, running small, plump hands through her Shirley Temple curls, she said, "Yes, that's what I told them."

"The statement used the word 'happened.' Is that your word?"

She looked around, as if not quite understanding what he was asking. Then she said, "I happened to go there at roughly the same time as my husband. Actually, I arrived a few minutes later."

"How much later?"

"I—I don't know. What difference does it make?"

"A witness says you arrived moments later."

"Well—" She shrugged. "I—I didn't ask Vince what time he'd gotten there. If people say it was just moments later—well, it must have been, that's all."

Dade looked at Vincent. "Is that your impression? That your wife arrived moments after you did?" Vincent looked at him, not answering. Turning back to Fanny, Dade said, "And what was your reason for going there?"

"I went there to see Sophie."

"You telephone first?"

"I—yes. Yes, I did."

"And talked to whom?"

The eyes widened slightly. "The line was busy."

Vincent turned to her. "Will you excuse us now?"

Ignoring him, Dade said to her, "So you just got in your car and went over to see her?"

"That's right."

"Fanny, I want you to excuse us now." Vincent said to her.

"Why did you say you went over to see her?"

"None of your business!" she said defiantly.

Vincent said to her in a low voice, taking hold of her arm, "Fanny, this has all been too much for you. Why don't you go in and have yourself a nice little drink and then when Mr. Cooley here and I are finished—"

She pushed Vincent away, her breath coming quickly, her eyes wide, staring at him. "Let me alone," she said. "I can take care of myself."

"Fanny—"

"I can take care of myself, which is a hell of a lot more than you can do!"

Dade said, turning to Fanny and rubbing a reflective forefinger across his jaw, "You told me Sophie wasn't expecting you. That must have been very awkward for you."

"What makes you say that?" The colorless eyes were watchful.

"Well, you'd only met her a couple of times in your life, that's true, isn't it?" Fanny took a step backward, looking at him as if she had suddenly caught sight of the glint of a blade. He went on: "And to go calling on her without any warning, not much more than an hour after she'd gotten off a fifteen-hour flight from Greece—"

Vincent said, "I want you to excuse us now, Fanny."

Backing away, she twisted her hands together and said to Dade, "I'm glad to have met you." Turning abruptly, she ran from the room. Reaching out, Vincent closed the door behind her, then turned back to Dade. They sat down again, as before.

Dade steepled his hands and looked at Vincent steadily. "Your brother was murdered. My client is accused of the crime. The alleged motive is robbery."

"I don't know what you're getting at, Dade." He shifted his position and flashed Dade another glance, the kind of look, it struck Dade, that a man might give you while shuffling a pack of cards, just before showing you a trick. Then, with a brief smile, as if his face for a moment ran ahead of his thoughts, he said, "We were close, once. Paul and I, we were very close. When we were boys. And when we were young men in out twenties. He ever tell you that, Paul?"

"I can't say as he did."

"We were the best of friends. 'Eteros gar autos ho philos estin,' 'A friend is another self,' as old Aristotle says. Well, that was a long time ago. It was such a long time ago that when, after being separated for so many years, he came back into my life like an interloper, kind of shouldering aside my memory of him, if you know what I'm saying, it was as if the brother I remembered, the one I had lived with all those years, was a man I'd made up. I didn't like him when I came to know him again. I couldn't understand what I'd ever seen in him. I just didn't want to be around him anymore. Well, this summer when Paul was away, I got to thinking. We're neither of us as young as we used to be. One of us could go any time. People do. We've both lived long enough to know that, Dade. Well, I thought, Why don't I give him a chance? I mean, Christ—! So, when he got back, I went over to see him. Does that answer your question?"

Dade leaned back in his chair, looking directly at Vincent. "You just missed Sophie. Was that by chance?"

"Sheer good fortune."

"I figured that somebody like Sophie would interest you. I mean, given her background, her knowledge of the ancient world."

"*Her* knowledge!" By now, Vincent was more drunk (as Dade afterward report to Ellen), if such a thing were possible. Like men of his background, when he began to be aware of his condition, he became if anything more studied in his speech and in his gestures, addressing Dade as if lecturing a class. "When I once suggested that the ancient Greeks were complete barbarians—I mean, imagine vaulting over the wall into the arena to suck blood from the wounds of a dying gladiator in the hope that it would cure epilepsy!—well, the poor woman was beside herself trying to defend them! Of course, it was the Romans who did that. The Greeks, as we both know, abhorred gladiatorial contests, but what interested me is that Sophie did not know it. What she calls her grand passion for her people and their splendid history is a subject about which she knows next to nothing. She once tried to defend homosexuality in *The Il-iad,* oblivious of the fact that there is no single reference to it in all the works of Homer. Of course, victorious armies 'routinely sodom-ized the vanquished,' as a writer for one of our news magazines so happily put it, but the enjoyment lay in humiliating the victim, what we call 'hate-fucking,' which is doubtless the origin of our gesture of derision with the middle finger, or, in the more robust style of the Italians, with the whole bent arm, one hand slapping the biceps. Later, their reputation degenerated, as did their practices, when their civilization fell into decay, which is probably what prompted the Hebrews to warn, 'Beware the Greek tree; it bears flowers but no fruit.' But all this came as news to the radiant Sophie. As I say, she knows absolutely nothing about history, neither that of the Greeks nor anybody else's. She knows one subject: herself. She talks about absolutely nothing else. She reminds me of an actress who was once quoted as saying to someone, 'Well, enough about me. Let's talk about you. How did you like my last picture?'" He managed to get halfway through a smile. "What my brother saw in her, I have no idea. Paul had no talent as a womanizer."

"She is very beautiful."

"I grant you that—as lovely as a work by Praxiteles. In fact, if instead of meeting her in the flesh, Paul had excavated her, I could more readily understand his longing to possess her."

"I had no idea you felt this way about her."

Vincent, as if suddenly sobered, abandoned his schoolmaster's tone and lifted his chin, eyes narrowed, looking down his nose at Dade. "She's just not my cup of tea, that's all there is to it."

"Oh?"

"I think your dislike has to do with your feelings for your late brother."

"Jealousy?" Vincent widened his eyes for a moment, throwing Dade a quick glinting look of mockery. He glanced at his watch, as if to call Dade's attention to the time.

Dade said softly, "I never got any impression that relations between you and Sophie were strained."

"Really?" Another flat, unemotional smile.

"I knew that you went to Paul for money when you needed it and that that made for difficulty."

"Well—!" Vincent moved toward the door, as if expecting his chance had now come to show Dade out.

"But that had nothing at all to do with Sophie, did it, Vincent?"

"Do you mind if we drop it at that?"

Dade said suddenly, "I put it to you that you took a dislike to her right after your brother was killed."

Vincent, his face mottled, reached out for the doorknob, saying, "Now, if you'll excuse me—"

"One last question: where did you get the thirty-five thousand dollars?"

"Come again?" Vincent's expression did not change, but a slight flush appeared on the grayish skin under the line of cheekbones.

"Monday night, you were on the hook for thirty-five thousand dollars. Now, two days later, you don't owe a dime. Where did you get the money, Vince?"

"I don't see why my affairs concern you. Now, if you'll excuse me—" Rising, he moved toward the door to open it. Dade blocked his way.

"Let me do you a favor," Dade said. "Let me tell you now what I'm going to say in court, so I won't spring it on you. For Paul's sake. May I do that, please?"

"Say what you have to say."

"Your brother brought back something from Greece. Something he thought would prove the so-called tomb of Agamemnon actually dates from the time of the Trojan War. You know as well as I do that the Greeks had been showing off what they called the grave of Agamemnon for thousands of years. We know that because when Euripides went to visit Mycenae, they showed it to him. They showed it to Pausanias about six hundred years later and he wrote a detailed description of it. I'm telling you things you know, just to refresh your memory, so's you can help me out—for the sake of your late brother, you understand. Pausanias mentioned that 'some remains of the circuit wall are still to be seen, and the gate which has lions over it.' They call that the oldest known coat of arms in the world. Schliemann said, 'We'll find his grave here. Right where Pausanias described it as being.' The scholars said, 'Bullshit.' Schliemann ignored them and said 'Dig here.' And what do you know? He found the graves—according to him—not just of Agamemnon but of his concubine, Cassandra, and the twin babies she had by him, both slain with their mother and buried with their faces covered with tiny masks of gold leaf. There they were, just as Schliemann said they would be. Of course, that couldn't be true. The scholars, as usual, knew better. But what if your brother was right? What if the grave was Agamemnon's? Proving that would make a man's name, wouldn't it? Make him famous in his own world for the rest of his life. Now, you're a scholar, Vincent. No, don't be modest. You've already shown me that much. Not a practicing scholar, true, but you'd know quick enough what it was Paul had brought back. Let's go one step further. Let's imagine you knew he was bringing it. You'd even found yourself a buyer for it. You went to Paul and said, 'Help me.' We know what happens to gamblers who lose and don't pay up. You were talking about having him save your life. 'Help me,' right? Now, if he turned you down, then you could have said to him, 'You had your chance.' "

"Get out."

"Tell me where you got the thirty-five thousand."

"I'm through listening to you."

"I'll say it to you in court. I'll say, Something's missing. That something was worth far more than thirty-five thousand to the right buyer. Your brother was killed, that something disappeared and two days later, your bills are all paid. Now, how are you going to answer that, Vincent?" Vincent turned his back on Dade, reaching for the doorknob. "I gave you fair warning," Dade said. "Your intimate knowledge of ancient Greece proves that you were quite able to understand what Paul was up to."

Vincent opened the front door. "That's enough," he said.

Dade started across the threshold, then stopped, frowning in thought. Turning back to Vincent, he said, "My client is accused of murdering your brother for a piece of junk jewelry nobody can seem to find. That's a funny coincidence, isn't it, Vince? A man is murdered and two things nobody seems to be able to describe both disappear that same night. What if they were the same thing, Vince?" In the half-light, Dade could detect the sudden rush of blood away from the head which makes a man turn pale and have to lean up against something for support, as Vincent did now, a hand out-stretched quickly to brace him against the doorpost "They were, weren't they?" Dade said softly. "Are you going to answer me?"

"*Hoi theoi sigay* . . ."

"I know. 'We learn speech from men, silence from the gods.' Don't try it, Vincent. They call it contempt of court."

The warm night air was heavy with the tropical scent of jasmine. As Dade started through the archway leading to the street, he heard footsteps and Fanny ran up to him. She seized his arm, her fingers digging into his flesh.

"Listen to me," she said. Her eyes were glittering. "I know what you're up to. Anybody but my client, that's the game you play, isn't it?"

Dade looked down at the hand clutching his arm. She withdrew it. He met her eyes. "You didn't happen to get to Paul's at almost the same time. You followed your husband there, didn't you? Why?"

"I—I was afraid for him. He was desperate. Because he couldn't pay. Before, he was always able to get the money somehow—don't ask me how, but it was never this much before. And they were going to go after me."

"How do you know that?"

"I was out shopping. I came in the back way with the groceries and as I put them down on the sink, I was about to call out to him when I heard their voices and the way they were talking frightened me. It was a man's voice. He said, 'Get it—' and when Vince tried to make a joke out of it and said, 'I can't,' I heard the man hit him and I heard Vince go crashing against a chair. 'Get it,' the man said, and

Vince said, 'If that's what they sent you to do, just do it, I can't help you.' Then the man said that his instructions were to talk to the little lady. I knew he meant me and that frightened Vince—I know you wouldn't know it to see the way he treats me—he does that in front of people, I don't know why—but he does care about me."

"When was this?"

"The day they were due back."

"What did you do?"

"I thought, They'll kill me. Then they'll kill him."

"And what did you do then?"

"I went back outside. I took the groceries back out to the car with me, so Vince wouldn't know I'd been home, and I waited. There was a car parked in front of the apartment house, an expensive car that I didn't recognize, and I waited until I saw a man come out and get in the car and drive away. Then, I went back into the apartment and pretended that I didn't know anything. We didn't talk. Sometimes, Vince does tricks with cards. That's what he was doing when I went back inside. His face was all bruised. He told me he had tripped and fallen. He gave me a kiss. I remember he put a finger under my chin and lifted it and looked into my eyes for a long time and then he smiled at me, that way he does, and pretended to give me a punch in the jaw, and I set about making the casserole we were having for dinner. I saw him looking at his watch. Then, sometime after six, maybe later than that, he said he had to go out for a little while but that he'd be right back and for me to go ahead and put the casserole in the oven. I did—and as soon as he left the house, I went out and got in my car and followed him. He went straight to Paul's. Sophie was out. Paul was there alone. Vince was surprised to see me. I pretended I was surprised to see him. I said I'd just stopped by to have a word with Sophie. He didn't believe that for a minute. Then Vince talked with his brother."

"Alone?"

"Some of the time."

"Could Paul possibly have bailed him out?"

"I don't know."

"And Sophie?"

"Sophie has nothing."

Dade tried to make out her expression in the darkness. She wrapped her arms around herself, shivering suddenly. He saw her eyes move, glinting in what little light came from a street lamp. "You say they talked privately?"

"Yes."

"For how long?"

"Just—just a few minutes."

"Where were they?"

"Upstairs."

"Could you hear anything?"

"No."

"And what happened then?"

"The two of them came downstairs."

"With anything?"

"No."

"Then?"

"We both left. I drove home, following him."

"And he went out again?"

"No! No, he was with me the whole evening!"

"Fanny, you don't want to lie to me."

"He was with *me!*"

"And if you have to get up on the stand and swear to that?"

"All right, then maybe I wouldn't say anything. I've always been told that a wife can't be forced to testify against her husband."

"It comes as a surprise to most people that that isn't always so. But in any case, silence can be a kind of testimony, Fanny. It's as good as testifying against him to have me call you as a witness and have you refuse to answer my questions about his movements." He put his face close to hers. "He went out after you got home that night, didn't he, Fanny?"

"Yes!" she cried out finally.

"Where?"

"I don't know."

"And how long was he gone?"

"A long time. I lay awake waiting for him to come home. He

didn't get back until almost midnight and then he just came to bed saying he was sorry to be so late."

"And is that when you knew that his debt had been paid?"

"He never said so!"

"It has been paid. You know that, don't you?"

"Yes." Still leaning against the stucco arch, she buried her face in her hands.

"My guess is, you knew it that night from the way he acted when he got back." He said softly, "You understand what the problem is, don't you? A man is desperate for money. He and his wife are both in serious danger. Then all of a sudden, he gets his hands on what he needs. He's going to have to explain where the money came from."

"Oh *God!*"

He patted her shoulder. "Talk to him. If he didn't come by it honestly, get him to call a lawyer. Before it's too late."

As Dade walked into their suite at the Bel-Air, the phone began ringing. Ellen answered it. "Yes," he heard her say, "he just returned. One second." Covering the mouthpiece, she said to him, "It's Irene. She's called three times now. She says it's urgent." He took the phone from her.

"Hello," he said. He listened. Then he said, "Yes. Yes, I am." And then, after a moment's pause, he said, "Yes, I can. Yes, indeed I can. Just give me directions."

After he put down the phone, Ellen said, "What is it?"

"She wants to talk to me."

"At this hour of the night?" Ellen looked at the clock. It was just after ten-thirty. "What's wrong?"

"It has something to do with her mother. That's all I know."

"How was brother Vincent?"

He told her the gist of his visit. "Back soon."

She put a hand on his arm. "Who's your money on? I mean, just make a guess, why don't you?"

"No."

"It seems poor form to bet on a hangman's noose but I've got a quarter says—"

"I'm sorry. No bets accepted."

"We won't make it a bet. Just think of me as—as a computer and see if you can beat my odds."

"I'm going to confide something in you."

"What?"

"No computer built can beat a grand chess master." He kissed her cheek.

"You son of a bitch."

"I'll remember you said that."

He found the address easily. It was on Sixth below Wilshire, one of the old residential blocks in Santa Monica, so close to the beach that, when the wind blew, there was sand on the sidewalks. It was a Cape Cod sort of house, built like all its neighbors on a knoll of ground which was planted with thick lawn and sloped down to the broad sidewalk and street. Brick steps had been set into the lawn. Dade climbed them. A redwood picket fence separated the walk from a rear garden. A gate, also made of redwood pickets, had numbers enameled on sheet metal fastened to it: "1212½" read the address. Pushing open the gate, Dade walked back along what had once been a narrow automobile driveway. Ahead of him was a garage which had been converted into a guest cottage. Lights shone from its windowed double doors now made into a wall. To his left and facing the rear garden of the house proper was the vine-covered shed roof of the front door of the cottage.

Irene was waiting for him and she opened the door as he approached. "Mr. Cooley," she said. She wore a long plaid jumper and her dark hair hung straight down to her shoulders. Holding out a slim hand, she said, "Thank you for coming." Her hand was cold. She looked very pale.

"You said it was important," he said.

"Yes." She folded her arms. She was trembling and trying to control it. She led Dade into the small house, closing the door behind him. Smoothing out her jumper, she gestured at a pair of canvas sling chairs in front of a metal fireplace which stood on a raised hearth of painted white bricks. Across from the fireplace was a little maple drop-leaf table with a couple of matching chairs. At the back of the room was the bar of a small kitchen.

He caught sight of a telephone on the kitchen bar and saw that it was off the hook. Pretending not to notice this, he waited for her to say something. She twisted her fingers together. When she volunteered nothing, he said, "Aren't you going to tell me what's the matter?"

Putting her hands flat on the table and looking at him directly, she said abruptly, "I understand the police want to talk to me. They want to ask me a question. If I answer it, my mother is the one who is going to suffer. Do I have to answer them?"

"I'm afraid so."

She took an uneven breath. "It's very difficult for me to talk about. Do you mind if I just take a moment—?"

"Take your time."

"Tell me, does he need anything? Manuel, I mean. Mother has been so terribly upset by all of this, she may not have remembered to ask. I've heard them say you sometimes have to pay off people in jail to get them to let you alone." She wet her lips. "I have a little money of my own and, I mean, if he needs it—"

"That's very generous of you. But it looks as if we'll have him out on bail in the morning."

"Oh, thank God," she said.

"You seem to be quite worried about him."

"Well, when people work for you, you feel responsible. If one of them falls ill and is taken to the hospital or something, you think about what has to be done for them and who is going to do it, just as you would about family. In fact, it's more so because one's relations usually have family of their own, whereas servants sometimes don't have anybody but the family they work for, isn't that your experience?" When he did not say anything, she went on: "It's just so crazy, isn't it? Somebody shoots Paul, Manuel finds the body and they put him in jail for it."

"That isn't quite what happened," Dade said.

"Oh, I know. He was presumably there at the time Paul was killed, so they thought he did it."

"You say if you tell the police what they want to know, your mother will suffer for it. Why is that, Irene?"

"They can't make me answer them. What can they do to me if I don't?"

"Why don't you tell me what's bothering you?"

She said suddenly, "Manuel had no grudge against Paul. Paul was very good to him. Paul was interested in his schooling—"

"Paul liked him, then?"

"Of course."

Dade pulled out one of the maple chairs for her. She sat down. Then he sat down opposite her. "And did your mother?" he asked in an ordinary tone.

"Mother is European." She corrected herself. "Well, her own mother was. She was Italian. She always used to say to Mother when she was a little girl, 'If you want to look beautiful, stand in the sun.' Her father was Greek, which is to say, from the Middle East. The Middle East is a very different place. I didn't know how different until I went there for the first time, when I was about fourteen, and I remember I saw a man standing on a street corner with his hands behind his back and at first, he seemed just like any other business-man one might see on the streets, but then, I stepped off the curb to cross the street and I saw his hands." She made a gesture with her fingers, as if trying to indicate the shape of what she was talking about. "He had a *komvoloyis* behind his back—you know, a string of those amber worry-beads they all seem to carry. It was really so strange, the first time I saw it. It was as if that one thing was a giveaway and I had this feeling that the people there were very dif-ferent from me, even though I'm part Greek. Then, I would be taken out into the countryside, traveling, and out in the villages they treated the women as if they were still in purdah. I can't tell you how awful it all seemed and how strange it made me feel! Not that they're not wonderful people! Oh, my God! During the war, my grand-mother says that the women in the mountains hid the rebels and when there wasn't anything for the men to eat, not a scrap, and the Nazis were searching for them everywhere, the nursing women fed the men from their own breasts. I remember when I was growing up hearing from my Greek grandfather that when the Greek dictator forbade the chorus to recite the *eleutheria*, you know, that famous ode to liberty that ends one of the plays—well, when they got to that part, they turned to the audience in silence and fourteen thousand people got to their feet and recited the lines. No, it isn't that I don't love them.

"When I first went to Greece, I went down into the basement of the Athens Museum, you know, where they have all those statues for graves that are the same—all in that kind of Egyptian pose, very rigid, with one foot advanced, arms stiff at their sides, a whole army of them. What do they call a statue like that? A *kouros*. Yes. A youth. There was one that was especially beautiful and I had learned enough Greek at school to read the inscription on it. It said, 'Here lies Kroisos, whom furious Ares slew, when he was fighting among the first.' I think his parents had put it up. I was so moved, I began to cry. I leaned against the statue and cried and a guard came up and hissed at me because I was touching one of the exhibits."

"The police want to know where you were the night your stepfather was killed," Dade said softly, still watching her.

"Oh, I know quite well what they want to know."

He sensed that she was going to be evasive with him again. Changing tack, he said, "I represent Manuel. I'm trying to help him. If you know something that might make a difference, won't you tell me about it? Don't you want to? Wouldn't your mother want you to?"

She made an impatient gesture, as if brushing his words away. "Europeans behave very differently with servants. They don't see them. They treat them—well, the way we treat appliances."

"How did they come to meet him, your folks? I suppose because his mother worked for Paul."

"She isn't his mother, by the way," Irene said abruptly. Dade turned toward her, surprised. "Do you know anything at all about his background?"

"Can't say that I do. I just met the boy for the first time this morning. You say she's not—?"

"Luisa's husband was killed when Manuel was about seven. Of course Manuel thought the man was his father, just as he thought Luisa was his mother. Luisa and her husband came from Guadalajara and moved in with her sister and brother-in-law Well, they had something like seven children of their own. Luisa couldn't speak a word of English and has never learned to. Well, then her husband was killed in some freak accident."

"What kind of accident?"

"He was electrocuted. After a storm, there was a downed power line. Sparks all over the place. He saw little children running toward it—you know how kids are—and he managed to get between it and them, trying to wave them off, and he fell across it. Manuel heard him screaming in agony. He went to the cemetery with the whole family, including Luisa's brother-in-law, who had always disliked him, as well as the children, because of the way their father had treated him. Manuel couldn't cry. He couldn't speak. The man he had always thought of as his uncle turned on him then, pointing at him and saying to the others, 'How can he cry when it wasn't even his father?' Manuel went to his mother afterward and said, 'Why did he say that?' and finally, she had to tell him the truth: She was sitting one day in the park when she was pregnant and all of a sudden another Mexican woman carrying a baby in her arms came up to Luisa and said she had to go across the street and telephone and would Luisa be kind enough to hold the baby for a few minutes? The woman never came back. Luisa waited hours. She didn't know what to do. She went home and told her family what had happened. They called the police to search for the mother. They couldn't find her. Then Luisa had a miscarriage. They told her she couldn't ever have children of her own. When they couldn't find the mother of the baby, she wanted to keep it. The family didn't want her to. They called it 'the little cuckoo'. Behind his back, the children still do. Luisa's husband went to the authorities with her and got permission for them to have custody. When her husband was killed, Luisa's brother-in-law felt she ought to go elsewhere. Where they lived they were crowded. And now, with the breadwinner gone, her sister and brother-in-law, what with seven kids of their own, wanted her to find a live-in job as a servant. What Luisa did was strike a bargain with them. She took the money she had been given as a settlement for the death of her husband and bought the house they were all living in.

Now she had a roof over her head for herself and Manuel. She let *them* stay there and she let *them* pay rent. Luisa wanted Manuel to learn, to speak English like an American. She wanted school for him. Manuel is her whole life. And this is the person they think killed Paul. Why would he have?" Looking up at him, she asked, "How is he taking it?"

"Well, jail for a boy who's only nineteen—"

"He's twenty-two."

"Oh?" Dade looked at her steadily. She tried to go on meeting his eyes but couldn't. She dropped her glance, coloring. There was a long silence. Then Irene said, "You might as well know. We've been together for a month. I met him when I had just come out to California, a few days before Mother went off with Paul to Greece."

Dade looked at her carefully. He waited for a long time. Then he asked, "Does your mother know about you and Manuel?"

"No."

"Are you sure?"

"Positive."

"How can you be positive?"

"Because she was out of the country all the time we've been together. The night they returned, Manuel was arrested. Mother has never seen us together."

"And Luisa? Does she know about you and Manuel?"

"How could she? She's never seen us together either. I've been very careful. One look would be all it would take. She wouldn't trust the situation. She wouldn't trust *me*."

"I see." Dade sat back in his chair, studying her. "But you haven't been to see him," Dade said.

"See him?"

"In jail. He was arrested Sunday night, now it's Wednesday, and when I saw him a few hours ago, you hadn't been there."

She got to her feet and walked away from him toward the kitchen. There, she leaned with her hands on the pass-through, her back to him. He waited. Finally, she said, still not turning around, "No, I haven't been there."

"Why not? Because you think he's guilty?"

149

She turned and looked at him, utterly shocked, all the color draining out of her face. Then she said, her voice a hoarse half-whisper, "I never said that! How can you put such words in my mouth? You don't know him or you wouldn't say that! All right, maybe he was defensive with you but you've got to remember, he's Mexican. They can talk all they like about Chicano or Latino or Hispanic or whatever other words they've made up to smooth over the truth, but you go down to the barrio and ask the people there what they are and if they answer you, if they trust you enough to answer you, they'll tell you flat out that they're Mexican, because that's what they are, they know they are and they know everything that goes along with that, everything people think, everything that's behind people's eyes when they look at someone like Manuel."

"I just asked you a question plain and simple because some things don't change, here or in Europe or in Greece or in Mexico. When a man goes to jail, the woman who cares about him goes to see him. Why didn't you?"

"He asked me not to. He made me promise not to."

"When did he ask you?"

"I really don't—"

"When?"

"What difference does it make?"

"*When*? He was arrested that night and was taken straight to jail. When did he have a chance to talk to ask you not to?"

She made her way slowly toward the chair opposite his and sank down into it, putting her elbows on the little drop-leaf table and digging her fingers into her lustrous dark hair. "Before he was arrested."

"*Before?*"

"Yes! He came to see me right after he found Paul's body. He told me everything!"

Dade looked at her sharply. "What did he tell you? If you want to help him, tell me exactly what he told you that night."

She looked at him, afraid. Then she laced her hands together and began speaking very softly and rapidly, telling him everything Manuel had told him already. "Then he left," she said. "He said to me, 'If anything happens, if they come looking for me, I want them to find me home in bed. As if nothing's wrong.' That's all I can tell you. Does it look very bad for him?"

"Tell me, did he have anything with him?"

"No."

"Are you quite sure?"

"Positive. Even though it was a foggy night and he showed up here in jeans and a T-shirt. What are you thinking of?"

"That junk jewelry he's supposed to have made off with."

"No. He had nothing with him."

"Is that why you weren't in your botany class that night? Because you were here with him?"

She gave him a startled look. Then she said, "Yes."

"But he couldn't have gotten here before, say, a few minutes of nine. That meant he expected you to be here and that you were waiting for him, doesn't it?"

She lifted her chin. "I didn't go to class because I wasn't feeling well. He knew I wasn't going. That's why I haven't been answering the phone. Because Mother told me the police found out I wasn't in class Sunday night and they're going to ask me why I said I was. That's why I had to see you. I don't know what to tell them."

"Tell them the truth."

"I *can't!* Don't you see, I can't let my mother find out. It would just destroy her."

"Why?"

"Because I want to marry him!" She looked at Dade, as if afraid that she had said too much. He turned away, thinking over what she had just told him. He did not say anything for some time. Then, finally, she broke in on his thoughts, saying, "That's why Manuel said not to let anybody find out about us, that it would just make him look bad—you know, as if he and Paul had had a fight about me and Manuel had lost his head. So, Manuel said to me, 'If anything happens, stay away from me. Don't let them find out.'"

Dade ran the tips of his left hand over his right palm, as if trying to read his own fortune. Then he said, "You'll have to tell them something."

"I'll just tell them I was here. That I didn't feel well and I cut class. And that when they asked me, I was so upset, I told them where I was supposed to be, forgetting I hadn't gone."

"Tell me again why you didn't go to class that night."

"I wasn't feeling well, and then after that quarrel between Mother and Paul—oh, I'm not giving anything away in mentioning it—I've already heard on the news that the neighbors overheard them yelling at each other—"

"One of the neighbors."

"Well, whatever. They were quarreling and there's no point in denying it."

"You picked them up at the airport, didn't you?"

"Yes."

"Were they quarreling then?"

"They wouldn't quarrel in front of me."

"But you just told me—"

"Yes, I overheard them quarreling at the house, but they wouldn't have known I overheard them. They thought I had already left."

"Why would they think that?"

"I kissed them goodnight and then I left the house."

"By what door?"

"The back door."

"Why the back door? Wouldn't you have parked in the cul-de-sac?"

"If you go out the front door, you can't lock it without a key. It's not the kind of door that locks when you pull it to. I don't have a key because it just didn't occur to anybody to give me one."

"Even though they were going off to Greece for a few weeks?"

"Luisa has one. If I had to get in for any reason, I'd call her."

"I see."

"And you say you left by the back door?"

"I always do when I'm over there. I use the back door because it locks when you close it. Well, as I said, I hadn't been feeling well and—well, as I started to leave, I remembered that there was some Alka-Seltzer in the kitchen and I went in there to get some. That's when I heard them quarreling."

"What did you hear?"

"I don't know. I don't eavesdrop."

"I just meant, what was the subject of their quarrel? You must have heard enough to pick up some hint."

"I don't honestly know. I really wasn't feeling at all well and hearing the two of them yelling at one another upstairs didn't help much."

"If they were yelling, you must have overheard at least a couple of words."

"Oh, it wasn't important! She wanted something and he wouldn't give in. When I left, she had started running a tub and I could hear her shouting at him. She was in the bathroom and I couldn't make out the words but she yelled out something like, 'Are you out of your mind?' After that, I just heard raised voices and I ran out the back way, as I told you. People quarrel. I don't think it had anything to do with anything."

He put his palms together, hands upraised, thumbs hooked under his chin. "You told me they weren't quarreling when you drove them home from the airport. Still, did you have a sense that they were upset? I mean, was there anything in the air? A silence, say?"

"Are you trying to get me to say they were having a fight from the moment I met them? Because they weren't!"

"I'm just asking you what I'll be asking in court—"

"In court?"

"Your mother happens to be the chief witness against my client. Therefore—"

"But the blood on his shoe—?"

"Your mother's testimony establishes the precise time he left the house."

The color left her face. She turned away. "I understand," she said in a low voice.

"Awhile back, I said to you that it would have been easy enough for you not to let anybody know about you and Manuel. After all, the police are only interested in why you told them you were in class the night of the murder. The answer is that you were at home, because you weren't feeling well."

"That's perfectly true."

"Someone with something to hide would have said no more and let it go at that. I mean, if you wanted to keep your mother from finding out about Manuel—"

"I didn't know whether the police knew yet."

"Why would they know?"

"He used to meet me every Sunday night and then bring me home after class. The other kids saw him. They wouldn't have thought anything about it before. And they don't even know my mother. There would be no reason for them to mention Manuel to her. But now, with Manuel in jail and everybody having seen his picture on television—well, the whole thing is bound to come out."

"I see, I see."

She began speaking to him rapidly with a note of urgency in her voice. "That's why I called you. That's why I had to talk to you tonight. If it comes out that we know each other—I guess it's bound to—that still doesn't mean that he was here. The night that it happened."

"And when I call you up to the stand to repeat what he told you that night, so that I can show that it was the same story he told the police?"

"I don't want you to do that. I've just decided. I'm not going to say anything about his having been here. I'll just say I was here all alone."

"And Manuel? He'll go along with your answering me that way?"

"Of course he will!"

"I can't let him do that."

"What are you talking about?"

"If I knew about it in advance, I would be obliged to let the judge know that my client intended to perjure himself."

"*What?* But I thought that whatever somebody said to his lawyer was confidential! I know it is!"

"Supreme Court just held otherwise, *Nix* vs. *Whiteside,* 84-1321, if you want the reference."

"But if Manuel wants to confide in you—!"

"I will put him on notice not to risk lying to the court. And the same goes for you."

"Then I won't testify?"

"You won't have a choice. I will need your testimony."

"No!"

"What you're just told me would greatly influence a jury in his favor."

"It would?"

"Yes."

"And you think I should tell the police he was here? And tell them about us?"

"You have to tell them."

"I can't let my mother find out about us. Not now!"

"Then tell them you don't want your mother to find out yet. They don't owe her that information."

She looked suddenly relieved. "Thank you," she said. Then her expression changed. She turned away, as if looking over her shoulder at something. "But she'll find out. At the trial," she said hollowly.

"If there is a trial," Dade answered.

"I don't understand. What would stop them from having one?"

"Finding that missing jewelry in the possession of somebody else."

"I don't understand! The papers say it was junk!"

"And if that's not true? And if Paul was killed for it?"

"Are you saying that it wasn't junk?" When he did not answer, she looked around, at a loss, then saying, "But then why would Mother tell everybody it was? I mean, it was hers, she ought to know better than anybody else, and—"

Dade said, "It's getting late and I'd best be on my way." He started across the room toward the door. She ran after him, seizing hold of his sleeve. He had the door open but she still clung to him.

"What are you saying?"

"I just asked the question, If Paul was killed for it, why?"

XXI

Shortly after eight the next morning, Dade was led to a holding cell used as an interview room. It was in a corridor adjacent to the courtroom where Manuel was to be arraigned. It was a small cell, with benches where bunks would otherwise have been placed. Between the benches, there was a wooden table. Manuel was waiting for him. He was dressed in a dark suit and wore a white shirt with a starched collar and a muted tie. When he saw Dade standing outside the bars of his cell, he got to his feet and said, "Good morning, sir—" and then broke off, as if something in Dade's expression had put him on his guard. He moved his head slightly to one side, looking at Dade out of the corner of his eye. The bailiff unlocked the cell, admitting Dade, then locked it again and walked away.

Nodding at Manuel, Dade sat down on one of the benches, sliding down to the center of the table and making himself comfortable. Then, clasping his hands on the table in front of him, he inclined his head slightly and said, "Sit down, Manuel." Manuel seated himself opposite Dade, also clasping his hands on the table in front of him. Manuel's dark eyes searched Dade's face apprehensively, as if he expected to hear bad news. Dade said, "I have a problem."

"Sir?"

"You haven't been forthcoming with me." Then, when Manuel

looked at him uncomprehendingly, Dade said, "I had a talk with Irene." Manuel closed his eyes and bowed his head. Dade waited for him to speak. When Manuel said nothing, Dade asked quietly, "You want to tell me about it?" Manuel's only answer was a slow shake of the head. Dade went on, saying in a low voice, "It's a good thing I found out now. Because the police, they're going to find out."

Manuel's head shot up, his eyes blazing. "How?"

"Irene will tell you."

"I said to her, 'Don't say anything. Whatever happens, don't say anything!' Why do you have to go dragging her into this?"

"It's going to come up. You know what that's going to sound like to a jury? First, you go after the mother, then the daughter."

"I didn't!"

"I'm telling you what it's going to sound like. It's going to sound bad. It's going to sound like a motive for murder. They're going to say that Paul Van Damm found out and was going to kill you, only you killed him first. That's how it's going to sound. That's what everybody's going to believe."

Manuel passed a hand across his eyes. "I've told you already—"

"I know what you've told me. I also know what you hadn't told me until I found it out for myself. When the police find out as well and start asking questions, how do I answer them? What explanation am I to make?"

Looking at Dade, he swallowed. He tried to speak. He moved his mouth but no words came out. Then, suddenly, Manuel's eyes filled and, clapping both hands over them, he turned away abruptly, his head bowed, his shoulders hunched. Dade said, "I have to know. Let's start with the lady."

Manuel swallowed. "She paid me, the lady," he said in a scarcely audible voice. "I'm sorry."

"It's all right, son."

"Then, I—" Controlling himself, he sat erect again and looked at Dade with reddened eyes. "I saw her. Irene. 'Rene. Irene, I mean. 'Rene is what I call her. I never thought someone like that would look at me. When she did—" He trailed off, looking away. "I couldn't tell her. I couldn't say anything to her about me having been with her mother." Dade nodded. "The mother, she wasn't around when it happened, with me and 'Rene. When it started, I'm saying. I didn't think. It was like she wasn't never coming back, the lady. But with 'Rene, I was crazy. I thought I'd die if I couldn't have her forever. When I said what I was feeling, she told me she felt the same way. All I wanted was just to be with her, to have her next to me all my life. I said, 'I'll work. I don't have anything but I'll work.' You've seen her place? You know how she lives? She said to me, 'This is all I want. You here, with me.' Then all of a sudden, this thing happened."

Manuel got to his feet, his dark eyes searching Dade's. "Does she know? About me and her mother?" When Dade said nothing, Manuel said, "She'll find out. She'll find out, now, won't she?"

"I'm afraid so."

Manuel stood before him, motionless. The muscles of his jaw rippled under the dark, glistening skin. The eyes moved. "What if I plead guilty? Then it won't come out, right?"

"And you won't see her again."

"I won't this way, either."

"Maybe. That's a chance you're going to have to take."

The arraignment began at 9:00 a.m. Luisa was there. Ellen sat with her at the back, while Dade joined Manuel at the defense table. Called to the stand, Lieutenant Persons responded to questions from the prosecuting attorney, setting forth the evidence considered sufficient to bind Manuel over for trial.

"Mr. Cooley?" MacBride asked.

"No questions of the witness at this time, your honor," Dade answered.

The prosecuting attorney made the expected remarks. He went on record as saying that Manuel was accused of having committed murder during the commission of another crime and that this could therefore be considered a capital offense. The District Attorney's Office strongly recommended against bail. MacBride remained motionless, his hands tucked under his robes, as if he were cold. Manuel pleaded not guilty. Dade requested bail in an amount commensurate with the means of the defendant. MacBride, not looking at Dade, ordered bail set in the amount of $25,000, gaveled, and Manuel was released. He shook hands with Dade, his face somber.

Persons came over to Dade. He said, "I found out this morning." He jerked his head in Manuel's direction. "About him and the daughter. You know about it?"

"I'm the one who told her to tell you."

"Real smart."

"Um."

"This puts another light on it, wouldn't you say? Maybe there was trouble with her folks. I mean, maybe the thing was junk—and grabbing it was just a cover-up."

"Um."

"Where's the kid going to be staying? With the daughter?"

"Home with his mother."

"The girl's mother from what I hear doesn't know anything. Is that your understanding, Mr. Cooley?"

"Isn't that why the girl asked you to keep it quiet?"

"No law says I have to."

"No law says you can't."

"You're asking favors."

"Sooner or later, you'll be asking them, too."

"I'll ask one now: when I have to come looking for your client, know where he is."

Dade nodded. Then he moved away and went up to Manuel. "Stay where I can find you."

"Yes, sir."

His mother ran to Manuel and embraced him. Dade took Ellen aside and said, "I want to know what Paul brought back with him in the way of proof. He can't tell me but she damn well can."

"Is it important? I mean, to Manuel's case?"

"A man is killed and that same night, two things nobody seems to be able to identify disappear: some costume jewelry and a scholar's proof that a body was Agamemnon's. I can't buy that kind of coincidence."

"Well, ask her."

"If I can catch up with her." His eyes moved toward Luisa. He said to Ellen, "That's just what I intend to do. Listen. Sophie always sleeps late. Tell Luisa to call me as soon as the lady is up." Turning away, Ellen spoke in a low voice to Luisa. Luisa looked at Dade, something unreadable in her expression. She nodded her assent.

When Dade and Ellen got back to the hotel, she said, "I just thought of something!"

"What?"

"You know what's wrong with this picture? Why was she playing that role?"

"Come again?"

"Don't you know what she was doing in *The Trojan Women?* She was playing Helen of Troy!"

"I don't understand."

"It's a bit part!"

"What are you getting at?"

"Why play Helen?—a name, incidentally, no more Greek than David is Hebrew, but that has nothing to do with anything. Sophie usually plays Andromache! After the Greek soldiers take away Andromache's baby, the last heir to the throne, so they can throw it to its death from the walls of Troy—that's the great scene, when Andromache has to let them take the baby away and can't say one word against the Greeks, not curse them, not cry out, not anything, or else they'll refuse the baby funeral rites. That's the role Sophie always plays. But, Helen? You know what kind of a role Helen plays? Once Agamemnon is victorious, his brother Menelaus shows up looking for the wife who ran off with Paris. The soldiers seize Helen and bring her before Menelaus. All she wants to know is whether she's to live or die. Then she makes one speech. She says her running off with Paris saved Greece, because if Paris hadn't chosen to give the golden apple to the Goddess of Love, Hera or Athena would have helped Paris to sack Greece and then made him king."

"Speaking as a lawyer, I find that argument ingenious."

"But think about it. All I want to know is, why on earth was Sophie playing Helen?"

"Well, hell, honey, Elizabeth Taylor played Helen of Troy at Oxford in Marlowe's *Faust* and that's no more than a walk-on."

"But she did it because Burton was playing Faust! That made sense. This doesn't. Find out why Sophie was playing Helen of Troy." Dade looked at her with surprise. Then, before he could answer, they were interrupted by a call from Luisa, who said Sophie was dressing and had ordered breakfast. "Shall I ask Luisa to tell her you're coming?" Ellen said.

"Hell, no. Ask Luisa to keep her mouth shut." Dade strode out the door, half-whistling under his breath. "I want to catch Sophie by surprise."

"Watch out for the Polish alphabet."

"Meaning what?"

"They say Modjeska could make an audience cry just by reciting it. My guess is, she'll try something of the same sort on you."

XXIII

He reached Carmelina just before ten and was about to turn down the 25th Helena when a car passed him coming out of it: Sophie's. She was the driver. At first, he almost did not recognize her because she wore no makeup and her hair was covered by a dark turban. She wore her usual dark glasses and a nondescript black cotton dress with a high collar. It was so unusual to see her devoid of makeup that he could not imagine where she was going. "Well, there's one way to find out," he told himself. He followed her. She drove down to Sunset and then headed east.

When she reached the San Diego Freeway she turned north, climbing up through the pass. Descending into the Valley, she turned off on Ventura Boulevard and, minutes later, drove into the crowded parking lot of a medical building. Dade could see her driving slowly up and down the lanes, searching for a place to park. Finding one before she did, he walked quickly toward the entrance to the building and went in ahead of her. Two banks of elevators faced one another. A teenage boy with the tall, willowy frame of a Masai got out of an elevator and started across the lobby, unconsciously moving in rhythm to the music to which he listened on the earphones of his Walkman. Going up to him, Dade took his arm.

The tall boy looked at him and said with a wide grin, "Hey, what's happening, man?"

Taking two five-dollar bills out of his wallet, Dade pressed one into the boy's hand and, nodding at the entrance, said, "A woman is coming through that door any second. When I let you know, you follow her, you ride up in the elevator with her, you hear what I'm saying?, and you follow her down the hall and see what office she goes into, then come back and tell me." He held up the other five-dollar bill. "Its buddy will be waiting for you down here when you get back."

"You want to serve her, right?"

Dade glanced up and saw Sophie about to enter the lobby. He tapped the boy's arm, at the same time turning away. He pretended to study the glass-covered directory on the wall. In its reflection he saw Sophie, still wearing her dark glasses, waiting for an elevator, the boy nearby. The doors to an elevator opened. Sophie got in, followed by two other people and then the boy. Dade waited. Then, after a few more elevator doors had opened and closed, the boy reappeared. Coming over to Dade, he said, "Three-twenty-three. That's your lucky number."

"And here's yours." Dade handed him the second five-dollar bill and took an elevator up to the third floor. The sign on the door to Suite 323 read FREDERICK BOXTON, M.D., INC., TRACY O'NEILL, M.D., INC., AND NATHAN BLINDER, M.D. "Blinder," Dade said under his breath. Underneath the three names was a single word in gold lettering: OPHTHALMOLOGY. Dade looked around. The hall was empty. Stooping down, he lifted the brass flap of the mail drop and peered into the waiting room. He caught sight of Sophie sitting by herself in a corner.

Straightening up, he frowned, then nodded to himself and, walking to the windows at the point where the corridor made a right angle, he rested his hands on the wooden strut in front of the glass pane and looked up at the line of hills that separated the Valley from Los Angeles. He listened for the sounds of doors opening. Every time he heard one, he stepped around the corner of the corridor, to a place where he could see without being seen. Each time, a stranger, a woman or a man or sometimes two people together, one leaning on the arm of another, stood before the bank of elevators.

He waited almost an hour. Then he heard the door open one more time. Something in the sound itself, perhaps in the slow, deliberate way the knob was turned and the door swung open, almost like the sound of an entrance being made, told him it was Sophie. He was right. She stood before the elevators, waiting, her head bowed, her face in her hands. She did not move. Then, there was the sound of a ping, the doors of a down elevator opened and Sophie stepped inside. As the elevator doors closed, Dade went into the doctors' waiting room and, taking out one of his cards, he scribbled a note on the back. Then, crossing to a frosted-glass panel, he knocked on it. The panel was slid back by a woman with red hair, pink-rimmed eyes which had almost no eyelashes and tortoise-shell glasses. An appointment book was open in front of her and she held a phone in one hand. Handing her the card on which he had written, Dade said, "I want you to take this in to Dr. Blinder."

The rabbit eyes looked up from his card at him. "I don't understand," she said.

"The doctor will."

Setting her mouth, she slid the frosted-glass panel shut. Moments later, the door to the examination rooms opened and the receptionist said, "Mr. Cooley, would you step this way, please?"

He followed her. She showed him into a tiny, empty office, then left him alone. He waited. After a minute or two, the door opened and a doctor in a white coat entered. He was a man in his sixties, with fine features, a freckled balding scalp and ophthalmoscopic lenses on wires protruding from the glasses he wore. He held Dade's card between his fingers. Without offering his hand, he said, "I'm Dr. Blinder. What is the meaning of this?"

"Allow me to explain," Dade said. Dr. Blinder entered the office, which had only room enough for a desk and two chairs. He went behind his desk and remained there standing, arms folded. Dade shut the door. "Privately," he added.

Looking down at the note on Dade's card, Dr. Blinder read, "'Think you can shed light on murder of Paul Van Damm.' What's this all about?"

"Are you acquainted with Mrs. Paul Van Damm?"

"I am not, sir."

"Do you have as a patient a Mrs. Hester Benson?"

"How does that concern you?"

Taking from his pocket the photograph he had removed from Sophie's collection of snapshots in her night table, Dade handed it across the desk to Dr. Blinder and said, "Is the woman in that picture the one you know as Mrs. Hester Benson?"

Dr. Blinder glanced at it and then looked quickly up at Dade, not understanding. "And if it is?"

"I have just shown you a picture of the late Professor Van Damm and his wife. Sit down, please."

Dade lowered himself into the visitor's chair. "Now, let's us talk."

"I couldn't possibly discuss one of my patients with you," Dr. Blinder said.

"Yes, yes, I understand."

Dr. Blinder said indignantly, "My relationship with my patients is privileged! Even if you subpoenaed me—"

"The law has changed, doctor. This is a case of murder. If I can show that you possess crucial evidence—"

"What sort?"

"My client has been accused of murdering Professor Van Damm. It's up to me to defend him, you understand? Now, without going into the case in any detail, let me just say this one thing: I'm searching for a motive—on the part of someone else."

"I don't really see how I can help you. I don't know any Mrs. Van Damm."

"The woman in this picture is better known as Sophie Galanos."

Slowly, Dr. Blinder sat down in the padded judge's chair behind his desk. "Sophie Galanos? I never recognized her."

"That's why she came to you, is my guess. In Beverly Hills, you go into a doctor's office and, if you're a celebrity, some other celebrity's going to recognize you right off the bat. See, nothing interests celebrities so much as other celebrities. Spotting them, they can tell right off the bat whether they're at the right party or the right restaurant or, for that matter, in the right doctor's office, get my point? They're very quick about it in that part of town. That's their livelihood, understand? Celebrities, they work harder at being recognized than anything. I think that's why Sophie came here. In this place, nobody's expecting to lay eyes on her and, got up the way she was, no makeup and the like, she'd be hard to spot. Now, I'd like you to tell me what it is you're treating Mrs. Van Damm for."

"You listen to me!" Suddenly, there were bright red patches in Dr. Blinder's cheeks. His voice shook. "I don't know how much you know about the business of medicine—and I mean, the business—but no specialty earns less money than ophthalmology! You see that waiting room out there? Those people pay small sums for visits here, mostly for nothing more than having their eyes refracted. We don't charge much. We can't. In addition, malpractice insurance is staggering. Now, you call me into a court of law and nobody's going to remember why I was there, just that I was, and with the damn TV cameras on—!"

"I know that! That's why I'm trying to help you!"

"God damn it—!"

"I'm trying to keep from asking you on the stand what I need to know. Just tell me now, privately, what, under the law, you'd have to tell me then!"

Dr. Blinder took off his glasses and rubbed his eyes. "Glaucoma," he said finally.

There was a flare of surprise in Dade's eyes. "How bad is it?"

"You know anything about glaucoma? Let me tell you something. The presenting symptom—that is to say, the onset—is characterized by subjective flashes of light or a halo around objects. That is what Osler referred to as 'the badge of the disease.'"

"Yes, I understand."

"Glaucoma, untreated, as I'm sure you must know, leads to almost certain blindness."

"I understand."

"The time occupied by the process has extraordinarily wide limits—I mean, it can take anywhere from a few hours to many years."

"Yes." Dade exhaled slowly, pulling at the tip of his nose.

"In her case, there was a gradual rise of intraocular tension which was slowly injuring the optic nerve. I had given her a form of pilocarpine to contract the pupils to the utmost and thus dilate the lymphatic canal of Petit."

"Pilocarpine," Dade repeated, remembering the pinpoint pupils in Sophie's eyes.

"At the beginning, hers was not a fulminate case. But then—" He paused. "Then we found out that the pilocarpine wasn't doing what we hoped. The alternative—well—. My patient felt that, given time, the medication would work. She also knew that the progress of the disease could take years. She was—counting on that."

"But you weren't?"

"No."

"You spoke of an alternative."

Dr. Blinder took a long time before answering. Then, in a tired voice, he said, "Iridectomy. In both eyes."

"A removal of the iris."

"To save her sight. Yes."

Dade said, suddenly understanding, "Gray-eyed Athena."

"I beg your pardon?"

Dr. Blinder lifted his head, glancing at Dade, and the light from his green-shaded desk lamp was refracted for a moment from the polished lenses of his glasses, giving him a blank stare, like a statue's.

"A year ago, her condition was grave. Six months ago, I had to tell her that no medication was having any effect, that the prognosis was, so far as we could tell, hopeless." He took off his glasses and rubbed his eyes. "She came to see me today to tell me that the change in medication I made a month ago seemed to be working. The intermittent flashes of light had disappeared, as had the halations. I was quite surprised. The medication is intended to relax the sphincter of the iris so as to reduce the degree of intraocular tension—thus, it makes the pupils contract. The symptoms themselves are not relieved at all. I examined her. The stony hardness of the eyeball had disappeared. The glaucoma was gone. This is something we sometimes see in cases of the acute, congestive type. Such a recovery is very rare indeed but it can happen. I told her the good news, took her off medication and discharged her."

"Amazing."

"She was quite shaken. Knocked her right off her pins. Good news can do that, just like bad news. We had to make her lie down for a little while before we felt safe in letting her go home alone. We asked if we could call someone to come and get her but she said no, insisting she was all right and saying she was late."

"Just let me ask you this: two nights ago, she still thought she was suffering from glaucoma, isn't that so, doctor?"

"Yes."

"Doesn't that mean she was still using pilocarpine?"

"Yes. She was today."

"Then, with her pupils contracted as a result of the medication, could she have driven on the freeway at night?"

"Absolutely not."

"Thank you, doctor."

When he reached Sophie's, he saw her car was gone. He was puzzled that she had not returned yet. He had assumed she would go straight home because she had gone out without her face on. Luisa showed Dade through the dark arched double doors that led from the foyer into Sophie's sitting room.

"I'll wait for the *señora*," he said.

"*¿Café?*"

"*No, gracias.*"

"*¿Una soda?*"

"*Nada, gracias.*" She started back toward the kitchen.

Dade went over to an armchair next to the bookcase and sat down there. In his mind, he could hear Paul's voice scratching away at his ear: "Learn a lot by going to the stacks and just reaching up and taking down books and opening them. Titles don't always tell you much. Nor does the information on the fiche." The fish, as Rose persisted in calling it. "I must consult the fish, Mr. Cooley." Dade was sure she did it to annoy him. On impulse, he took the photograph of Paul and Sophie out of his pocket and looked at it, as if he needed to be reminded of how Paul had looked. He had been a spare man, of middling height. The photograph showed a man with a strong jaw and a long nose and a straight line of a mouth. There were laughter lines around the eyes. They showed white in the tanned skin. The eyes looked straight ahead. He was bald, with a dolichocephalic skull. Someone had held a gun to the bald skull (the powder marks had been found to prove it) and blown out a scholar's brains in less than a second. Dade got to his feet. It occurred to him that perhaps Sophie carried cosmetics with her. He had no more time to give to waiting around for her. He started out of the room. As he went to open the front door, he heard a phone ringing. Luisa scurried down the hall from the kitchen door.

"*Por favor. Venga. El teléfono es para usted.*"

"*¿Para mí?*" He pointed at himself.

She shook her head. "*Es un profesor.*"

He went into the kitchen. The receiver of a wall phone lay on the unglazed yellow tile of a counter. He picked up the instrument. "This is Dade Cooley," he said into it. "May I help you?"

A voice said, "This is Millard Sykes. I'm calling from the University of Arizona. Can you tell Professor Van Damm I tried to reach him?"

Sidestepping the question, Dade said, "Are you the one with whom Professor Van Damm had an appointment on Tuesday?"

"Correct. The point is, I set aside time to accomodate him. Now, I've got people all over the place mad at me—you know, this facility is like the telescope for astronomy students who make appointments a year in advance to use it and if it happens to be overcast on your particular night, well, you're just out of luck, but if he'd just telephoned—"

"Professor Van Damm was killed the day he got back here from Greece."

"Oh, my God."

"You said facility. You're not in the Classics Department then?"

"No, physics."

"Physics?"

"That is correct."

"I wonder if you can tell me why he wanted an appointment with you."

"He wanted us to date something for him."

"Date something?"

"May I ask your role in this, Mr.—?"

"The name is Cooley. I am a family friend of many years' standing. No one seems to know why he wanted to see you. Can you help me out with that question at all? You say he wanted you to date something?"

"Let me explain what it is we do here. We work on carbon-14 dating. On a Tandetron Accelerator Mass Spectrometer. The old process was complicated and required a fairly large sample of the material to be dated and took some considerable time. This new process, which was developed in 1982, is altogether different. We can date a sample as small as three or four milligrams. We are able to date a fragment of organic material within forty years, with a sixty-five percent degree of accuracy. If you double that number—that is, if you allow us a latitude of eighty years—our degree of accuracy rises to ninety-five percent."

"Extraordinary. And what was it Professor Van Damm wanted you to date?"

"He wanted us to examine something previously thought to date from around 2300 B.C., to determine whether instead his sample could have come from a *later* period, say from 1250 B.C."

"I see," Dade said slowly. "And what was the sample he wanted you to date, may I ask?"

"Some strands of hair."

"Strands of hair? From what?"

"He didn't say. That's all I can tell you."

"Thank you, Professor." As he was putting down the phone, Dade looked out the kitchen windows and saw Sophie crossing toward the house. Trapped in the kitchen, he waited and then heard Sophie let herself in with her key. He listened. He knew that she must have seen his car parked in front of the house. Relieved, he heard her go quickly up the stairs.

Thanking Luisa, he went back into the sitting room and sat down to wait for Sophie. "1250 B.C." he said under his breath, remembering that that was the presumed date of the Trojan War. The Trojan

War? "Strands of hair?" he said to himself. But the body Schliemann had thought was Agamemnon's had no hair on it at all. Agamemnon's?

In a little while, he heard a sound and turned to see Sophie, wearing a long mauve caftan, standing in the doorway. Now, she wore makeup. She had discarded her dark glasses. He went over to her, greeting her. She turned to look at him with her large, dark eyes. He saw that the pupils were once again normal. Something in his presence seemed to disturb her.

"Why are you looking at me that way?" she said.

"Congratulations are in order, I think," he said.

She looked at him full, her eyes brilliant with alarm. "What are you talking about?"

"I followed you. I know."

"You followed me?"

"Did Paul know?"

She nodded. Then she crossed the room toward the windows, no sound but the silken rustle of her gown. She sat down on a low stool covered in bargello in shades of rose. A shaft of sunlight made her hair shine like spun gold. She said, "I knew someone once who suffered from it. I knew I had to get help right away but I wanted to keep it a secret. In my position, once something like that gets out—well, you know, for someone like me, when you can't work any more—I suppose you know that after she lost her hearing, Margaret

Sullavan killed herself. When the doctor told me what I had and then six months ago, when he told me how bad it had gotten, I was— well, I guess I was as numb then as I was today when he told me that it had just gone away. That it was all right." She rubbed her long, white hands together for a moment or two and then, on impulse, stretched out a hand and put it on one of Dade's. "Feel," she said. Her hand was ice cold.

"You should rest."

"I know. I thought maybe I would go away, after this is all over. Driving home, I said to myself that I ought to go on a trip." She took a quick breath. "But I have no money. I'll have some when Paul's insurance comes in but I can't spend that because I'll need the interest to live on. Oh, I have a little money, a little bit here and a little bit there, like all actresses, but not enough to get by on. I should have married a rich man but men like that only want someone like me the way they want a Lamborghini or a Picasso. I could never bear the idea of that. Well, six months ago, before we were married, when the doctor told me that I was going blind, I decided to kill myself. I decided that I would get into a hot bath and open my veins. They say such a death is absolutely painless. Well, I made up my mind. I went into the bathroom and started running the hot water. The phone rang then. It was Paul, saying a friend had just brought in some fresh corbina he'd caught off Baja and wouldn't I come over and grill it over olive wood with him? When I didn't answer right away, he began to press me, saying, 'What else were you going to do?' She started to laugh. Peals of laughter shook the room, like the ringing of bells. "I almost said, 'I was about to kill myself!' Anyway, as it happens, I was hungry, I hadn't eaten all day and being Greek, I simply adore fresh fish and the long and the short of it is, I said I would go, got dressed and drove over there—over here, that is— with those awful sparkles in front of my eyes the whole way." She sat motionless, her eyes meeting Dade's. "Oh, Dade, he was so kind, I can't tell you. He was very sensitive. You know, we always used to talk. He would ask me things about traditions in our theater." She put her palms on the edge of her stool, pressing down so that her back arched, at the same time lifting her chin to reveal the pure line of her throat. "Most people don't even know the plays were sung like operas, but the music is lost. Nobody remembers the melodies any more." Getting to her feet, she walked away from him and began to sway back and forth, taking small steps, her head on one side as if listening to the flutes and drums, keeping time, clapping out the dactyls of her speech as she quoted one of Helen's lines:

Grant I may speak ere I die. I am innocent!

"The way we play is very fast, the verse's meter gives us the pulse of the work, sets the pace for the dancing chorus, with the feet of the chorus stamping on the earth to arouse the spirits, faster and faster. You cannot imagine what it is like to play in a Greek theater, out of doors in that hollow like the palm of God, thousands and thousands of people there watching and listening, so close, so close. Paxinou said once to my teacher, 'You can hear them breathe!' Imagine!"

Dade watched her. She gave him a radiant smile and then took his hand. "Paul thought the world of you. You made him very happy. Take that with you."

"Thank you," he said.

"Well, we cooked our fish and we talked. Paul knew something was terribly wrong and he asked what was the matter and I broke down and told him about the glaucoma, and he told me he loved me and asked me to marry him and let him take care of me. I was so afraid—of blindness, of dying, of darkness, of everything. He kept saying, 'Let me take care of you. I want to.' I said yes."

"And Manuel?"

She let out a coarse laugh. "The condemned prisoner always gets a hearty meal!"

"Was the trouble with your eyes the reason you canceled the film?"

"Yes."

"Did Sam Kellerman know about your condition?"

"I never told him. I never told anyone." She crossed her arms.

"But he wouldn't have rested until he'd found out, isn't that so?"

"I guess so. Why do you ask?"

"I have a more important question I want to ask you now. Paul told Clinton the night you returned that he had brought proof back with him that Schliemann was right about his dates."

"What proof?"

"That's what I want you to tell *me*."

A line appeared between her blond brows. "I don't know."

"You must have had some idea."

"I was rehearsing most of the time. When we were together, we took picnics and went sightseeing."

"You have to know what he was bringing back with him. You must have seen it and asked him about it."

Suddenly, she lashed out at him. "I was going blind!" she shouted. She put a hand to her mouth. "I'm sorry. He didn't bring anything back with him. And I don't know what in the world you're talking about!"

She stood with her feet apart, fists on her hips, and said in a throbbing voice, "Listen to me! I thought my career was over, that I had no more reason for living—and then this, today! Where is my gratitude? Oh, my God, where is my gratitude?" Her voice broke. Her eyes filled with tears and she turned her back on him almost angrily. "Get out of here! Leave me in peace!" Softly, her back still turned to him, she began to cry.

He started for the door, saying to himself, "It's the goddamned Polish alphabet! She almost had me!"

In the hotel's parking lot, he found Harm stooped down by the bushes, giving scraps to a cat. "Is that your cat, Harm?"

"I just feed it."

"How's the job hunt coming?"

"It's not."

"You in good health?"

"Yes, sir?"

"Drugs, record?"

"No and no."

"I may think of something."

"Sir? I mean, honest?"

Dade nodded, going on into the hotel.

Ellen was sitting at the desk in their suite, making notes on a pad. "Where were you?" He told her. "Glaucoma?" She was horrified.

"But she's all right now."

She shook her head slowly. "Incredible. My God." Then, her glance sharpened. "So *that's* what it was?"

"What what was?"

"The answer. I mean, why Helen of Troy!"

"I don't follow you."

"If her eyesight was that bad, she wouldn't have been able to handle herself on that huge stage, in the glare of those lights. But Helen of Troy makes her entrance escorted by soldiers, she stands in one place while she plays her scene with her husband and then his soldiers lead her off, 'lead' underlined three times. I guess in her mind she thought it was the last time she was ever going to appear on a stage and I suppose that's how she wanted to be remembered— as Helen of Troy. And then to come home, facing something like that, and have your husband killed." She shivered.

"Why lie to the police about where she was?"

"What do you mean?"

"She didn't make that drive. She couldn't have. She lied, all right."

"But it didn't give her an alibi for the time of Paul's murder."

"It's an alibi for something."

"What?"

"To cover up where she really was. In case somebody asked."

She walked over to a coffee table and picked up her purse, checking the contents and then adding a fresh packet of Kleenex. "You know, I think you've just come up with what Sam Kellerman meant. That they had to get married. He must have known. Once she dropped out of his picture, he wouldn't have rested until he found out why!"

"Tricky but no cigar."

"Yes! She needed someone to take care of her and that's what I think Sam meant when he said what he said. It was the best compromise she could make."

"*Compromise!*" He whipped out his notebook and scribbled down the word. "Compromise: to settle, to put in jeopardy!"

"Bravo!"

Dade pointed at her. "The matches," he said.

"What matches?"

"The Greek matches Tinka was using. Sophie couldn't have brought them."

"Well, maybe Mrs. Kanavarioti picked them up herself. I mean, people do travel."

"She's a poor woman. I think Greece is a little beyond her means."

"Maybe the box has been there for a long time."

"It was a full box. A new box. And as I told you, she was using it. I'd just like to know where it came from."

The phone rang. Dade answered it. His face changed. He said "Yes" into the phone several times and then "Right away," and put down the phone. "I have to go," he said. He started toward the door.

"What is it?"

"That was Persons. I have to get over to the county hospital right away."

"But what happened?"

"It's that man from Paul's department, Harry Slaughter. He's critical. And he's asking to see me."

"I'm going with you," she said. He hurried her out the door. As they went down the thick-carpeted corridor, she said, "Will you tell me what happened?"

"He was out jogging—"

"A heart attack?"

"No." He looked at her and said, "A drive-by shooting." Her mouth fell open. Dade signaled and Harm went running for their car.

XXVII

As the street started uphill, they entered what looked like an entire city of a hospital set in the rubble of the slums.

A receptionist at a long desk greeted them with a professional smile. Moments later, Dade and Ellen got out of the elevator on the second floor. Sergeant Burns was standing outside the open door of a room. He caught sight of them and hurried over to the bank of elevators. "Mr. Cooley, sir," he said. "They asked that you wait till they call you." Then the ferret-face of Lieutenant Persons peered around a corner.

The lieutenant came up to Dade. "Same gun," he said. "Same gun used to kill Van Damm. Just heard from Ballistics."

They walked together down the wide hospital corridor. The lieutenant said, "Some connection. But what? I know you didn't know this Slaughter, but what about Van Damm? Any enemies?"

"Didn't have an enemy in the world. Not that I'm trying to pretend he was a saint—" A look of surprise came over Dade's face suddenly. "Halo. Nimbus," a voice in his memory whispered. "Dónal!" he said. "Listen to me, Persons. Paul was going to see him in Greece!"

"Name?"

"Fitzgerald. Dónal Fitzgerald."

"Occupation?"

"Retired professor of classics. Paul's mentor at Oxford. Old by now. Must be in his mid-eighties."

Burns whipped out his notebook. After Dade had spelled the name for him, Burns said, "Can you give us an address or a number?"

Dade shook his head. "Call Interpol. As I remember, he lived on that island where they left Philoctetes." The name eluded him.

"Left who?" Persons asked.

"The man they needed to win the Trojan War and had to go back for. He had been bitten by a snake and the wound stank so much, the Greeks left him off there to get rid of him. But later, well—see, he had Hercules' bow and arrows and without them, the Greeks couldn't win. That's how they killed Paris."

Burns gave him a dazed look. "Can you spell—?"

Dade waved him off. "Forget it. Nothing to do with anything." Dade remembered suddenly. "The name of the island is Lemnos." He looked at his watch. "Ten hours ahead of us."

"Middle of the night there now," Persons said. "We'll call first thing."

"First thing is right now, Lieutenant," Dade said.

A nurse hurried up to them. "We're ready," she said.

Dade followed her down the corridor, the lieutenant falling in step with him. "How bad is he?" Dade asked him. Dade looked at his watch. It was almost two.

"From what they say, he can't last much longer."

"When did this happen?"

"Around half-past twelve. There was a witness. An old guy driving down San Vicente to go to the market. Slaughter was running down the center strip and the poor old guy saw him hit and ran straight into a lamppost."

The nurse pulled up short at a door where a police officer was stationed. Nodding at the door, Dade said, "He was involved with some girl who worked in the Classics Department. Maybe she should be sent for."

"Name?"

"The department will know."

"Any more you can tell me?"

"She's about fourteen."

"Figures."

Dade entered the room alone. Behind a screen, Slaughter lay on a bed, tubes in the backs of his hands and one taped underneath his nostrils. Monitors kept track of his vital signs. A starched nurse who was sitting beside him got to her feet and, nodding at Dade, rustled past him and out of the room.

Dade sat down on the white metal chair at the edge of the high bed and leaned toward him. Slaughter's eyes were fixed on the ceiling. They had a look of surprise in them. His mouth was open and his breathing was uneven. Several times, he stopped breathing altogether and then the breathing would begin again, gasping, laborious.

"Harry?" said Dade. He watched the man's expression. It did not change. Dade got to his feet and leaned over the bed, his face above Slaughter's. "Harry?" he said again, "you know who I am? You wanted to talk to me." When there was still no reaction, he put a hand on the muscular shoulder and said, "It's me. Dade Cooley." The eyelids flickered. The breathing grew more rapid. Dade saw that the eyes were trying to focus on him. Under the tan, the skin had a pallor. The lips started to move. Dade could see Slaughter trying to lift a hand with tubes in it taped to the side of the bed. Dade put his hand over Slaughter's. "Take it easy, Harry," Dade said.

"Dade Cooley?" The voice came from his throat, the lips not quite able to close and form consonants.

"That's right." Dade squeezed his hand again.

The eyes swam out of focus. "You there?" he said. He tried to lift himself up.

Dade pressed the man's hand. "I'm right here, like you asked. What is it you want to tell me, Harry?"

Slaughter started to say something but he spoke in a whisper and so softly, Dade had to put his ear next to the man's mouth. Slaughter's breathing grew labored. Then he said, "I found out."

"What?" Slaughter tried to speak again. Dade could hear nothing but the sound of air escaping from the man's throat. Dade listened, pressing down with his left hand on the calloused hand taped to the side of the bed. "Found out what?" Dade said.

"About the *kraydemnon*," Slaughter whispered, his voice disembodied, like a voice at a seance. Dade looked at him intently. Now, Slaughter met his eyes. The disembodied voice emerged once again in a whisper from the throat. "That's what she brought back."

Now, the jaw hung slack. Out of the corner of his eye, Dade picked up a change in the blips on the screen which monitored vital signs. He heard footsteps outside the door, the rubber squeaking of a nurse's shoes. Then the nurse came hurrying in, checking her patient's pulse. Swiftly, she put on her stethoscope and listened to his chest as a bell rang on an intercom and a voice on a speaker said, "Room two-five-four, Code Blue. Room two-five-four, Code Blue."

Dade said, "Harry? Harry, can you hear me?" He held Slaughter's hand. He felt what seemed like an answering pressure.

"Expired," the nurse said.

"I'd swear he can hear me."

"Maybe he can. They say hearing's the last thing that goes. But he won't be able to make any answer."

Dade went out of the room. In the hall, Persons came toward him. On the intercom in the hall, they could hear the Code Blue announcement being repeated and then saw interns and nurses racing down the hall, pushing a rattling tray of instruments like a shopping cart ahead of them as they ran.

Ellen joined Dade and Persons. Together, the three of them walked toward the bank of elevators.

The lieutenant said, "He talk to you at all?"

"Yes."

"He say who shot him?"

"No."

"Now, wait a minute." The lieutenant pointed a finger at Dade. "You try covering for that kid—"

"He didn't tell me who shot him, Lieutenant."

Lieutenant Persons was suddenly angry. "I know what you're going to say! That whatever he told you is inadmissible!"

"Deathbed accusations are admissible, Lieutenant."

"Then what accusation did he make? I want to know what he said! I've had it with all this bullshit about the law and what can and can't be said—always by the book, always the same damn question: Was there even that much of a mistake in procedure? Not, What happened? Not, What's the truth? Not, Who's guilty? Christ, no, just, Was it by the book? Now, what did he say? I want to know what he said!" The veins in his neck were throbbing. The lieutenant beckoned to Burns, who was following them back toward the bank of elevators. Burns stepped forward and, at a word from the lieutenant, took out a notebook. Dade repeated what Slaughter had said. The lieutenant and Burns both stared at him. "When you asked him if he could tell you who shot him—"

"I didn't ask him that, Lieutenant."

"Well, why the hell not?"

"He was already dead."

Down the corridor, they could see the Code Blue team slowly leaving Slaughter's room.

"What's that word?" Burns asked.

"*Kraydemnon.*" Dade spelled it for Burns.

"And what is it?" the lieutenant asked.

"It's what you people have accused my client of stealing. The so-called junk jewelry."

"What does it look like?"

"I've never seen it. But I'd sure as hell like to."

As they all left the hospital, Dade and Ellen walked toward their car. Dade looked up, squinting up at the cloudless expanse overhead. "A high sky," he said to her. "You know that expression?" She shook her head. "I once heard Joe Garagiola quote Nobe Kanawa, the Dodgers' groundskeeper's definition: 'It's a high sky when a ball's at its apex and you can't tell whether it's going up or coming down.' Right now, that's how I feel."

XXVIII

At Ellen's request, Dade drove down La Cienega to Beverly. "What's there?"

"The Irvine Ranch Market."

"What's got into you, honey, our market is Room Service."

"I'm going to make a dish to take by Sophie's."

"But under the circumstances—"

"Under the circumstances, I am going to take something by. I've already called Luisa and told her."

"Honey—"

"You listen to me!" Ellen turned to him with a warning glint in her eyes. "We've been here two days and I haven't so much as taken by flowers. I'll do as I see fit! Furthermore—"

"Furthermore what?"

"Furthermore, I am getting claustrophobic! Hotels are fine for people on a tour but I just can't live in one!"

"It's a fancy place! Tell me one just one thing that's wrong with it."

"You've already named the one thing. Look, if you're actually going to defend Manuel, that means we—meaning, I—have to go out and find us a place to live. We can't just live in a hotel. You're not Scott Fitzgerald."

"Watch yourself."

"I mean, if this were only going to be for a day or two—"

"Hm."

She turned abruptly, staring at him. "What does 'Hm' mean. What are you keeping from me?"

"Nothing."

"Hm," she said. "Well, I'll hm you."

In the market, they walked by racks filled with cherimoyas, chayote, star-shape carambolas, prickly pears, New Zealand tararillos which, cut open, looked like russet kiwis, pepino melon, little taros and something a sign identified as the dasheen of coco yam. Ellen went to the fish counter and chose carefully, getting monkfish, thresher shark, squid and mussels and then picked up onions, potatoes and baby carrots, as well as garlic, plum tomatoes, parsley and a jar of bay leaves and, finally, limestone lettuce, a small bottle of cold pressed olive oil and balsamic vinegar.

"We'll need a baton of French bread. Go get one, there's a dear."

"What are you making?"

"*Kaccavia*. An ancient fish soup the Greeks say they introduced to their Marseilla Phocaem colonies. Bouillabaisse to you, kiddo."

"Sophie will be very grateful."

"Hm."

"What does 'Hm' mean?"

"I thought *you* knew." She nudged him and said, "Go pick us up a bottle of Retsina."

At the checkout stand, he pulled out his notebook and whispered, "You hear what that woman ahead of us in line just said?"

"What?"

" 'Charge'! Charge: to entrust, to blame! Yes, indeedy, this is old Dade's day."

When they got back to their suite, Ellen headed for the small kitchen with her groceries. The phone rang. Ellen answered it. She listened for a moment. "It's the desk asking whether you're in to Lieutenant Persons."

"Is he on the line?"

"No, he's in the lobby."

"He drove all the way out here without checking first! What's going on?"

"Yes," she said into the phone. "Now you can try your 'hm' out on him, dear," she said to Dade.

There was a knock on the door. He crossed the room and opened the door. Persons stood there, Burns beside him. Persons' blue pin-striped suit was rumpled and his tie was askew. "You look to me like a man who could use a drink. So do you, Burns."

Ellen poured two tall glasses of Dad's Old-Fashioned Root Beer. Persons drank thirstily, then he said, "Sergeant Burns here just came from the premises occupied by the victim."

"Everything's okay. Lived there alone," Burns said.

Persons took a snapshot in a brown leather frame out of his pocket and said, "This was behind the bureau on the floor. That the girl you told us about?"

"I've never seen her," Dade said.

"One in that picture's about the right age," said Persons.

Dade took the photograph and glanced at it. Then he took the snapshot out of the frame and looked at the back of it, examining the small red print along the edge. "This isn't the girl."

Persons said, "How would you know? I mean, if you've never seen her?"

"Because I recognize the girl in this picture. Furthermore, it's five years old." Handing it to Ellen, he said, "It's a picture of Sophie's daughter." Ellen nodded in confirmation, then returned the picture to Dade, who put it back into its frame.

The two men looked at him expressionless. Persons finished a last draught of his root beer, rose and carried the glass over to the sink, rinsed it out and upended it on the drainboard. He declined a second.

"We had Interpol place a call to Fitzgerald in Greece."

"Reach him?" Dade asked.

"Man's dead," Persons said. Dade shook his head. Persons scrutinized him. "Friend of yours?"

"Yes." Dade clasped his hands together. "How did he die?"

The lieutenant said, "Man was terminally ill. With something that leads to successive amputations."

"*Obliterans.*"

"Well, he went out for a swim off the island where he lived. His wife told us about it. Just swam out beyond his strength, with his wife there on the shore and her watching. Suicide and no doubt about it."

"He know about what happened to Professor Van Damm?"

"Wife said they read about it. She said Fitzgerald killed himself the next day. That would have been yesterday—Tuesday."

"Could his wife tell you anything? Any trips he made, for instance?"

"One to Berchtesgaden."

"*Berchtesgaden!*"

"To make a visit to the salt mines there, she said."

Dade's jaw dropped. "When was this?"

"Oh, a good six months ago, according to her. She didn't sound all that bright."

"She isn't."

"Talked with an accent."

"Greek."

"Didn't seem to know much about him."

"Didn't. More of a nurse than a wife, that's why."

"I understand," Persons said.

"She tell you anything else?"

"Just that he had just been waiting to see Professor Van Damm, is how the wife put it. He was in a lot of pain but he wanted to see Van Damm and he kept hanging on, waiting to see him. Then, once Van Damm showed up, they saw one another, and that was it. We asked the wife—the widow, I mean—why he wanted to see him— Van Damm, that is. She didn't know. The appointment was at that Greek theater they got over there."

"You mean Epidauros?"

"Right. Fitzgerald and his wife attended the performance Sophie Galanos gave there. That was the only time Fitzgerald saw Professor

Van Damm, the widow says."

"And the *kraydemnon*? You happen to ask her about it?"

Persons nodded. "She never heard of it."

The phone rang. Ellen answered it, then turned toward Persons, holding the receiver out to him. "It's for you," she said.

"Thanks." Persons took the phone from Ellen and said into it, "Persons." He listened. Then, he looked at Dade as if for his reaction. "All right," Persons said finally. "Stay on it." He walked over and put the receiver back in its cradle. Then, turning to Dade, he said, "Can you tell me the present whereabouts of your client, Mr. Cooley?"

"What seems to be the problem, Lieutenant?"

"He's disappeared. Along with his car."

"Who says?"

"His own mother." Dade turned away, not saying anything for a few moments. "I'd like to question him."

"As soon as I hear from him, I'll have him to get in touch with you, Lieutenant."

"I'm putting out an APB on the kid."

Irene had a little vegetable patch at the side of her cottage. Dade could see a trail of ants and squash blossoms and the ferny tops of carrots and what looked like French sorrel. He squatted down and crumbled the friable soil in his hands, sniffing at it. "Good soil," he said under his breath. Then he looked up at the sky. It was yellow with smog and the air was very close. He went over and rang a goat's bell hanging from a leather thong on the door. Irene came out, a surprised look on her face, letting the screen door bang behind her.

"I wasn't expecting you," she said.

"I should have called."

"It's all right. Won't you come in?"

"Vegetables."

"Hadn't you seen them?"

"I was only here at night."

"That's right."

"Is Manuel in there with you?"

"No, I haven't seen him."

"Since when?"

"I haven't seen him since the time I told you about. When he came here that night."

"You mean, after he got out on bail this morning, he didn't come see you?"

"He telephoned."

"When?"

"This morning. Right after he got out."

"What did you talk about?"

"I told him about how the police had wanted to talk to me. About there not having been any class on Sunday night. I told them the whole story, as you said. I told him I had. I told you you said it would help him, when the time came."

"And what did he say?"

"Just that we shouldn't see one another until this is over."

"When's he calling you next?"

"I don't know."

"When he does call you, you tell him I want to hear from him right away, you understand me?"

She looked at him, puzzled. Then she opened the door and invited him to come in. He looked at his hands, which were dirty from poking around in the soil. "You've got some ants. What you want to do is grind you up some grapefruit rind and make you a little trail around your beds. That'll keep them out."

"Will it?"

"May I just wash up?"

"Right this way." She escorted him into the bathroom behind her kitchen. It was opposite a closet and behind the bathroom and closet was her bedroom. He washed his hands, drying them reflectively. The bathroom was tiny. Not enough room to swing a cat in, he said to himself. When he emerged from the bathroom, he said, "This is a very cozy place to live."

She showed him the bedroom. The windows were small, set high up and gave out onto the branches of trees and the sky. The double bed was covered with an old-fashioned quilt. He eyed the room. Together, they went back into her living room. She sat down on the raised hearth.

"What's the matter?" she asked.

He held off answering her, saying instead, "When you do hear from him again, you tell him I said for him not to talk to anyone else who's involved in this business. I don't want him seeing anybody connected with this case, you understand me? No ifs, ands or buts, you hear what I'm saying? It's his neck and I don't want him sticking it out."

"What's happened? What's wrong?"

"You stay near that phone, Irene, and when you hear from him, you tell him to call me. If he can't find me, I want him to go over to the Bel-Air and wait in the room for me. I'll tell them at the desk to let him in. Will you tell him that for me?"

"I want to know what's going on?"

"I've told you what you need to know. Now, just do as I say."

"I will."

He took the framed photograph out of his pocket and showed it to her. "That's you, isn't it?"

She took it from him. "Yes." She looked at him with surprise. "Harry gave you this? Why?"

"No."

"He keeps it on his bureau. What are you doing with it? Do you mind telling me?"

"You must have been about fourteen or so when this was taken."

"Yes. I was out here to spend summer with my mother. He was very sweet to me. He had a pool where he lived then and I used to go over and swim there every day."

"And you only fourteen! I'll bet your mother didn't half know!"

She gave him a smile. "I had this absolutely terrible crush on him at the time! I didn't tell her how I felt and I didn't tell her where I went—and I'll tell you something else—I know what they say about him but he never tried to take advantage of me. He felt the same way about me as I did about him, I could tell. It was one of those absolutely perfect summers. Everybody should have a summer like that once in a lifetime, particularly when you're very young and your skin tingles all over and if anybody just touches you, it's like getting a shock. Mother, of course, did find out and she was simply beside herself. She was furious."

"And now?"

"It's been over for a long time. She knows that." She smiled a little. "Later, you remember how you felt but you can't really connect it to anybody. When I saw him again it wasn't there any more. Music could bring it all back—a particular song, say—but he couldn't." She looked at him puzzled. "How did you say you got that picture?"

"The police gave it to me."

"I don't think I understand."

"He was in an accident."

"A bad accident? Where is he?"

"Yes, it was a bad accident."

"Where is he?"

"They took him to County General."

"I'll go right now." She started toward the door, snatching up her purse from the table.

"No."

"What does 'No' mean?"

"He's dead, honey."

"Oh, my God, no! Was it a car accident?"

"Somebody shot him, Irene."

"Shot him? Why would anybody—that's crazy! Do they know who did it?"

"He was out jogging and somebody shot him. That's why I came here. Right now, the police want to talk to Manuel."

"About what happened to Harry? Oh, but that must be some kind of mistake. Wait—" She ran to the pass-through and snatched up the phone.

Crossing quickly to her as she started to punch out a number, he stopped her. "Who are you calling?"

"Luisa. To see if he's there."

He took the phone from her and put it back in its cradle. "He's gone, Irene. I'm afraid he's disappeared."

"Who told you such a thing?"

"That's what Luisa told the police."

"Disappeared? I don't believe it. Why would he do such a thing?" She broke off, clapping a hand over her mouth. "Oh, my God." She grabbed Dade's arm. "What do they mean, 'disappeared'? Are you trying to tell me the same thing happened to Manuel?" She turned deathly white. Dade made her sit down.

"I didn't say that. Nobody said that. Don't go meeting trouble halfway."

"But I don't understand. Manuel didn't even know Harry Slaughter!"

"There is a connection."

"What?"

"The same gun was used. The same gun used to kill Paul."

She remained sitting where she was, a frightened look in her eyes. Excusing himself, Dade left the garden cottage.

XXX

Ellen was making tea. Dade had the newspaper spread out on the counter and was glancing through it. "'Andes Climbers Find Frozen Body, Possible Inca Shrine,'" he read. "Four hundred years old."

"Explorers recently found the frozen remains of a mammoth thousands of years old," Ellen said to him. "And still edible, I hear."

"They're not planning to eat this fellow. May I ask what on earth suggested such a connection to you, my dear?"

"I just like to keep my end up. And what were they planning to do with him, the Inca?"

"Execute him. Execute!" Out came the notebook and pencil. "Execute: to put to death legally; to put to death illegally! He was apparently a sacrificial victim."

"Oh?"

"That's nine!"

"Victims?"

"Opponyms!"

Ellen shook her head. "That isn't one. Killing is killing! How about *pharmacon*? Plato uses it to mean both medicine and poison." He scratched it out impatiently.

"This here's an English game, honey. When's dinner?"

"Later."

"I had no lunch."

"Good."

Gesturing at the bar stool across the counter from her, she poured their tea. "Who was Fitzgerald?"

"Doctor Dónal, as we used to call him—" Dade broke off, his face suddenly wreathed in smiles. Brandishing his notebook at her, he cried out, "Doctor: to cure, to adulterate! Oh, Dónal! You would be proud of me this day." He sipped his tea. "He was an Oxford don and Paul's tutor. Me, I got to know both of them after the war." Dade eased himself onto the padded leather stool, leaned against its curved back and pushed off from the counter, turning in a slow circle.

"Don't," she said. "You're making me dizzy."

"I knew a lieutenant in the Army in Germany who had been in Korea the year before and used to fly all over the place in a helicopter with the commanding general, who was making inspection runs. He'd yell out, pointing down at the ground, 'Look at that, Tupper! No latrine screens!' Well, when he finally ended up at Army Headquarters where I met him, it used to be Lieutenant Tupper's particular pleasure to tuck his feet up under him and have his secretaries take turns spinning him around in his swivel chair."

"You're going in circles."

"This here is a swivel chair."

"I mean, in your talk. Get back to Fitzgerald!"

"He was an Irishman, an American, with a lantern jaw and a kind of a trace of a grin that never left it. Well, come the war, he served abroad as a sergeant in the American Army, in the same unit as Paul. They were both in G-2. They had met at Oxford, at a performance of *Ralph Roister Doister* when Dónal suddenly keeled over, fell out of his chair and cut open a big ugly gash on his forehead. They all thought he'd had a stroke until Paul got a load of his breath and said to him, 'Quick, where are your rooms?' and Paul got him back to Lincoln College, Dónal yelling out, 'Comedy horseshit! My idea of comedy is the Marx Brothers or Maxwell Anderson!,' after which he passed out, Paul put him to bed and then left the room, taking care to sport the oak on his way out. Well, nobody was ever more out of place than old Dónal as an enlisted man in the American Army. He did his best to blend in. Once, on a bet, he and Paul went for twenty-four hours straight on nothing more than two four-letter words apiece. After the war, since his German was fluent and he was in Intelligence, he was stationed in Bavaria as part of a team searching for art treasures the Nazis had stolen. Dónal had an absolutely uncanny knack for finding things. He'd come to a farm and when what was almost a kind of second sight told him he was onto something, he'd point to the nearest manure pile, for example, and say to the men assigned to him, 'Look under there.' And more often than not, they'd find stolen works of art.

"Well, finally, a story reached his ears that he might find himself a Crackerjack of a prize in the salt mines under Berchtesgaden. He showed up at the entrance to the mines with his men late one night and wanted to be shown around, but it was pitch dark and they were told all the miners had already gone home and the place was shut up so there was no way for him to get down the shaft. He knew that once the word was out that the Americans were going to search the mines, well, since the miners knew the Nazis were finished, millions in art treasures could vanish in as little time as it would take for a miner to change himself into a thief. He let it be known that he had jeeploads of cigarettes and chocolate for anybody who cared to help him out. In no time at all, he began to see twinkling little lights rising up over the heights in the distance and then spilling their way down the hillsides, the lights from the miners' lamps they all wore on their helmets.

"Well, Dónal and his men and the miners they recruited got into those toy cars you ride down that narrow track down into the salt mines—a terrifying ride when you go hurtling at top speed around curves and downhill in absolute darkness—and then down at the bottom was this enormous chamber with a vast black lake, and they were all ferried across it, just like the souls of the dead being ferried across the Acheron by Charon. When I went there once, I remember that the only way to get back was up an elevator in a shaft cut into solid granite—one mile of granite, imagine!—and so claustrophobic, Hitler himself only rode in it once to get back up to Berchtesgaden at the top. Anyway, that's where Dónal found works of art looted from every museum in Europe. He saw to it that every damn thing was given back. That's what he lived for."

Ellen looked at Dade sharply. "There's your answer. Paul went to see him and came home with something! But came home with what?"

"Something that cost Paul his life." Getting to his feet, Dade walked up and down, pulling at the tip of his big nose and making a shushing sound under his breath, his brows drawn together. Then, as if trying to get away from the whole subject of Paul's murder and Fitzgerald's career, Dade said, "By the way, when I went to the lavatory—"

"This last time, dear?"

"That's the time. It struck me that I might take up collecting euphemisms: bathroom, convalescent home, adult bookstore, and the like. If you'd like to go in on it with me . . . "

"You know, at times it's all I can do to refrain from describing you as simply impossible. I make what I think is an important suggestion and you are such a self-centered lout—!"

" 'Sticks and stones . . . ' as my friend Merda Chaffee was wont to say. That was a favorite of hers. Merda was ever one for an enthymeme—"

Ellen was halfway through her tea when she put the cup down on the counter so suddenly, she almost spilled it. "Enthymeme!" she cried out. "Enthymeme and Schliemann!"

"What are you talking about?"

"That's where it was! It's your friend Merda and her enthymemes that made me think of it!" She looked at her watch, then said, exasperated, "I have to get to the library. I need a copy of one of Schliemann's books. It's in there. I can see it." She grew excited. "You know how, when you remember having seen something in a book, you can even remember which side of the page it was on and how far down the page?"

"What have you remembered?"

"Where I read about the *kraydemnon*. It was in Schliemann!"

Grabbing her by the arm, he hurried her to the door, his eyes alight. "Tell me on the way."

"Where are we going?"

"Paul's office." He hurried her out of the room.

As they drove toward the campus, Ellen said excitedly, "Remember when Susannah said if you learn two things at the same time, they get linked somehow in your mind? She learned it from that teacher they simply loathed—she had the Ex-Cel class but was a supercilious disciplinarian and whenever she sent a student out for a glass of water so she could take one of her antacid pills, the student, by prearrangement—and it was your precious Jonah that started the whole thing and don't you forget it—would always get the water from the toilet and then the whole class would watch, eyes fixed on the teacher's face, as she drank it down. Well, anyway, she's the one Susannah learned it from and the point is, the day I learned the word 'enthymeme' is also the day I read about the *kraydemnon* in a book by Schliemann!"

Dade led Ellen down the corridor to Paul's office and unlocked the door for them.

He turned on the lights. The room was musty. Ellen scanned the books on the shelves. Dade said, looking around, "The German books are over here."

"Come on! I read him in English!" She ran her eyes up and down the stacks. "I don't understand his shelving system."

Dade looked over her shoulder. "It's geographical. Look." He pointed to a shelf to his right, reached by a library ladder on rollers. "There's Mycenae."

"I don't want Mycenae. That's not where it is." Then she caught sight of something. "There it is," she said. She took a large book bound in black leather and stamped with gold down from a shelf. The book's spine read "Ilios: *Schliemann*." "You know who he's like?"

"Who?"

"Schliemann. Rabbi Glueck. There was Glueck, disguised as an Arab and tramping all over the Holy Land with nothing to guide him but his Bible, and he ended up finding King Solomon's Mines! Well, Schliemann had the same faith in his Homer and my land, Dade, he found *Troy*! That, in the face of the fact it had been lost for thousands of years and nobody was even sure it had ever existed in the first place."

Carrying the volume over to Paul's desk, she sat down in his chair, pulling Dade by the wrist and making him sit down on another chair next to her, where he could read over her shoulder. As she opened the thick volume, the pages separated at a place where there was a bookmark. It was a photograph wrapped in tissue paper. She was about to start leafing through the book when she squeezed Dade's wrist and said, "This is it! Look! And he's even got it marked!" They began to read an entry in Schliemann's journal:

> Troy, June 17th, 1873
> Since my report of the 10th last month I have been especially anxious to hasten the great excavation on the north-west side of the hill. . . .

Ellen reached out a hand and ran a finger down the thick paper of the page, scanning the words.

Dade said, "What is it?"

"Sh." Then she caught sight of something and pointed at it excitedly. "Here!" They both went on reading:

> In excavating this wall further and directly by the side of the Palace of King Priam, I came upon a large copper article of the most remarkable form, which attracted my attention all the more as I thought I saw gold behind it.

Ellen turned in her chair and looked at Dade. "It's here," she said. "It's here somewhere." They continued reading. There followed a list of treasures and Schliemann's effort to identify them with passages in Homer. Ellen took Dade's hand excitedly, scanning the book's page, murmuring under her breath and then stopping again. They read:

> It is probable that some member of the family of King Priam hurriedly packed the Treasure into the chest and carried it off without having had time to pull out the key; that when he reached the wall, however, the hand of an enemy or the fire overtook him, and he was obliged to abandon the chest. . . . That the Treasure was packed together at ter-

rible risk of life, and in the greatest anxiety, is proved among other things also by the contents of the largest silver vase, at the bottom of which I found the splendid gold *kraydemnon*. . . .

At that moment, Ellen caught sight of something and, exclaiming in triumph, pointed at a footnote. She said to Dade, "*This* is what I remembered!"

What Dr. Schliemann discovered can hardly have been the *kraydemnon* of Homer, which was a large veil or mantilla, such, for instance, as the sea-goddess Ino gives to Ulysses, to buoy him up on the water (Od. v 346). This would rather seem to be, as Mr. Gladstone has suggested the order of the words implies, something worn *over* the *kraydemnon*.

They looked at each other with astonishment. Ellen said, "You see, Schliemann made a mistake and called it the '*kraydemnon*' when he wrote the account in German! This footnote is in a later edition, a translation. The only reasonable explanation is that the dresser called it by that name because *Paul* did—he probably used it as a cover name!"

She turned a page. There was a photograph of Schliemann's raven-haired twenty-year-old Greek wife. She wore a kind of chaplet, almost like a cloche of the twenties, but made of gold, which hung like a fringe of golden bangs across her forehead, with longer chains hanging down to the shoulders. Matching bands curved over the hair and joined the headband, giving the whole thing the look of a fitted crown. From all the bands were suspended countless gold ornaments, amulets that must have tinkled when she walked and flashed in the sun. The most famous face in all history had been framed in gold.

Ellen looked at Dade. Her blue eyes widened with amazement. "That's what Paul brought back from Greece! Oh, my God!" she said. "That's what it is, Dade! It's the diadem of Helen of Troy!"

XXXII

Unwrapping the photograph he found in the book, Dade read Paul's note on the back. It identified the picture as a Trojan Grey Minyan cup, which had been found by Schliemann in what he had claimed was the tomb of Agamemnon. Paul's small handwriting noted that "despite the fact that the work has been smoke-damaged, the design of the headdress has never been found anywhere before or since." Snatching the photograph from Dade, Ellen turned it over and stared at it intently. It was a picture of a cup. Painted on it was the portrait of a woman wearing the diadem. Smudged with smoke, the woman's features could not be distinguished.

Dade said, hands flat on the desk, holding the thick book open with his thumbs, "Homer refers to the gifts Agamemnon brought home to Mycenae. The loot from Troy. Now, if this cup Paul found in the tomb was part of that loot—"

"But that diadem is supposed to date from about a thousand years before the Trojan War!"

Dade stood up suddenly, as the truth hit him. "But if there were strands of hair in the diadem which can be carbon-dated at 1250 B.C., *the time of the Trojan War*—No. I don't believe it."

Ellen let out a cry of delight. "Well, I *do! That* must be the proof he said he was bringing home with him! If he was right, that would prove that the body could have been Agamemnon's, just as Paul thought. Since the body was given a royal burial, it stands to reason that if it was buried so many hundreds of years after the others and just after the end of the Trojan War, it's almost a sure bet that being able to date the one-of-a-kind diadem shown on that cup would date the body! Poor Paul!" She sighed. "And to think that he was killed for that, Dade."

"He was killed for fifteen million dollars' worth of what are called 'the jewels of Helen'! The diadem!"

"He was right, Dade. I know it."

"Then do Paul's shade a favor and write that thing for him. You got about everything you need."

"Except the diadem."

"Details."

Dade reached across the desk to the phone under the green-shaded banker's lamp. Pulling the instrument toward him, he rested his hand on it for a moment, eyes half-closed in thought. Then he lifted the receiver, punched out 411 and, when the Information operator came on the line, asked for the office number of Judge Harvey Morgenstern. When Dade got the number, he called it, saying to Ellen, as he glanced at his watch, "It's almost five-thirty. I won't reach him."

The phone was answered by Morgenstern's secretary. Dade gave her his name.

"Mr. Cooley," she said, "he went out to get a bite to eat with his law clerk. We're going to be working late."

What was her name? He snapped his fingers at the empty air. Then it came to him. Audrey. "Audrey," he said, "that is you, isn't it?"

"That's right, Mr. Cooley."

"Do something for me."

"What is it?"

"I'm a couple of minutes away from there." In his mind's eye, he could see the Federal Building on Wilshire, just a few blocks south of campus. "I need five minutes with him right away. I don't want to say that it's life and death but I don't want to find out afterward that it was. I'm in Paul Van Damm's old office on campus." He gave her the number.

She said, "We'll get back to you the minute he comes in."

"I'll wait for your call."

Putting down the phone, Dade telephoned Persons' office. The switchboard operator said, "I'm afraid he's gone for the day, sir."

"I want you to find him. He can reach me at this number. Tell him it's urgent." He gave her his name and the direct dial number of Paul's office.

He put down the phone and got up and looked out the window at the late afternoon sky. He waited, wondering. Was any of it true? Of course, in the recently deciphered Hittite tablets, there was what some scholars believed to be a reference to the contemporaneous Trojan War. There was even a mention of Paris, called—as was the case with the double-named Trojans to record the tinge of their Asiatic background—by his Greek name, Alexandros of Ilios, "Breaker-of-Men."

The diadem had been found not in Troy VI—the Troy of the Trojan War—but in Troy II, at a level a thousand years earlier. But anybody trying to stash a treasure chest when the town was being overrun by the enemy may have known of a way to get down thirty feet or so from what we now call Troy VI to Troy II, where there was a ready-made hiding place in the Trojan wall—which is where Schliemann claimed to have found it. And was that where he found it? The find spot was still in dispute. He said impatiently, "Maybe I'm a fool for believing any of it. The damn thing's probably centuries before her time."

Ellen answered shortly, "So are the crown jewels Elizabeth wears! For all we know, it was an ancient royal crown Paris gave her."

Dade wet his forefinger and made a mark in the air, nodding at her. "Dónal," he said. "He must have gotten a line on it and then found it. What he wanted was to get it into Paul's hands." Dade thought of Paul, murdered for his dreams. Had Helen sat on the walls of Troy as Homer said, and told the old king the names of the

Greek heroes as they emerged from their tents in burnished armor, taking the field? He imagined the sight of the Trojan warriors as they rushed out of the Scaean Gate. They must have looked like the USC football team—and not much older. Most wars were fought by teenagers anyway.

He walked over to where Ellen still sat at the side of the desk, the book open on her knees. She put a slip of paper between the pages to mark her place, then closed the book and lay it on the desk. Putting a hand on her shoulder and kneading the muscles at the back of her neck, "I owe you," he said. "Name your reward."

"May I?"

"Let's hear it."

"I don't want to make the *kaccavia* for Sophie. I mean, under the circumstances—"

"Your wish is granted."

"But the fish won't keep and to waste all that food—"

"I tell you what I saw in the hotel's parking lot?"

"What?"

"There's a kitty lives there. Hungry." He patted her shoulder and then started pacing up and down the small office, plunging his big hands into his pockets and jingling his change.

Ellen said, glancing at the phone. "They'll call."

"They damn well better."

Dade took down a volume of Plutarch and, leafing through it idly, said, "Listen to this: he says Alcibiades was like a chameleon, who could turn every color but white. Remind you of anybody we know?"

"Are you speaking of Sophie?"

"Oh, meow, meow, as my kitty says." He looked at his watch, restlessly.

"That must have been one hell of a war," he said. "Lots of other wars back then. How come that's the one they never forgot?"

"I don't know. Somehow it ennobled them. First time in history you ever hear of the wounded being carried off the battlefield."

"And all for a woman. At least, that's what they said."

207

He took down a volume of *The Trojan Women* and leafed through it. He came to Hecuba's speech denouncing Helen, and read a line of it to Ellen:

> Such magic hath she, as a cup
> Of death!

"And still has."

"You make her magic sound like a curse."

"Isn't it?"

Half an hour later, the phone rang, startling both of them. It was six o'clock. Dade answered it.

"Mr. Cooley, is that you? This here is Persons."

"Can we get together right away? Privately?"

"Want me to come out there to the hotel?"

"If you can make it."

"Be there in half an hour."

"If I'm not at the hotel when you get there and you need to reach me, try me at this number." Dade gave Persons Judge Morgenstern's name and number.

There was a moment's pause. "Yes, sir, Mr. Cooley," the lieutenant said.

"Lieutenant," Dade said, "may I suggest that you put Sophie Galanos under close surveillance?"

"Miss Galanos, sir? Is there something—".

"I'll explain as soon as I see you."

"Yes, sir."

Dade then called the Bel-Air Hotel to tell them he was expecting Lieutenant Persons and to ask if Manuel had called. He hadn't. Dade looked up at Ellen, shaking his head.

"Are you worried about him?" she asked.

"Yes."

The woman at the message desk came back on the line, saying someone had tried to reach him: Jonah. Dade phoned him. "Jonah?"

"Papa, I checked up on the Van Damm insurance. It's all in order."

"Thanks very much."

"There's been a change, by the way."

"I don't understand."

"The professor's widow relinquished ownership."

"Any idea why?"

"The widow wanted to borrow on the policy."

"I see."

"That takes time. She didn't want to wait, so one of the agents suggested she take the policy to a bank and give them title, and then she could borrow from them. See, you can't put a lien on someone's insurance policy. It's not an instrument subject to being attached."

"Yes, I understand that."

"This way, Mrs. Van Damm just applied for a loan on the paid-up policy and when the insurance is paid, she can take some of that money and repay the bank and have the ownership transferred back to her."

"You happen to know the amount involved, son?"

"The girl said it was thirty-five thousand dollars."

Dade swore under his breath. After he had put down the phone, he told Ellen what Jonah had said. "And when was the last time we heard that particular sum mentioned?" he asked.

"Vincent!" she exclaimed, remembering. "But why would Sophie ever have given it to him?"

"Well, we'll ask each of them that question when the time comes."

"They won't tell the truth."

"I don't care! Let them tell their stories and then let's find out how much they can make a jury believe."

Then the phone rang again. Morgenstern himself was on the line. "Dade?"

"Harve."

"I read you were in town. Any chance you two can come by and see us? Olga, she'd love that."

"Soon as we can. Once we're quit of this. Meanwhile, I need your help."

"What's wrong?"

"It's a federal problem."

"I don't understand."

"I'm in Paul's old office on campus. Can I stop by and see you? I can be there in five minutes."

"Come now."

Dade put down the phone, turning out the desk lamp. "Let's bring the Schliemann," he said.

They drove out onto Gayley, the street which ran along the western boundary of the campus, drove a few blocks south to Wilshire and then west for another couple of blocks to the Federal Building. Leaving the car in the lot, they went toward the precast concrete structure, with a dozen floors of symmetrical windows, all of them as narrow as bowman slits. They took the elevator up to the fifth floor and went down an empty corridor to Judge Morgenstern's office. Audrey greeted them and led them past where the law clerk sat working late in the glow of a desk lamp. When she showed them into Morgenstern's office, the judge got up from his desk and ambled over toward them. He was a tall, gangling man. He raised his black eyebrows over the black frames of his glasses and gestured at a pair of armchairs. They seated themselves.

"Drinks would be fine. You don't have to come for a meal, just make it drinks. Who gives a damn about Olga's feelings?"

"When we're quit of this," Dade said.

"You said that."

"Then we'll have dinner. We'll talk law. Lots of law in this."

"That so?"

"You knew Paul."

"I'd met him. Some fund raiser. We're always hitting each other up for money down here. Tit for tat. Getting to be our whole social life. Knew him's too much. Say met him."

"Read about the case?"

"I have. Something missing, as I remember. Motive, wasn't it?"

"Yes. Here it is." Dade took the book from Ellen and showed him the picture. "The diadem of Helen of Troy."

"Get out of here." The judge took off his heavy dark-framed glasses, then clasped his hands and looked across at the two of them with naked, veined eyes. "What makes you believe that's what he was killed for?"

Dade told Morgenstern what Slaughter had said. That he had found out Sophie had secretly brought the diadem into the country. "Deathbed accusation," Dade said.

Morgenstern nodded. "Admissible. What's this diadem worth? Anybody got any idea?"

"Some private collector once offered fifteen million to have the gold death mask of Agamemnon stolen for him. In that class, I'd say."

Harve Morgenstern said, "You telling me fifteen million dollars' worth of art was brought into this country? No law against that. No duty on bringing in works of art, either."

"As such."

"Meaning?"

"The diadem belongs to the Berlin Museum. Knowing Dónal and Paul, Paul intended in all good faith to return it to them."

"Then why bring it here first?"

"Wanted to have some kind of test run. Something to date it."

"Anything of a criminal nature in that?"

"As a matter of fact, the results of such a test would only have been helpful to the Berlin Museum—in dating the thing. But the point is, the diadem was and is stolen property."

"Stolen?"

"Yes. Bringing it into this country was a federal crime. According to Slaughter, Sophie's the one who did. Then, once it was here, it was stolen again."

"You saying that's why Paul was killed?"

"The police say so. That's why they've charged my client with murder. If I can find out who has that diadem, I can clear him."

"So, what do you want from me?"

"A federal warrant to take Sophie Galanos into custody as a material witness in a federal crime."

"Well, you've got grounds." Judge Morgenstern pressed a buzzer on his desk and when his secretary's voice came over the intercom, he sent for his law clerk, a thin stooped scholarly-looking young man, not long out of law school. Harve Morgenstern told him to prepare a bench warrant to have Sophie Galanos taken into custody for questioning.

Dade said, "I'll tell Lieutenant Persons to pick up the warrant. How long will you be here?"

"All night, the way things look now. Anything else you want?"

"A favor."

"What?"

"Make a call for me, Harve. Call the FBI and arrange for a wiretap. It's a case involving an international art theft, so they have to oblige."

"A wiretap where?"

"I'll let you know as soon as I find out."

"Come again?"

"If Sophie plans to sell off the diadem, she had to have made her plans long ago. What I have to find out is, who was in on those plans?"

"How do you know the diadem hasn't already been sold off?"

"As of tonight, I learned she's been arranging to borrow on her late husband's insurance, so she can't very well have sold it yet."

A buzzer interrupted them. Audrey's voice on the intercom announced Lieutenant Persons on the phone for Dade. Harve Morgenstern handed Dade the phone. Persons was waiting at the hotel. Dade said into the phone, "I'll be there in ten minutes."

Harve Morgenstern said, "I'll call the FBI and have them coordinate with Persons. You'd better get out of here."

XXXIII

They went through the garden directly to their suite. Dade called the desk and asked that Lieutenant Persons be sent in. Ellen started making the *kaccavia*. "I knew it," Dade said. He protested. "You said—"

"Use up, wear out, make do."

"So much for kitty."

"I've saved kitty some. She can't eat this much."

"Poor kitty! Luckless plight. Plight!" Out came the notebook and pencil. "Plight: condition, good or evil." He clapped with joy and recited,

> A villous moon hung over shadrack row,
> A scabrous and a dipsillary moon,
> A mordicle, a tissel glistered there,
> Beneath which sported Pooh-pooh the Tansing bear.

"Carroll?"

"Cooley." Dade pulled off his jacket, hung it over the back of a chair and then loosened his tie. When there was a smart rap at the door, Dade showed in Persons, Burns at his side.

"You want more root beer?"

"If you have it," Persons said.

"We need the space in the refrigerator. They sneak back in and fill it up again each time we go out. We'd appreciate it if you would help us keep ahead." He poured out two more root beers.

Looking at Ellen stirring the pan of fish on the stove, Persons said, "It looks like we're interrupting your dinner."

"No, no." Dade gestured at Ellen. "The little lady just likes to keep busy."

"What are you making, ma'am?" Burns asked.

"It's a surprise. The surprise part is the way I serve it to him." Ellen smiled. "I hope you gentlemen can stay for that part."

Dade sat down in a padded armchair at the small dining table and indicated with a gesture at the three empty chairs for the others to join him. He put Paul's book down on the table. "First of all, Persons, I want something from you, in exchange for the cooperation I'm shortly going to be giving you."

"What?"

"I want you to call the DA tonight and get him to drop the charges against my client."

Persons looked at him as if he thought Dade were joking. Persons let out a half-hearted laugh. "I can't do that!"

"Well, of course you can. When you hear what I've got to tell you, he'll not only be glad you suggested such a thing, he'll be downright grateful."

"He will, sir?"

"You write this down," Dade said to Burns. Burns exchanged glances with Persons, while he took out his notebook. "If this thing were ever to come to trial, I'd get up in court and accuse somebody else of stealing that so-called junk jewelry. Now, I know it didn't used to be possible to do something like that. There was a rule created in 1924 by the California State Supreme Court that barred defense lawyers from blaming the crime on someone else. Well, the California Supreme Court just changed its mind and said that all the defense has to do to accuse somebody else is to raise a reasonable doubt of the defendant's guilt. You both understand me?"

"What's this reasonable doubt about your client's guilt?" In a few words, Dade told them about the diadem. "Wait a minute," said Persons, holding up his hand like a schoolboy in class. "You telling us this thing was supposed to have been the property of Helen of Troy? I mean, that's a little like saying it was Sleeping Beauty's, isn't it? You're talking about people out of fairy tales. And you want me to go to my district attorney and tell him this? You're kidding, right?"

"The treasure exists," Dade said to him. "We have photographs of it. It was in the museum in Berlin. The Germans moved the treasure during the war because of the bombings. First they moved it to the Prussian State Bank in Berlin and then they hid it in an air-raid shelter under the Tiergarten."

"Can you spell that word, please?" Burns asked.

Dade complied. "It means zoo."

Persons flushed. "You say, the zoo?"

"That's where they hid it. That is the last place it was known to have been. Well, it all disappeared in the bombing raids on Berlin. Not so much as one single gold coin from the treasure has ever been found. Until now."

"You want me to go to my district attorney and tell him that some kind of gold crown that belonged to someone in a fairy tale, was hidden under the zoo in Berlin and then disappeared like more than forty years ago is what we're after and he's to believe that?"

Dade handed the book to him with Ellen's marker keeping his place. "You'll need this with you. Now, understand, here's the evidence. We'll go by names." He ran through his list, ticking points off on blunt fingers, explaining briefly what role each person had played: "Mrs. Ogilvy, who overheard the argument; Clinton, who told us Paul was bringing home proof; Harry Slaughter, who told us Sophie had secretly brought the diadem into the country; Vincent, who found out something that was worth thirty-five thousand dollars; Dr. Blinder, who told us Sophie never could have made the drive that night to see Tinka; Sykes at Arizona, who was standing by waiting to carbon-date what Paul had brought home; and Dónal

Fitzgerald, our finder, who met with Paul the day before Paul was killed."

Persons rested his elbows on the table and put his face in his folded hands. Then, lifting his head, he said, "I still say it could have been that kid."

Dade tipped back in his chair. "It was one thing, Lieutenant, when you accused my client of committing murder in order to steal a piece of junk jewelry. But as things stand now, you'll end up in court having to accuse him of committing murder in order to steal one of the most famous treasures in history. You'll have to show he had knowledge of it, as opposed to others who damn well did know what it was."

"It could be the same thing as I said before. Not much more than a smash-and-grab kind of crime. The kid didn't have to know what it was!"

"The DA could get himself laughed out of court."

"It's not for me to say."

"It's an elective office. No man invites ridicule. You go tell him what I said. You tell him we have to move tonight."

"And you think that's going to make him drop the charges against your client?"

Dade said, "No. What's going to make him drop the charges is what I'm about to tell you. Either Manuel is guilty or he's not. If he is, once you drop those charges, he'll try to get back the diadem from wherever he hid it and make a run for it, while he still can—and your DA may well end up with both your suspect and what he killed for. Your way just means the kid will stay in jail until he rots. Unless, of course, he tells us all where it is—which strikes me as about as stupid a thing as I ever heard of. I mean, Bert—may I call you Bert?"

"My name is Ralph."

"I'm well aware of that. I already have a couple of other friends named Ralph but none called Bert. I don't know why you have to pick on every little thing I suggest to you—"

Persons burst out laughing, turning away. Finally, he said, "Okay. I give in."

"Thank you," he said.

Persons said in a tight, controlled voice, "I mean I will ask my captain to talk to the district attorney."

"Not, one hopes, in that tone, my friend." Dade took out his watch and consulted it. "It's almost seven. You have your captain—"

"He's out of town. My captain."

"Then act in his stead."

"I can't."

"Yes, you can. That's what 'lieutenant' means. An officer who takes the place of a superior in his absence."

"Mr. Cooley, I just don't have enough to go on."

"Yes, you have. A federal judge, Judge Harvey Morgenstern, has issued a warrant for taking Sophie Galanos into custody for questioning as a material witness in a federal crime—which it is, since it appears to involve the theft of a national art treasure from another country."

"Mr. Cooley," he said, "I've got to call for legal advice."

"I'm giving you the best in the world. Which is: Do your duty."

"You say this judge has issued a warrant to detain the lady?"

"He's waiting now for you to pick it up. Take her into custody as a material witness. *But don't talk to her!* She's allowed a call to an attorney and to a bail bondsman. You monitor those calls to make sure they're made only to those people. Bail will be denied until she has been charged with some crime. A smart lawyer will show up before that arraignment with a writ of habeas corpus. Since the crime of which the lady is to be accused is one of international import, habeas corpus will not obtain, because there is extreme probability of flight from lawful prosecution. It's that simple. Detain her. Then, I want you to keep her incommunicado."

Persons surrendered. "Okay, okay!" he said.

"I want you to call me after you get the DA to drop the charges against the boy, but first, right after you've picked up that warrant. In addition, I want you to make public the fact that those charges against my client have been dropped."

Persons said, "You want me to cancel the APB, too? The one on the kid."

"No, we've got to find him. For his own sake, as well."

"We have the girl's place under surveillance, in case he shows up there. And I think he will."

"Unless she goes somewhere to meet him" Dade said. "I'm going to Sophie's house as soon as I hear from you."

On his way to the door, Persons said under his breath, "We're not supposed to talk to her, but it's okay for you?"

"You can't, once she's been read her rights. All I'm doing is taking my best shot. Once you take her into custody, it's too late for any more best shots."

"When do you want us to take her into custody?"

"As soon as I'm through. Call me when you've got that warrant." Dade opened the door to show them out. "Morgenstern is getting us a wiretap order from the FBI," he said.

"To tap her phone?"

"No."

"Whose?"

"That's why I'm going to see her. To find out who's in this with her. That's the phone we're going to have to tap."

Persons said to Burns, "Get on the radio. We have her under close watch. Keep it that way." Persons and Burns left.

Ellen went back over to the stove, lifting the lid from the pot. A cloud of aromatic steam was wafted toward Dade. "Ready in about fifteen minutes," she said.

"Let me take a shower." He arched his back. "Poor Paul!" he said. "Built castles in the air but she destroyed them. 'And, like another Helen, fir'd another Troy.'" He left the room, gesturing like an actor leaving a stage, meanwhile stripping his shirt off and unzipping his trousers.

XXXIV

Persons called half an hour later, with the warrant in his possession. He said he was standing by to take the lady into custody and did Mr. Cooley want it kept quiet?

"Quiet? I want it on the news the minute you take her into custody." Dade looked at his watch. It was five minutes of eight.

"I hear you," said Persons, telling Dade the charges against Manuel had been dropped and a statement to that effect had already been released to the press for the eight o'clock news.

Dade left immediately. He had no sooner reached the 25th Helena when he caught sight of Sophie's car nosing its way out of the cul-de-sac. After that, he saw a car parked down the street on Carmelina. He began following her at a distance. At Sunset, she drove east. He became aware that the car he had seen was now following them. Her driving was erratic and at first, he was afraid she might cause an accident, but then he noticed that other drivers avoided her. He followed her as she drove past Grauman's Chinese and alongside dirty sidewalks set with gold stars lettered with the names of people in the film industry, many, the scuffed names their only surviving memory. The traffic was heavy. After they had driven some blocks, Dade was puzzled that she hadn't taken a street like Fountain, where the traffic moved swiftly. It struck him that she was driving like someone whose mind was elsewhere, and he began to wonder whether she had any particular destination in mind.

Then she drove south on Vermont to Beverly, bumping over abandoned trolley tracks. After that, she went west to Santa Monica. When she reached the ramp curving down from the bluffs of Ocean Avenue to the Pacific Coast Highway, she swung across the highway, left her car, and then started out on foot for the Santa Monica Pier. Dade followed her and caught up with her as she stood at the railing. In the distance, he spotted the unmarked surveillance car.

Sophie was looking out over the breakers crashing below them and when he touched her elbow, she turned with a frown on her face. Then, recognizing him, she raised her eyebrows in surprise and said, "What are you doing here?"

"Sophie," he said, "let's you and me have us a little talk."

She looked puzzled for a moment. Then she said, taken aback, "Did you follow me here? Did you actually follow me again?"

An offshore wind had come up. It blew their hair. Resting a hand on a rail damp with salt spray, Dade said, nodding at a building facing the shore, "Let's us go over there and have us a drink."

She said, thinking, "But that means you've been following me since I left the house! How dare you? How dare you!" She shivered, hugging herself.

"Come on," he said. "It's cold out here. I don't know what you're doing out on this pier, anyway."

"I came here to think. When I want to think, I want to be near the ocean."

He offered her his arm. "Let's us go have us a drink," he urged her again. "And a little talk."

The large, velvet eyes searched his face. "About what?"

"About that trinket you brought back with you from Greece."

Her composure remained. Her face showed nothing. But she was watching him. "What trinket?" she asked. Without answering, he offered his arm again. This time, she took it.

He led her across the street toward the Gate of Spain, a penthouse bar on Ocean Avenue. They got into an exterior glass elevator and rode it up to the bar. The room was dark. A headwaiter showed them to a booth overlooking the water. A waiter came over to them, offering them menus. Dade said, "Owner of this place passed on to his reward some while back, leaving twenty-three great-grandchildren. Nice man. I like saying 'passed on to his reward.' It speaks to the soul, don't it? I mean, when you say 'died,' you could as well be talking about a flower or a pet rabbit." He looked at the menu. "You want something?"

"No."

"Ouzo?"

"I don't care."

He said to the waiter, "Ouzo for both of us." They sat in silence until the waiter returned with their drinks in tall glasses and a pitcher of water. Dade added water and the clear liquid turned milky. He lifted his glass. "*Ya sou,*" he said. They sipped their drinks. Finally, Dade said, "Where did you get it? What you call that junk jewelry."

"Some little shop in the Plaka." She named the ancient part of Athens, at the foot of the Acropolis.

"What little shop?"

"What does it matter?"

"It matters because I think you're in a good deal of trouble."

The dark eyes searched his face. "How am I in trouble?"

"Your husband was killed. Nobody could figure out why. Now, there's a motive."

"What motive?"

"The diadem. The one Paul thought belonged to Helen of Troy."

She remained motionless, as before, her eyes still fixed on his. "I don't have the slightest idea—" she began.

"I'm doing you a favor," he said to her softly. "Do you understand what I'm saying to you? I'm giving you a chance to tell me your side of the story—before the police come knocking on your door. They don't take kindly to people they find out have been lying to them." He watched her face closely. Her expression remained unchanged. The degree of control she had over it surprised him. She did nothing but remove her turban and touch her thick blond hair with a slender hand.

Then, frowning and pursing her lips slightly, she turned back to Dade and said, "What gave you such a crazy idea?"

"Harry Slaughter told me you brought it back."

"How would he know?"

"From the draft article in Paul's desk. I think that's how he found out. I guess he was planning to get his hands on it and do the same thing with it Paul had in mind."

"Why don't you ask him?"

"I can't, Sophie."

"And why not?"

"He's dead."

"He's not dead." She spoke in a matter-of-fact way, like someone correcting a stranger's pronunciation of her native language. "He's not dead," she went on. "What's the matter with you?"

"He was shot to death this afternoon. The person who shot him could have been you."

She half-rose, her face ashen. "Oh, my God!"

"The police will want to question you."

"I didn't do it! Dade, I didn't do it! Oh, Christ, God, what am I to do? It must have been Manuel." He got to his feet and made her sit down again, then signaled the waiter for another round of drinks. She said, "I went to Manuel in jail because I thought he killed Paul and I said to him, 'Manuel, I want to help you. I will help you. I don't know what went wrong. I don't know what made you do such a crazy thing. Just tell me the truth and I swear I'll help you.' He just stared at me, not saying anything, not even thanking me for offering help." Her scarlet lips were parted, her breathing rapid. The luminous eyes searched his in the half-darkness. "My God, what got into him?"

"I've got one chance of getting him off."

"What?"

"Showing them who did do it. Making out a case for the one other suspect they've got under surveillance."

"Then there is another suspect?"

"Yes."

"Who is it?"

"You."

Sophie looked at him with her eyes wide and her mouth open, touching her fingertips to her breast, too incredulous to speak. He continued to stare at her in silence. Finally, composing herself, she shook out her blond hair, which she wore loosely in a long chignon. She said, speaking without emotion, as if she were answering a question about what time it was, "You think they're crazy enough to believe I'd kill my husband in order to steal from myself?"

"Given a reason."

She opened her purse and took out an enameled cigarette case. Removing a long, Egyptian cigarette from her case, she held it for Dade to light for her. He picked up a box of matches from the ashtray. Then, exhaling and sitting back against the velvet cushions of the booth, she looked at him through her thick lashes and said, "And who will give it to them?"

"I will."

There was a flare of surprise at the back of the dark eyes. Throwing her cigarette into the ashtray between them, she clasped her hands before her on the table, squeezing them together so that he saw the knuckles whiten, and said in a voice she was now having trouble controlling, "Are you threatening me?"

"I'm simply telling you what I propose to do—which is give them someone else in exchange for Manuel. Maybe *he* saw *you*. Maybe he's kept his mouth shut all this time out of loyalty. And maybe that's why he wouldn't even answer you when you went to see him and tried to get him to talk to you."

"No!"

"It may not seem like it, but I'm trying to help you."

"Help me?" She let out a short, bitter laugh.

"The evidence I have is like a loaded gun pointed straight at you. Cooperate or you'll end up in prison."

"No!"

"You were heard arguing with Paul before you left the house the night he was killed. Arguing about what? I kept asking myself. Today, I got the answer. From Professor Sykes."

"No."

"You were arguing about what to do with the diadem, weren't you? Paul wanted it to make his name. My guess is, you wanted it to make your fortune."

She said, "I thought you had some feeling for me. For Paul's sake."

"For Paul's sake, why don't you tell me the truth? Or don't you dare?"

"I'll tell you! I'll tell you!" She sat very still, letting him look at her for a long time, as if she felt secure in the knowledge that the only thing he would be able to see was her beauty. He remembered Homer's description of Helen with her girl's face as she confronted her husband after ten years of war. What had she said? She had asked what her fate was to be, life or death, and, struck by her beauty, he had been unable to lift up his hand against her.

Finally, Sophie said, "Paul told me about it the night he asked me to marry him. *That* was the real reason he wanted to see me. It was all a risk. He needed me to help him get the diadem out of Greece. I was the perfect person to do it. I knew it was worth millions and millions. I lay awake at night, making plans, working out everything, about how to get the diadem here. And how to sell it afterward. I didn't tell Paul about my plans to sell it until we were back in this country. He had never quite trusted me. How wouldn't even let me be part of it unless we were married—I suppose because he had some crazy notion that, once we were married, everything we had was jointly ours and I somehow couldn't harm him."

"'. . . had to get married . . ?'"

"What did you say?"

"Nothing." He pulled at an earlobe. "You knew Dónal Fitzgerald, didn't you?"

"I met him," she said. "Once." She looked at Dade blankly.

"Tell me about that meeting, will you do that, please?"

"He was friends with Paul. He must be eighty-something. Once, a few years ago when Paul and I were traveling together, we went to a castle in Ireland, down to the catacombs where there were a lot of knights from the Middle Ages buried in full armor—the bodies were all laid out on shelves. I don't know what it was about the place—I mean, Ireland is damp, not dry, like Egypt—but these bodies weren't decayed, they were, well, *weathered*—cured, one might almost say, like old leather. They were desiccated and for some reason kind of brownish but just perfectly preserved, even the fingernails, which looked as if they'd grown after death, although people say that's just the flesh receding, and I remember one of them was lying in his armor on his shelf and sort of looking out at me, the eyes slits, as if he were pretending to sleep while all the while watching me, and one hand, the right hand, extended a bit, palm upward, and Paul, sort of as a joke, bet me I wouldn't shake hands with this knight-at-arms and I said, 'Of course I will!' and I took the knight's hand in mine and at that instant something quite terrible happened to me, I don't know what it was, I can't possibly describe it to you, I felt almost like Persephone going down into the Underworld with Hades, and after that, always belonging there for a part of every year. Dade, it was as if that dead knight had drawn me into the limbo in which he lived, that half-world, that twilight, so that part of me could never escape again. Oh, I know all this sounds absurd and I suppose I'm making too much of it, but I'm just trying to explain how it was when I first met Fitzgerald."

"And then about a week ago, he came to see you at Epidauros, isn't that so?"

"Yes."

"Why?"

"It was part of the plan I'd worked out. I was to be backstage in my costume, part of which was a copy of the diadem made from the photograph Schliemann took of his own wife wearing it."

"Where did the copy come from?"

"Sam Kellerman had it made when he was going to do *The Trojan Women*."

"Must have cost a pretty penny."

"Don't you think they spent a fortune on Elizabeth Taylor's jewels in *Cleopatra*? Sam wanted the picture to be authentic. You can't fool a camera the way you can a stage audience."

"So Sam had it made for you."

"He had it made for the actress who was to play Helen of Troy. I always play Andromache. But when it came time to do the film, I just couldn't. Because of my eyesight. That's why it was canceled. Then, when the Greek Classical Theater asked me to appear this season, I had a brilliant idea. I told them I was only up to a brief appearance because of my health. I didn't tell them anything about my eyesight. I offered to play Helen. Our problem from the start was to figure a way to smuggle the diadem past customs out of Greece and then past customs again into *this* country. I knew I would only have one chance. That's when the whole thing came to me. All I needed was to borrow the copy of the diadem Sam had gotten the studio to make. But it was locked up in the prop department and when all this came up, the business with Dónal Fitzgerald, I went to Sam and said I was playing Helen at Epidauros and could I wear it there and he, well, sort of borrowed it for me."

"Just like that?"

"Of course not! We hated each other! Didn't you know that?"

"Why?"

"Some years ago, we had a terrible fight. I was under contract and Sam wanted me to do a really awful picture. Something I hated that he couldn't risk admitting he'd bought by mistake. He wanted me in it as insurance. When he wouldn't back off, I threatened to go to Zukor. Well, it just so happens that Adolph Zukor was always a fan of mine. Imagine, Zukor was still head of Paramount, even though he was ninety and still went to the office every day. When I warned Sam off, he just snorted and said, 'Zukor thinks he's had a good day if he's found his glasses by three in the afternoon!' Right then, I went to Zukor and told him every rotten thing Sam had ever said about him. Zukor just kept nodding and smiling. Then I discovered the battery in his hearing aid was dead. He never heard a word I said, but his secretary did. It got back to Sam. I won but Sam never forgave me. So, when the time came, I had to beg him to borrow the diadem for me. I pleaded with him and then, all of a sudden he gave in and said, 'All right!'"

"Tell me why."

"I got on the good side of him."

"Which side was that?"

"Oh, come on, Dade!"

"I want to know why he lent you the studio diadem."

She looked drained. "I told him the truth. And if you dare to say something like, 'That must have been a refreshing experience for you—'"

"And after you told him the truth?"

"He took pity on me."

His eyes glinted. "Why do you lie where the truth would serve?"

With a sudden gesture of surrender, Sophie lifted her magnificent head, in the bar's dim light, her hair as gold as the diadem itself. "All right, all right. I cut him in on it. I promised that when we got back with it, with the original—"

"What is this 'we'? Are you trying to suggest to me Paul was in on it?"

"Of course not. It was just between Sam Kellerman and me. It was nothing but a straight business deal. I will say that he kept up his end. He did everything I needed."

"Including dropping dead at the right time."

"Yes. Poor bastard! They say the plate of revenge tastes best cold. Well, I'll tell you something. I don't have any appetite for it at all." She pushed her drink away.

"After he lent you the copy, Sophie, what happened then?"

"He lent me the copy and we took off for Greece. I told Zoë Polykleides it was fake, just junk. Which, of course, it was."

"When she talked to me, she called it the *kraydemnon*."

"Because Schliemann did. And Paul just went right on calling it that because we couldn't call it by its real name!"

"Then?"

"Fitzgerald was to come backstage to congratulate me afterward. At that time, the exchange was to be made."

"And was it?"

"Yes." Her expression was suddenly shadowed. "As I say, I had never met him before. But when I did, he looked somehow familiar. Then, he held out his hand. I took it. His hand was cold. I know you'll think me crazy for saying this, but I swear it was the hand of that dead knight in the catacombs. And then he looked at me. And the way he did made me feel that he knew exactly what I was thinking and feeling and that it was in some awful sense true. I know that's crazy. I can only tell you that that is how I felt. I was sick with horror. All of a sudden, there I was, wearing the golden diadem of the woman over whom they had fought the Trojan War."

He laced his fingers on the table in front of him, eyeing her. "Go on."

"I got dizzy. I almost fainted. Paul and I got on the plane in Athens that night and flew back to the States. I had taken the studio copy of the diadem with me and brought back the real one. The problem was getting it through customs, not so much here as there. The Greeks won't let you take any artifact out without certification. Never mind that it wasn't Greek but Trojan—in their minds, everything in Greece is Greek. So what I did was arrive in Athens wearing it, pose for the press as I got off the plane and then pose for the press again as we were boarding the plane to fly back here. Only that time, I was wearing the original.

"I didn't tell Paul until we were back home that I had arranged for us to sell the diadem. There really were golden hairs in it. Not Schliemann's wife's—she had black hair. These were golden hairs, just as Fitzgerald had told Paul. At first, I thought it couldn't be true. How could hair last that long? But then I remembered seeing this fall of hair on an unwrapped mummy in the Louvre." She took a shuddering breath, fingertips to her eyelids. Then, collecting herself, she went on speaking.

"Once the hair was carbon-dated and authenticated, all this in secret, mind you, we were going to get fifteen million dollars. Well, why not? Paintings sell for that. One sold for far more than that a while back, one by an artist I never even heard of. Paul intended to give the diadem back to the Berlin Museum where it belonged. I said to him, 'Paul, listen to me. All your research will be documented and attested to and you can publish it and no one can ever doubt it' 'And the diadem?' he asked. 'We'll say it was stolen. You will be vindicated, you will triumph, you will be remembered—but meanwhile, we're going to be rich, Paul! We're going to live and live and have everything in the world!' I was so happy, Dade! My God, here I was, going blind—at least, that's what I thought then—and in spite of it, I couldn't feel anything but happiness!"

Her face changed, became hard, bitter. "But he wouldn't listen to me. He said he would call Clinton, that he would go public immediately with the whole story, and that after that, whoever might have been interested in buying the diadem wouldn't dare touch it. I said to him, 'If you do that, the Berlin Museum will go to the State Department and demand the diadem back and you won't ever get to Sykes at Arizona—they won't listen to you, you know what those European museum people are like, they won't listen to anybody. They'll laugh at you!' And you know what he did? He hit me! He—hit me!" She began to cry. Controlling herself, she said, "He told me to call the buyer and tell him the deal was off. I explained to him that I had never even met the buyer, that I couldn't call him, that all I had was a time and a place where we were to meet that night, right after our return, and that I would have to go to the buyer and explain in person what had happened. He didn't believe me. I said, 'Then come with me.' He wouldn't. He wouldn't leave the diadem in an empty house and he didn't dare leave the house with it to go somewhere with me to meet a stranger, a stranger he was afraid might be dangerous. I said to him, 'Then you have no choice.' After that, I went out."

"That was the argument Mrs. Ogilvy said she heard you two having, is that correct?"

"Yes."

"And where did you go?"

"To meet the buyer."

"Without the diadem?"

"Well, we had to talk first."

"About what?"

"He would have to be assured that he was buying the actual diadem Schliemann found."

"Wouldn't he have checked the museum markings?"

"Pardon me?"

"Museums make secret marks on their most valuable acquisitions. That's how they're identified. Did your buyer have access to those marks?"

"Well, of course he did!"

"How do you know?"

"The man's not a fool."

"But you are. You don't even know what I'm talking about. You're nothing but a goddamned liar, Sophie. Now I want to know where you went when you went out. And don't say to Tinka's. You couldn't possibly have made such a drive. Not with those drops in your eyes."

"I'm not going to tell you."

"Try making that answer to me when I put you up on the stand. You won't be able to hear a pin drop in that courtroom. Now, where were you for those three hours?"

"I couldn't stay in the same house with him. I had to get away. I had to think."

"Where were you?"

"If only you understood how I—"

"One last time: where were you?"

"With Manuel."

"Where?"

"In a motel."

"What motel?"

"Just a few minutes away. A motel in Santa Monica. Some place where there are separate units."

"How did you get there?"

"I drove."

"With those drops in your eyes?"

"It isn't that far. I took back streets. I parked on the street. I saw Manuel's car parked in front of a unit. He met me there. The people who run the place never even saw me."

"Name?"

"Oh, some stupid name." She put a hand to her head. "The Welcome Inn. As I say, they didn't see me."

"And why were you meeting Manuel?"

"Don't ask stupid questions."

"One more time: why were you meeting him?"

She turned away, the back of one hand half hiding her face. Then she said, "He was to take me to the buyer. I couldn't drive by myself. But once Paul had become so impossible—well, I just had to postpone meeting with the buyer. I called him. I said, 'You'll just have to be patient. You have to give me time until I can bring him around, and I will. I will.'"

Dade took out his notebook. "You just told me you didn't know the buyer's number."

"I just said that to Paul."

"How much did Manuel know about all this?"

"He didn't know anything."

"How much had you told him?"

"Why should I have told him anything?"

"Could he have found out what you were up to?"

"I don't know. I suppose he could have."

"Where did he think he was going to drive you?"

"Where I told him to drive me. It isn't his place to ask questions."

"And you left the motel when?"

"Around seven-twenty."

"An hour before you got home? You said this place was just a few minutes from where you live!"

"Will you let me explain? I got outside and my car wouldn't start. Manuel waited for me. He went back into the court, where there's a public phone, and called the Three A's. They said they'd be right over. I made Manuel leave because the place is on Santa Monica Boulevard—I had parked there and not in front of the unit—and I didn't want someone driving by and seeing us together."

"He left, then?"

"No, he went back into the room to wait until the Three A's showed up."

"They showed up when?"

"I don't know. Ask them. All I can tell you is, it took them forever. Their truck didn't get there until well after eight."

"Was there anything wrong with your car when you got into it that night?"

"Nothing."

"It had been sitting in the cul-de-sac for how long, the whole time you were away?"

"Yes."

"And did you have any trouble starting it that night?"

"No."

"What about the lights?"

"It was dark. I switched them on. They weren't at all dim, if that's what you're getting at."

"Did they tow the car?"

"No. They tried to jump-start it and when they couldn't, they were going to tow it. Then they looked to see if I had a loose battery cable and sure enough, that was all there was to it. They tightened it down, the car started and, seeing that I was all right, I guess, Manuel drove away."

"And so what you're telling me is, as a result of this trouble with the car, you didn't get home just after seven-thirty, as you had planned, you got home an hour later."

"Yes."

"Just when Manuel was due there?"

"Yes."

"Did you know Paul was expecting him then?"

"Yes. Manuel had told me."

"And then?"

"After I got home, I saw Manuel running out of there. I went upstairs and found Paul dead and the diadem gone. I didn't say anything to the police about the diadem. What could I say? If there was a chance of getting it back and making that sale, that chance would be ruined once the truth was out, and no amount of truth would bring Paul back." She shuddered. Opening her hands, she said, "There. That's what happened. Oh, I know what the police will say. That I killed Paul to keep him quiet and hid the diadem and plan to sell it after all this quiets down and then leave the country and go somewhere where they can't lay hands on me. That is what they'll say, isn't it?"

"That's one of the things they'll say. Right now, what I want to know is, who else knew about it?"

"I don't know."

"What about Vincent?"

"Vincent?"

"He knew, didn't he? Isn't that why you had to give him the thirty-five thousand?"

Her face crumpled. "I don't know why I even go on talking to you."

"Because right now, I'm the only wheel in town, you know that, don't you?"

"I understand."

"Now, here's a last question and then I'll let you go. I'll want you to think very carefully before you answer this one. I know you'll lie to me but I'm prepared for that. Make it a good lie. Who knows? Maybe I'll fall for it."

"What do you want to know?" she said with an edge of scorn in her voice.

"My question is, how did Dónal Fitzgerald communicate with Paul about getting the diadem out of Greece?"

"Fitzgerald wrote to him."

"You got the letters?"

"Paul burned them."

"And how did Paul communicate with Fitzgerald?"

"In the same way."

Dade whistled and said under his breath, "That went by me like a dirty shirt."

"What?"

He shook his head. "Fitzgerald was much too clever to make such a stupid mistake. He knew letters have a way of falling into the wrong hands. You're nothing but a goddamned liar. Catch you out at one lie and you turn around and try me with another, to see if maybe I won't like that one better."

"How dare you!"

"Tell me about the letters."

"He wrote in code! The letters he sent Paul were in code!"

"And that's why Paul had to burn them?"

She said impatiently, "I don't care what you think!"

Dade got to his feet abruptly, pulling a bill out of his wallet and throwing it on the table. "You will," he said. "By God, you will."

"All right," she whispered. The youth seemed to run out of her face. She turned quickly away, as if she had felt it happen and wanted to hide the sight from him, but not before he saw lines of strain suddenly appear around her eyes and mouth. "All right," she said again.

Dade sat down slowly. "How?" he said.

"Someone came to see him."

"Who?"

She moistened her lips. "I don't know."

"Whoever came to see Paul knew everything. Now, who was it?" His eye fell on the book of matches he had used, now lying on the table next to the glass ashtray. He suddenly remembered the box of Greek matches on Tinka's table, the matches Sophie could not have brought since she had not been there. Then he saw the answer. He picked up the box of matches, turning it over in his fingers.

"Tinka," he said. Sophie slumped against the velvet backrest of the banquette, Dade said, "She was the go-between for Dónal and Paul. If you made plans to sell that diadem, it was with her help It had to be, since she knew about it and if you tried anything without her, she could have shut you down with one call to the police. You knew Paul wouldn't go along with your plans, so you two were going to handle it all yourselves and split the profits with Sam, you and Tinka, weren't you? She felt she was entitled to a share, for Paul's son, right? You had to call her. You couldn't risk cutting her out." She lowered her golden head in silent assent. Dade rose, offering Sophie a hand. He led her across the room to the exit.

As they descended in the exterior glass-walled elevator to the street, Sophie noticed a crowd in the dark on the sidewalk below them. There was a flashing blue light on the turret of a squad car. Sophie said, "I think there must have been an accident."

The elevator descended swiftly. It came to a halt and they stepped into the lobby of the building and started out the doors to the street. Persons and Burns stepped toward them. As Persons' hand shot out, showing Sophie his badge and then gripping her by her elbow, a battery of lights was suddenly turned on and, in the whitish glare of quartz floods held aloft by gaffers pacing men with hand-held news cameras, Sophie took a step backward, her face full of alarm. Over the sound of cameras whirring and the metallic clicking of countless shutters, repeating like echoes, Persons said, "Mrs. Paul Van Damm, also known as Sophie Galanos, I am now taking you into custody as a material witness in connection with matters related to the murder of your late husband!"

XXXVI

Microphones were shoved in their faces, cameras focused on Sophie in tight close-up shots. Persons took a card encased in yellowed plastic from his wallet and began reading Sophie her rights.

"Let us through, please," Burns yelled out at the crowd as Persons began steering Sophie, still holding her by the elbow, toward a squad door, its lights on and its doors open, the engine running and a scarred-face deputy seated behind the wheel.

Reporters began shouting questions. "Is Sophie Galanos being placed under arrest?" one reporter yelled out. When Persons said nothing, the reporter, holding a microphone with the call letters of a local network television station, called out, "You used the word 'custody.' Does that mean the same as 'arrest'?"

Sophie shrank away, as if the questions hammered at her like blows. In the dark, they could all hear the pounding of the surf and see the phosphorescence of the breaking waves. There was a tang of salt in the damp air and a hint of iodine. The chorus of questions grew louder, some addressed to Sophie, some to Persons, some to Dade, and despite the fact that no answers were given, the questions were shouted out in a cacophonous chorus, as if the important thing were to ask the question, to raise it, not so much to get it answered. The cameras, resting on shoulder pads, were swiveled around and aimed at reporters, their faces stark in the harsh light, as the reporters uttered their questions in brief, terse sentences. Then one voice rose above the noise.

"We have just received a report, Miss Galanos. There seems to have been a major change in the investigation of your late husband's murder. Do you have any comment on the report that the charges against Manuel Garcia have all been dropped?"

Sophie heard the question. She seemed to sway on her feet. Her eyes looked around fearfully. Persons and Burns held her elbows, supporting her. She looked at the crowd surging around her in the glare of lights. An officer helped her into the back of a squad car, separated from the front by a metal screen. Her head turned toward Dade. Her eyes met his. Her mouth was open in disbelief. Then Burns slammed the back door and the squad car drove away, its turret light rotating and its siren starting up, then rising.

Persons hurried over to Dade. Reporters converged on them. Taking Persons' arm, Dade led him rapidly across the boulevard and then down to his own car, the reporters flanking them and calling out questions.

"Tinka Kanavarioti," Dade said to him.

"The woman she said she was with?"

"Yes. Stake her out. Tap her phone."

"We're ready."

"Down the block from her there's a 7-Eleven store on the corner. Across the street is a laundromat with some empty rooms above it. I'd like for us to hole up in there."

"I'll call San Berdoo. When do you want to go?"

"Now." The lieutenant's eyes slid over to meet Dade's. "The DA went along for one reason. You scared him. I said, 'Look, if it turns out you made a mistake, you just rearrest him. What have you got to lose?' 'My job,' he said. I sure as hell hope you know what you're doing."

"Bet on it."

"I did. Everything."

Dade drove back to the Bel-Air Hotel, Persons following him. Dade got out of his car. Harm loped up, glowing. "Saw you on the late news a few minutes ago, Mr. Cooley!" Shaking hands with Dade as if congratulating him, "Boy! Boy!" he said.

Dade said to him, "Ever think about being on the force?"

"Being a cop?"

"Think about it, will you?"

"Yes, sir."

Burns got out of the squad car and opened the back door of it for Dade. Dade said, gesturing at Harm, "Sergeant Burns, here's a fine upstanding young man who's thinking about going into police work."

Harm said, "Who's thinking about what?"

"You are." Dade gave him a push. Burns held out his hand. Dade said, "This here's Harm Watmough."

"You call me," Burns said, "at Headquarters. Robert Burns, like the poet." Burns took out a card and handed it to him.

"I'm not much on poetry," Harm said.

Dade got in beside Persons and they drove off.

XXXVII

Dade filled Persons in as they drove. Nodding, Persons said, "This Tinka's the go-between?"

"Was and is."

"What makes you think she'll make her move tonight? This Tinka woman?"

"What choice has she got?" Dade laid it out for him. "Up till now, the smart thing to do was nothing. But with Sophie in custody, we've got a kind of hot potato situation, wouldn't you say? Get rid of it while you can."

"You think she has it?"

"Or knows where it is."

"Let's take our best shot."

"We've got one big thing in our favor," Dade said.

"What's that?"

"Tinka doesn't know we've connected her to it. She has no way of knowing."

The squad car swooped down the on-ramp onto the San Diego Freeway south, siren wailing. They raced past stopped cars, their drivers motionless, as if they were frozen in time. On both sides of the freeway, fields of the city's lights stretched out toward the dark night sky. Moments later, they were heading east on 10. They cut a swath through the traffic ahead of them. It parted. They heard the squawk of the radio. Burns picked up his microphone and replied, his words unintelligible to them.

Then, half-turning in his seat, Burns said to Persons, "Lieutenant, an unmarked car will meet us at the San Berdoo off-ramp, Orange Show Road and follow us."

Persons met the reflection of Burns' eyes in the rear-view mirror and nodded slightly. Persons turned toward Dade. The headlights of the stopped cars, flashing on his face as the squad car sped by them, exaggerated the deviated septum of his nose and shifted his features, giving him the look of a sketch by Picasso.

Persons glanced at his wristwatch. "Getting on for ten," he said.

The watch was a diver's watch. "You dive," Dade said.

"Right."

"Ever been to Greece?"

"No, sir."

"Damn shame. That you didn't get to see it."

"It's still there, I hear."

"Fish are gone."

"What?"

"You heard me. Those damn fools fished it out by dynamiting."

"You're kidding."

"Would you like to hear a joke?"

"Sure."

"What has four legs, is green, and if it fell out of a tree on you, would kill you?"

"What?"

"A pool table."

"That's a good one!" Burns said. He laughed. "That's really funny!" He pounded on the wheel.

"You liked it, did you?"

"Yes, sir, I did!"

"Would you like to hear it again?"

Burns half-turned, looking puzzled at Dade. Persons said, "Watch the road."

It was shortly after ten when they saw overhead the lighted sign for the next three exits. The first read "ORANGE SHOW ROAD: ½ MILE." Burns turned off and raced down the curving off-ramp. An unmarked car began following them. They drove up the street into San Bernardino, following the route Dade himself had taken the night before. Burns spoke into the microphone in the car. The radio crackled into life. A voice said something they couldn't understand. Burns said, "All quiet."

Dade said, "Make a right here and then a left at the signal."

They approached Tinka's street. On the corner ahead of them, they could see the lights of the 7-Eleven. Burns drove on past it, made a U-turn and parked on the thoroughfare in front of the laundromat. "Here okay?" he asked.

Persons nodded. All three of them got out of the car. They saw a door at the top of a flight of stairs leading up to the vacant quarters over the laundromat. They went up the stairs. A plainclothesman showed them his I.D. His name was Fisher, Herbert T. He wore cowboy boots and dirty jeans and a black leather jacket over a ripped T-shirt. He had curly black hair and an angular face and the two sides of it didn't quite match. Of course, Dade said to himself, nobody's do, but his was way the hell off. He wore rimless glasses that sat sideways on his nose.

Dade offered his hand, pronouncing his name. The plainclothesman repeated what Dade had read on his I.D. "What's the 'T' for?" Dade asked.

"Nothing. My mom, she wanted me to have an initial like Truman. She liked Truman." He glanced at Persons. "7-Eleven, Lieutenant?"

"Later."

Fisher went over and sat down on a wooden kitchen chair with broken rungs. The room was dirty. A rug had been yanked up from the floor, leaving carpet tacks sticking up everywhere, catching on their shoes. The windows were thick with dust and grime. Drawn by the light of a street lamp, a moth fluttered up and down a window pane. Against the wall across from the windows which looked out at the 7-Eleven store opposite was a once-green couch with burn holes in the upholstery. Another man in work clothes and sneakers sat on the floor. He wore earphones and sat in front of a small radio. He pointed at the rolled-up shades at the tops of the windows. "We had to leave them that way. If you sit on that couch, you can't be seen from the street." He pointed to a door. "Bathroom. Window in there faces onto an alley." There was a ceiling fixture in the room with three bulbs in it but the lights were not on. Dade thought, they would not be turning on any lights. They could be there for hours. He sat slowly down on the couch. Some of the springs were broken. The plainclothesman with the earphones had lank dark hair and the complexion of someone who had suffered from acne through-out adolescence. His features were regular but a certain self-consciousness about his appearance in the presence of a stranger be-trayed itself in the way his fingertips played briefly over his face. He introduced himself. He was a detective sergeant. His name was Foley. He touched a finger to the right earphone, pressing it to his ear, listening to Mike, the stakeout. "Where is he?" Persons asked.

"In a car," Foley said.

"Where?"

Foley told him: When word came on short notice to find a place where they could stake out Tinka's house, a detective on duty in San Bernardino remembered that the week before, a local kid named Bye-Bye had been caught in a raid on a rock house. He was out on bail. What the detective remembered was that he lived across from Tinka's house and always parked his car there on the street. He worked as a clerk in a neighborhood liquor store. Around nine that night when Bye-Bye got off work and started to get into his car, the detective clapped a hand on his shoulder, saying he had a warrant to take Bye-Bye down to the station for further questioning. He was to go with the detective in a waiting squad car. Bye-Bye asked permis-sion to drive his own car home because it was parked on a street where overnight parking was forbidden. We'll take care of it, the detective had said. Mike, the stakeout, stepped forward and then held out his hand for the keys. With him was the wire man who had already placed a tap on Tinka's phone. Moments later, Mike and the wire man drove off and shortly afterward parked on the dark street where Bye-Bye left his car every night just around that time—across the street from Tinka's.

"Luck," said Foley.

Mike, the stakeout, sat in the car and watched Tinka's house with binoculars. In the back of the stakeout car, the wire man listened to the tap on Tinka's phone.

Foley said, "I can't have him here. I can't listen to two guys at the same time." There was an intent look on Foley's face. Persons turned to him, waiting. They could all hear a faint, scratchy voice, like the voice of a doll: the stakeout reporting in. Tinka was still up. Her lights were on and Mike reported he could see her move in and out of her living room.

Foley said, "Mike reports she's out on the porch calling her cat." Another crackling interrupted him. When it was over, Foley said, "She's gone back inside. She's watching television again." Mike reported that she had been watching it from the time he arrived. Then he said to Foley that she had gone out again onto her porch with a saucer of milk, set it down and called her kitty, as he put it. The kitty came up on the porch and ran to the saucer. It had a bell around its neck and was clearly practiced because it was able to run in such a way as to keep the bell from making any sound.

Persons said, "Tell Mike the cat's not the one we have under surveillance."

Foley said, "He's off the reservation."

It was also reported that the lady had earlier made a snack for herself before they arrived and had carried it into the living room and she had eaten at the table in front of the television set. Foley reported that Mike said, "'A can of cat food is what she had. The cat gets milk and she eats his dinner, how do you like it?'"

"Cut it out," said Persons.

"Fuck off, Mike," Foley said to him.

"How do you like that, stealing from a cat?" they heard Mike's scratchy voice coming faintly over the radio.

"Fuck off, Mike," Foley said.

244

Burns said to Foley, "What has four legs, is green, and if it fell on you, would kill you?"

"I'll bite."

"A pool table."

Foley threw Burns a look. "You shithead," he said.

"I laughed"—he pointed at Dade—"when he told it. I didn't just laugh, I pissed."

"Can it, guys," Persons said.

From time to time, Mike reported on Tinka's movements. She was sitting in a chair in her living room in front of the television, watching a movie. By now, it was after ten-thirty. Occasionally, Tinka dozed off. It was such a still night, Mike reported that he could hear her snoring.

Through the dirty windows, they could see the colored blur of the 7-Eleven neon. Dade folded his hands over his middle and closed his eyes. He made himself not look at his watch. Time slowed down to a trickle. Dade closed his eyes again. He began to think about *The Trojan Women*. Fragments came back to him. Andromache mourning the loss of her husband, Hector of the glittering helmet, and the loss of her sister, Polyxena.

Her death is sweeter than my misery.

Once again, he heard the swelling voices of the Chorus singing, describing the Trojans as they dragged the Horse up the ramp:

A towering Horse with golden reins—
O gold without, dark steel within!

And then, as she sends her baby away to its death, begging the child to come and kiss her goodbye, Andromache's terrible cry:

O Helen, Helen, thou has drawn thy breath
From many fathers, Madness, Hate, red Death . . .

He thought, How they had hated Helen, all of them, both Greeks and Trojans.

An hour dragged by. They all knew that because Foley held up a hand for silence and they could all hear the toy-factory voices coming from his headphones, like somebody humming through tissue paper on a comb. The sound stopped. Foley said, "Mike says the guy on the phone tap reports her phone just rang. Time: eleven-forty-three."

"Go on," said Dade.

"Mike says wrong number," Foley answered. "He says she was asleep watching television and the phone had to ring a while before she waked up."

"What was said?" Dade asked.

Foley spoke into his microphone. "Repeat what was said." Scratch, scratch. "A wrong number," Foley said, repeating what Mike had learned from the man on the tap.

Persons glanced at Dade. "What do you think?"

"There are no wrong numbers in this game."

Persons turned on Foley. "You tell him to report in right now. That jerk on the tap. Everything. Or I'll kick his asshole right up into his guts. Tell him what I said."

Foley got on the radio. "Now hear this. The lieutenant says—" Squeak, squeak. "Okay. I copy," Foley said. Then, to the others, "Bright-eyes reports following. Old lady says hello kind of slow and female voice says, 'Is Arlene there?', and the old lady says, 'You've got the wrong number.' Click. End of transmission."

Foley leaned forward, trying to read Persons' expression in the dark room. The faint neon glow gave all of them an insubstantial look.

A sound like chalk on a slate. Foley's hand shot up. Nobody moved. Foley said, "Mike the stakeout says she's just left the house. She left the lights on."

Persons said, "Watch it. She's got a car. She may get into it."

"Left on foot," Foley reported.

"Carrying anything?" Dade asked sharply.

246

His question was relayed to Mike, who answered, "A shopping bag."

Dade said, "She could have it with her." They all reacted, stiffening.

Hearing something more, Foley said quickly, "Headed this way." They all looked at each other.

Persons nodded at Fisher. "Now," he said. "And keep her in sight at all times."

It was eleven-forty-five. Fisher hoisted himself out of his chair and went out the door. They could hear him walking slowly down the dark stairs. Once, it sounded as if he had lost his footing. A few moments later, Persons got to his feet and then beckoned Dade and drew his attention to the street. Below them, they could see Fisher cross the street at an angle unsteadily. He lurched into the 7-Eleven. After a while, they saw him emerge again, a store clerk waving him off. Fisher remained where he was, swaying on his feet in front of the place. The clerk tried to push him away from the front of the store. Fisher lost his footing and fell against the building. He took a pint bottle in a paper bag out of his back pocket and drank from it. He slid slowly down the wall, squatting on the sidewalk and leaning against the building. The front door of a nearby house opened and an old lady in a wrapper let out a small dog. The dog explored the trees along the dark street and then hesitated, sniffing at Fisher.

"Do it," Foley said under his breath. "Do it, dog." The dog moved away and urinated halfheartedly on someone's lawn. The door opened again and the old lady standing in the lighted hallway called, "Here, Queenie." The dog ran back inside the house and the door closed.

They all waited, poised, watching out the windows. Fisher had keeled over on one side and lay with his knees bent and his arms around him, as if for warmth. Tinka appeared, walking slowly down the street, almost with a sailor's rolling gait. She wore a shapeless tweed coat with a ripped lining which hung down in the back. She was carrying a brown paper shopping bag. They saw Fisher turn his head, keeping her in his sight. She went into the 7-Eleven, took empty bottles from her grocery bag and returned them, and then bought a quart of milk, two bananas, a package of cigarettes and a copy of *The Inquirer.* When she emerged from the store, she carried her groceries in her shopping bag. She started back up the street in the direction of her house, walking past the exterior pay phones. Then Tinka stopped, taking the purse from under her arm and rummaging in it as if she felt that she had forgotten something. Then, they saw her turn and go to a pay phone. She reached up and deposited her coins.

Dade went rigid, furious, starting to move away from the wall, then catching himself just in time. "Christ," he said under his breath, punching a fist into a palm. His face fell. He had been outsmarted. He said, "She knows. God damn it, she knows." Then they saw Tinka replace the receiver without speaking, moments after having punched out a number. She started back up the street again toward her house.

Foley said, "Shee-it!"

Minutes ticked by. It was almost midnight. Then, scratch, scratch. Foley said, "Suspect driving out of her garage. Car banged-up '79 Volvo sedan. License California Idaho Farmer Louis two-three-six-seven. Chase car one standing by. Suspect's vehicle heading east on Lapeer."

Dade said, "Now! Come on! Let's get out of here!"

Dade, Persons and Burns ran downstairs. They got into their car. Burns listened to the radio for a moment. He gunned the car's motor. "Back on 10, headed west."

Now, they heard Burns' radio clearly. "Chase One to Chase Two. Come in."

"Chase Two. Have sighted suspect's car. May I have this dance?"

Burns picked up his microphone. "You're on. Chase Three, do you copy, come in, Chase Three?"

"Chase Three, El Monte, waiting at on ramp."

Burns said, "Remember the high-tension lines. You'll lose signal there for a few minutes."

"Will keep visual contact."

The freeway was crowded. Across the center divider they saw a waterfall of lights pouring down the hill, coming toward them. Persons said, "Where the hell do these people come from, will you tell me? Here it is twelve-twenty in the morning. Now, who goes anywhere at twelve-twenty a.m.?"

They drove in silence. Walls covered with vines along the freeway screened tracts of houses which stretched away into the distance on either side. The radio chattered.

Burns said, "This is Burns. Repeat, please." He bent forward, intent, listening. Then, when the radio cut out, he half turned toward them and said, "That girl. I mean, the daughter. She took off."

Dade said, "When?"

"Just now."

"Stay close," Persons said.

Burns relayed the message. Nothing more happened for about half an hour. Then messages came from the chase cars as they traded places. They reported that the Volvo was now traveling south on the San Diego. Burns eased over into the right lane, getting reading to loop up on the San Diego himself. The radio sparkled, breaking up sentences and words. Burns swore. "They lost that girl!" he said. "They fucking lost her!"

Persons snapped, "Where did they lose her? Get backup. Talk to me!"

Burns gave a location south of Santa Monica and called for backup. Then he said, "A lot of traffic. The men who had her under surveillance said the girl stopped for a light and when they caught up to her car, it was parked at an intersection, empty." Dade swore under his breath. They drove south, lights scattered in the darkness all around them. Then one of the lights seemed to come toward them. It was a plane coming in for a landing.

"The airport," said Dade.

Chatter, chatter. Burns listened to the radio they could scarcely understand, and, half-turning in his seat, told them that Tinka had taken La Tijera, a boulevard that made a half-right off the freeway, toward the airport. They took a right on Century and headed straight toward the airport. Tinka's car was visible ahead of them. She turned left into a parking structure opposite the TWA terminal.

"Here," said Dade. The three of them got out of the sedan, leaving it parked illegally. A traffic cop ran across the street toward them. Burns flashed a badge at him. Dade strode ahead into the TWA terminal.

Burns said, "Maybe not this terminal."

"There she is," said Dade.

They moved over to a cart of luggage and examined the bags, their backs to her. Tinka went to the counter and stood in line for a moment. When her turn came, a uniformed woman behind the counter punched buttons on her computer. She handed Tinka a ticket in an envelope. Tinka, carrying a small handbag, walked the length of the lobby and went through the metal detectors and then made her way toward the escalators.

They waited for several more people to climb on the escalator and then rode it up, Dade facing the way they had come, as if looking for someone he was waiting for. Were Tinka to turn around, his back was to her.

They got to the top. Announcements were being made about a flight for New York now loading at Gate 35. Ahead of them, they saw Tinka go into the ladies' room. Several other women followed her.

Dade waited behind a pillar. Then, a girl in a blue dress with white cuffs and long dark hair walked quickly by, her head turned, looking at things for sale in the lighted windows. She carried what looked like a cosmetics case. It was blue-and-white leather. She went into the ladies' room. A moment later, Tinka came out, carrying the blue-and-white cosmetic case.

"Now," said Dade. Persons and Burns moved toward Tinka, seizing her arms. Persons began reading her her rights.

Behind them, Dade suddenly caught sight of the girl in the blue dress coming out of the ladies' room and hurrying toward the down escalator. Dade jabbed a finger in her direction and yelled at Burns, "Get her!"

The girl started running down the moving steps. Burns chased her. There was a flash of metal. Dade shouted out, "Burns! The gun!"

Burns leaped up, his body arcing in a flying tackle and crashing against the girl's as the two of them fell heavily onto the moving metal stairs. Dade ran toward them, followed by Persons, pushing the handcuffed Tinka ahead of him. Women screamed. Dade, Persons and Tinka had now all gotten onto the escalator. Ahead of them, Burns had seized hold of the hand which held the gun and he was smashing down on the edge of a step with all his strength. There was a scream of pain. The gun clattered out of the girl's hand and in seconds, Burns had both hands pinned behind her body, handcuffing them. All five of them continued moving slowly down to the lobby floor on the escalator. Opposite them, a line of moving spectators rose on the adjacent escalator, traveling crosswise, motionless, as if transfixed by what they were watching. Then a woman began screaming without stopping.

A man said, "My God, he's killing her! Do something, somebody!"

"Police!" yelled Burns. "Police!" He pulled out his wallet and held up his badge to the crowd. "Police, understand everybody?" Then he grabbed at his victim's head and wrenched it around so that they could see it. Dade reached down and took hold of the long hair and pulled it. It came off in his hand. "It's a wig!" Burns yelled. "It's a lousy wig!"

Dade said, "Good to see you once again, Manuel."

Burns yanked the boy to his feet. He began to read Manuel his rights, yelling them out. Persons pounded a fist in a palm, yelling, "Son of a bitch! What did I tell you? From day one, what did I tell you?"

Suddenly, Manuel kicked Burns viciously in the groin. Burns clutched at himself in agony. Then, with a fighter's instincts, he backhanded Manuel savagely with the edge of his hand. Blood began to pour out of Manuel's nose and mouth. Burns yelled out to the crowd, "Police brutality! Details at eleven!"

Dade turned and caught sight of Tinka's face. She looked like an old doll. As the gypsies say, Your future is getting shorter, he thought.

The five of them went through the heavy glass doors and left the terminal. Limping, Burns let out a shrill whistle. Plainclothesmen from a chase car parked behind theirs ran toward them. Persons said to one of them, "You ride with Burns. Let him take them in. It's his collar."

A girl's voice screamed, "No, don't!" They turned and saw Irene running toward them from the terminal.

Manuel shouted at her, "Get away! Get away!"

She ran up to Manuel, throwing her arms around him. "I was here," she said. "I was waiting. Oh, God."

He looked at her, then tried to wipe the freely flowing blood away from his face with his shoulder, but couldn't reach further than his chin. Irene pulled out a handkerchief and blotted at his face. "Oh, God," she said.

"Get away!" he said to her.

Persons signaled to the second man from the chase car. "Bring her in," he said.

"She hasn't done anything," Manuel said.

Burns began to shove Manuel toward the squad car. "Give me a reason," he said, giving Manuel a quick rabbit punch in the kidneys. "Come on, what are you waiting for?"

Persons said to Burns, "Knock it off."

Irene was crying silently. She threw her arms around Manuel, burying her face in his neck and trying with all her strength to keep Burns from separating them. "Don't leave me!" she cried. "Oh, God, God, please don't leave me alone!"

XXXVIII

After quickly checking the contents of the blue-and-white cosmetics case, Persons put it in the front of their squad car, telling the driver to get Headquarters on the radio and put in a call to the FBI on a stolen goods pickup. Then he said to Dade, "Now it's their baby." Dade and Persons got in the back of the squad car. Dade had asked to be dropped off at the hotel. It was just past two in the morning. Their driver swung out of the airport. On the top of a tower, a beacon rotated against the night sky.

Persons said, "Son of a bitch. It's not as if you hadn't given the kid every break." Dade said nothing. He sat with his eyes closed. Persons turned away. "I'd like one thing. Okay if I ask you?"

"Go ahead."

"I shouldn't be asking favors of the kid's attorney—or former attorney—"

"I'm still his attorney."

"Then, off the record, think about asking the kid to enter a guilty plea, will you do that for us? I'll talk to the DA and see what kind of a plea-bargain situation we can set up but I mean, for Christ's sake, I don't look too good, begging the DA to drop charges against him and then rearresting him a few hours later. Of course, we did catch him with the goods, and that's a big plus, not just for me but for the department. Let's just put this whole thing to bed, okay?" Dade pursed his lips. "Is that a yes?"

"I'll tell my client what you said."

"Okay, okay. And the lady? Want me to hand custody over to the FBI?"

"Not yet."

"Mind telling me why?"

"When I get there. In an hour, say. By the way, just so's we'll have us a full house, what say about rousting Brother Vincent out of bed and having him and his wife join our little party. And bring Luisa."

"Are you kidding?"

"Am I laughing?"

"No."

"And that's the way it's going to be, kid." The driver pulled up in front of the hotel. Dade got out of the squad car. He said, "Do something for me."

"Sure."

"I'm bringing my wife down to Headquarters with me. I want to show her that diadem before the FBI takes off with it. Fix it up for me, will you?"

"You got it, Mr. Cooley."

They shook hands.

XXXIX

It was three-thirty in the morning when Dade and Ellen arrived at the Criminal Courts Building. Dade said to her, "Looks to me like we're going to be around here till the last dog is hung." Inside, Dade asked to see Sophie Galanos. While Ellen waited for him on a bench in the corridor, an officer led Dade down the hall and into a small windowless interrogation room. It was empty except for a table and a couple of oak armchairs. There was an overhead light covered with steel mesh. A door at the back of the room opened and Sophie was brought in by a guard, a hand clamped on her upper arm. When the guard had closed the door after him, Sophie stared at Dade, her eyes hollow in the glare of the overhead light, and said in a hoarse voice, "You bastard."

"Sit down." She remained standing for a moment or two, then seated herself.

"Why are they keeping me here?"

"For questioning."

"About what?"

"The diadem. Incidentally, they've recovered it."

She got to her feet, a shocked look on her face. "What do you mean?"

"Manuel had it. They caught him with it."

"No."

"It's true, all right, Sophie. And the gun. Paul's gun."

"When did this happen?"

"About an hour ago. At the airport."

"What did he say?" Her lips were parted and she was breathing slowly, as if with an effort.

"I don't think he's been questioned yet."

"He hasn't said anything?"

"Not so far as I know, Sophie." He studied her.

She said, the fingertips of one hand touching her throat lightly, as if in an unconscious effort to call his attention to herself, "I told you. I said all along that he was guilty. I was never sure that he knew about the diadem. Now, it's clear that he did. He killed Paul for it, didn't he?"

"How did he find out about it?"

"I don't know."

"If he knew about it, somebody had to tell him, wouldn't you say?"

"I don't know how he found out about it."

"You were sleeping with him. The police don't know that yet. But they'll find out. Then they'll put two and two together."

"I didn't tell him about it! I don't know how he found out about it!"

"Let's go ask him."

"You ask him."

"Let's ask him together."

She threw him a venomous look. "I don't want to see him again!"

"Let's go," Dade said. He escorted her into the corridor. There, he saw Persons coming toward them. Dade took him aside and said, "I want to know how Manuel found out about the diadem. Let's all go upstairs and ask him." Persons nodded, then walked away and spoke to one of his men.

Sophie clutched at Dade's arm. "What will happen to me?"

"To you?"

"Because I brought it into the country. Tell me. What will they do to me?"

"Under international law, the diadem is the property of the German nation, to whom Schliemann gave it, and the Berlin Museum has the right of custody. You told me Paul intended to return it to the museum."

Sophie held onto his arm, half-supporting herself. She sighed and said warily, "Paul intended to. I told you I planned to sell it. Can they try me for that?"

"With nothing but my unsupported word? They'd need Tinka's testimony. Any lawyer would warn her not to incriminate herself."

"Are you saying they won't try me?"

"You cannot be put on trial for supposed intentions. There is no law against bringing objects of art into this country. But there is a law against smuggling in stolen property. It belongs to the German people."

"Then give it back to them! You're the one who has it. I don't. Paul was going to give it back to them! You know he was!"

"It was smuggled into this country—either by you or by Paul or by both of you together. No way now of proving a case against you, Paul being dead. I mean, he can't testify against you."

"Then what will happen to me?"

"The FBI is now in communication with the Berlin Museum. The diadem will be returned to them and you, I'm sure, will receive their public thanks."

He saw points of light out the back of her eyes. "Then it's over. It could be over. Is that what you're saying?"

"At this point, it isn't the diadem they're concerned about."

A door opened and Burns came into the corridor, escorting Irene. Burns came up to Dade and spoke to him in an undertone. Dade answered, holding up his hand as if to stop him. Irene hesitated in the doorway. Dade could see that the open door blocked her view. Dade stepped over to her.

She said to him, "Where is he? Make them let me see him."

Ellen came toward her, saying, "Your mother's here." Ellen led Irene into the corridor, gesturing toward Sophie.

Sophie moved toward Irene, saying, "It's all right. It's all over now."

"What do you mean it's all right? Where is he?" She looked around, as if expecting to see him.

"Where is who?"

"Manuel. I went to meet him at the airport. We were going away together."

"You were going away with Manuel?" Sophie looked horrified. "What are you talking about?"

"I love him. And he loves me!"

"Does he?"

"What is that supposed to mean?"

"There's someone else. There has been for a long time."

"It isn't true!"

"It is."

"How do you know? How could you possibly know?" Sophie looked at her, saying nothing. She kept looking at her until, suddenly, Irene covered her face with her hands. Then she sat down slowly on a bench in the corridor. "No," she said. Sophie still looked at her, not speaking.

Persons said, "They're ready with him."

Escorted by Persons and Burns, Dade and Ellen went upstairs with Sophie. Irene ran after them, taking hold of Dade's sleeve. "Make them let me see him. Please."

Dade looked at Persons, who nodded. Together, they were shown into the same room where Dade had first seen Manuel. Tinka was waiting in there, a matron at her side. Sophie looked at her with surprise. Tinka's face was blank. At the sight of Tinka, Irene said, "Mrs. Kanavarioti?" Slowly, Irene turned to look at her mother.

Sophie reacted with surprise when she saw Vincent and Fanny standing across the room. Fanny appeared not to have been given time to put on her makeup. Her face was colorless and puffy with sleep. Vincent was composed, even subdued. He did not even look up when the six of them filed into the room. His eyes were half closed, incurious, as if he somehow still imagined himself back in bed with his plump wife in their little stucco bungalow high above the lights of the city. No one spoke to them. They themselves said nothing, not even exchanging glances. A sergeant with a stenotype machine on his knees sat inconspicuously at one end of the long table.

Then the door at the back of the room opened and a guard led Manuel in. He was shackled. He did not look up.

"Manuel," Irene said. She went to him, putting her arms around him. She whispered, "She said—" Her eyes moved in Sophie's direction. Manuel did not look up. "I didn't believe her," Irene whispered. "Don't worry. She can't touch us." She kissed him. He looked out at all of them with the eyes of an animal caught in a trap. Holding Manuel close to her, Irene said, "It's going to be all right. Say you know it's going to be all right." Her eyes searched his face. He didn't say anything. Burns made her move away from him.

Dade said to Manuel, "What we want to know is how you found out about it." Manuel remained silent, carefully not looking at anyone.

"Manuel?"

The boy looked at Dade. "I don't know what you're talking about," he said.

Dade said loudly, "What the hell is this? We just picked you up at the airport with it and you don't know anything about it?" Manuel continued to meet Dade's eyes. The look in the boy's eyes was cool, almost insolent. When Manuel made no reply, Dade said finally, "Let's take it from the top. Let's go over it together, shall we do that Manuel?" Dade folded his arms. "You got to the house at eight-thirty that night, didn't you, Manuel?" Dade's gaze sharpened. "You knew Sophie was on her way home. You had to have known. You had just left her minutes before."

Irene said, "What? Oh, that can't be true!" Manuel swallowed audibly.

Dade waited for some reply. When there was none, Dade went on: "You let yourself into the house. You were very quiet. What did you do then, go upstairs? Professor Van Damm would have been surprised to see you, wouldn't he?"

Manuel made an effort to speak. Then he said, "He sent for me."

"Paul was always sending for him!" Irene said. "Manuel told me he did! I told you that! He wanted Manuel to take him to James Clinton's!"

"And just drive him over there with fifteen million dollars' worth of treasure in a case on his knees? Or was he going to leave it in the house until he got back?"

"What treasure? What are you talking about?"

Dade said sharply, "The one person Paul wanted to see was Professor Sykes at the University of Arizona. There was no conceivable reason for him to take the diadem over to Clinton's." Dade stabbed a finger in Manuel's direction. "I say he never sent for you!" Dade shouted at him.

"Diadem?" Irene echoed, her eyes on Manuel. He did not look at her.

Manuel said, "I swear—"

Dade interrupted him. "You've done enough swearing. Surprised is right. He would have been astonished to see you there." A fleeting expression, a startled look, passed over Manuel's motionless face. "How would you have explained your presence? Well, the easiest thing in the world would be to tell him Sophie had sent for you—just as you later told us *he* sent for you. 'Oh, she's out? Well, is it okay if I wait for her, sir?' That's about what you said, isn't it?" A tremor passed over Manuel's face. He bent his head. "What were you waiting for?" Dade's eyes raked the room. "It's so simple, isn't it? The diadem was upstairs."

"What diadem?" Irene asked.

"Your parents brought back something of great value from Greece," Dade said to her. "Worth a fortune. That's why Paul was killed." Irene swung her head around and stared at Manuel in disbelief. Dade said to Manuel, "My guess is, Professor Van Damm had the diadem on the desk in his study. Where else would a scholar examine something?"

"I don't know what you're talking about!" Manuel shouted.

"You were just picked up with it at the airport and you don't know what I'm talking about? Not to mention the gun Professor Van

Damm was killed with, and Harry Slaughter as well, and you don't know what I'm talking about?"

Manuel let out a sound like the cry of a wounded animal and began yanking at his manacles, as if he thought he could free himself with brute strength alone. The guard seized him roughly by one arm, slamming him up against the wall. Dade said, "That's enough!" The guard let go of him. Manuel lifted his shoulders and then bent his head down toward his manacled hands, rubbing at the dried blood on his nose with the back of his hand. Dade took a long breath. "Yes, yes. You were going to steal it. That's what you went to the house for. You knew when you went there he was home alone. You knew you'd be there ahead of Sophie because you disabled her car before you left her."

"I didn't! I didn't!"

Dade's eyes bored into him. "You knew if you stole it, he could identify you. You had to kill him. But then what? You were the obvious suspect. You had a key. So what were you waiting for? You were waiting for Sophie." Dade's eyes fastened on Sophie. "He was waiting for you! This whole crime was set up to frame you, so as to leave him in the clear!"

"It isn't true," Manuel said.

"You planned to kill Paul the moment Sophie entered the house. Seize the diadem and run off, letting it seem that she herself had killed him. You ran down the stairs and ran out of the house. You knew she'd seen you. You figured you were safe. She couldn't possibly say a word about the diadem or else she would lose all chance of ever getting her hands on it. Is that how it happened Manuel?"

Burns grabbed Manuel by the hair and jerked his head up. "Answer the man!" Burns said.

Irene was staring blankly at Manuel. His eyes turned in her direction. "It's not true," he said.

Irene grabbed Manuel's arms and turned on her mother, crying out, "If Paul was killed for this—this whatever it was, *you're* the one who killed him!"

"Irene!" Sophie cried out. "You can't believe such a thing!"

261

"You're not going to let them blame him for what you did!" Irene shouted at her mother. "You're not going to take him away from me!" Sophie stared horrified at her. Beside herself, Irene began screaming at Sophie. "You can't let him pay for what you did! I love him! I love him! I can't stand any more of your lies! You—*actress!*" she cried. "You have no feelings, you never have had any of your own! They're always, always somebody else's feelings!"

Dade said to Manuel, "Why did you shoot Harry Slaughter?" Manuel shook his head slowly. "Why did you think it was necessary to shoot him? What was the reason? Because he knew what you'd killed Professor Van Damm for?"

Irene cried out, "Manuel didn't even know Harry Slaughter! I told you that!"

Dade broke off and walked away from Manuel, looking in Ellen's direction. There was a long silence. Then, moving back toward Manuel, Dade put his face close to his and said, "You know what I just put you through? That's how easy it would be for the district attorney to make out a case against you in court—a case any jury would believe." Dade took a quick breath. "That's why I did it," he said. "To make you understand what danger you're in. I'm your attorney. The one who's trying to save you. I can't do it all by myself, Manuel!" Dade put a hand on the boy's shoulder. "You were caught with the diadem in your possession, Manuel. You went to the airport to meet Mrs. Kanavarioti and gave it to her."

As if against his will, Manuel's eyes sought Tinka out. The others followed his glance, looking toward her. She stared at them, almost like the Goddess of Discord, her eyes protuberant, fixed, like the eyes of a woman in the midst of casting a spell.

Dade said in a low voice to Manuel, "Where did you get it?"

Irene cried out, "Tell them Manuel!" Irene pointed at her mother, her eyes blazing. "If she gave it to you, then tell them so! You can't protect her any more!"

"Where did you get it, Manuel?" Dade repeated.

There was a long silence. Manuel looked around at all of their faces, like another Paris. A clinking sound made him glance down at the manacles on his hands.

Dade's eyes were fixed on his. "Son," he said, "I'm your attorney. I'm still your attorney. You want to talk to me, say, privately?" Dade waited, still looking steadily at the boy. When Manuel would not meet his eyes, Dade took a step back and then said to all of them, "Well, maybe it's time I spoke my piece, all right?"

He turned to his left, letting himself look briefly at each of the people in the room. The stenotypist was half-turned away, bent over his machine. To Dade's left, Sophie and Irene stood some distance apart from one another. Little eddies of silence seemed to emanate from Sophie as if she were as capable of communicating with all of them with words or without, just as an actress can dominate a scene by turning her back on an audience. Irene looked her mother up and down once, briefly, and then, as if they had nothing further to say to one another and never would have, she turned back toward Manuel, resting her hands on the high back of a chair, her dark eyes waiting, expectant, to meet his.

He still kept silent, still stared down at his manacled wrists. He was flanked by Persons to the left of him, Burns to the right. Next came Tinka, once Paul's young mistress, then widowed by her poet husband and now reduced to the semblance of a shapeless bag lady. It was like a joke, as if Fate, backstage, had whispered to her, You'd better change. In this next scene, you play an old lady who supplements her diet with cans of cat food. Hurry. To her right stood a matron with beefy arms and a ring of keys fastened to her thick belt. Last came Fanny and Vincent, their backs to the wall, almost as if they were leaning against it with fatigue. From time to time, Dade had seen Fanny look around her with birdlike, imploring glances, reacting at times with alarm but clearly without really understanding anything she was hearing. When she looked at Vincent, he did not meet her eyes. He was like a man completely absorbed in pretending that nothing going on concerned him at all. Dade thought that this would be how Vincent looked playing poker. Ellen was seated near Dade. He moved closer to her chair and then rested his forearm on its back.

Then Dade said suddenly, pointing directly at Vincent, "You went to your brother's house when he returned for two reasons. First: you wanted to make sure for yourself that he had brought back the diadem." Vincent's face wore the expression of a player studying the cards he had just been dealt. Dade said, "I won't ask you for confirmation. I won't ask any of you. I've had enough lies from the pack of you. I'm going to put it together all by myself—and in front of you so's you can see the hand I'm holding. That's to save us all time."

Dade rubbed his eyes with the heels of his hands. "Second: and for money. The thirty-five thousand was what you were going to demand that same night to buy your silence as a down payment, right, Vince? And that same night, you went out to tell the boys who had put the arm on you that you were sure you'd get the money to them in a day or two. A man can bargain with them. 'Touch my wife and you won't get a cent. Give me two days and you'll get all of it.' Was that roughly how it was, Vincent? Yes, you knew it was there. And you knew exactly what it was."

Fanny swayed on her feet and her complexion now had a grayish pallor. Seeing this, the matron seized hold of her arm, making Fanny cry out in alarm. The matron made her sit down. Fanny leaned on the table and put her head in her arms. Vincent moved over behind her and rubbed the back of her neck.

Dade put his fists on his hips and, looking around at them all, said, "Two people show up just when a man is murdered. Each of them knows the other is going to arrive there. When I learned that, I said, How did they both happen to show up just when Paul was killed? Coincidence? And then I said, No, frame. Frame. But who was framed—and by whom? Did Sophie plan to frame Manuel? She had no reason. Did Manuel frame Sophie? Why should he try to? If he'd found out about the diadem and planned to steal it, all he had to do was go there earlier, kill Paul, steal it, and hide it. But the coincidence of the two of them showing up just at the moment Paul was killed still said, Frame.

"Sophie had no idea Manuel knew anything about the diadem, so why should she suspect him? But she must have suspected him. That's why she wanted to have him arrested right away—while there was still time for her to get him to tell her where it was—in exchange for her help. She couldn't afford to mention the diadem—and didn't.

She thought no one knew about the diadem—no one but Tinka—and if the police thought he had been killed when he surprised an intruder, well, it happens all the time. Why should she say any more? Still, why were they both there at exactly the moment that Paul was killed? Something kept saying, Frame. Frame! Sophie, she didn't even have an alibi. She almost had one. Tinka was Sophie's alibi. That's where poor Sophie was for three hours—according to her—off seeing her friend Tinka. Didn't make sense, did it? Sophie got home just at the moment Paul was killed—so what kind of an alibi was that?

And then it occurred to me that it was the perfect alibi—not for Sophie! For *Tinka!—who didn't think we'd ever find out that Sophie never drove to her house that night—and couldn't have!*" Dade jabbed a thick forefinger in Tinka's direction. There was a sudden brief stir in the room, heads turning as everybody looked straight at Tinka. Tinka's face showed nothing.

"Paul had worked in Army Intelligence and Tinka worked in the same building with him. He had gotten her a job there as a scrubwoman. Or was she more than that? Were her mop and pail only part of a cover? Did she have that one indispensable gift of a secret agent—the power to dissimulate under all circumstances, to the end of one's life, if necessary? You," he said, confronting her suddenly, "you were right in the middle of this whole thing! And you have no alibi! We know that much now!" She continued to look at him as before, saying nothing, as if denial were beneath her. "Tell us, Tinka," he said to her, pointing at Manuel. "You used him. We caught you two together. Are you also going to use him to shield yourself from being accused of a murder that you committed?" She gave a little sigh, folding her hands, her face with no more expression than a Buddha's. Turning to Manuel, Dade shouted at him, pointing at Tinka, "Is she the one, Manuel? Did you get it from her and then, when she sent for you, go with it to meet her? Manuel, *talk to me!*" Manuel said nothing, as if he and Tinka had rehearsed—and practiced again and again—and then entered together into a conspiracy of silence.

Suddenly, Dade swung around and walked to the other side of the long table. Going up to Manuel, he grabbed him by both arms, at the same time calling out over his shoulder to Burns, "Bring her in now."

Burns ran to the door, went out and returned moments later with Manuel's mother. She was trembling. She tried to get Manuel to look at her but he would not.

"Bring her over here," Dade said sharply. *"Venga!"* Ellen jumped to her feet, starting to go to Luisa to comfort her. Dade waved her back and said, "No, don't. Luisa, come here." When Burns had brought her up to Dade, Dade waved him off and then, stepping behind her, put his big hands on her shoulders and, pushing her forward, said, "Tell her, Manuel. Tell her you're going to spend the rest of your life in prison to protect someone else—hoping one day to cash in on your silence—*and make her live with it!* I want to hear you say it to her. I want to watch you do it to her, Manuel."

There was a long silence. Then Luisa stretched out a slender hand and touched her son's cheek with her fingers. That broke him. He covered his face with his hands.

"All right," Dade said to him. *"Where did you get it?"*

Manuel lifted his head. And then he said almost under his breath, "She gave it to me." His eyes met Irene's. She looked at him. She just looked at him.

"Thank you," Dade said to Manuel. "That was the one thing I had to have. To save your neck." Dade pointed at Irene. "You were the one waiting for Sophie to return. Probably waiting there the whole damn time while she was gone—because for this to work, it had to be perfectly timed—and you had no way of knowing when she'd be back. What did you do, go on pretending to be sick, lying on your mother's bed, Paul's gun hidden under the pillow, lying there where you could watch the cul-de-sac so that you could watch your mother return? Then what did you do? Run over to Paul's study, calling out to him over the music, 'Oh, how beautiful! Let me see it—in here, in the light!' And then kill him as your mother returned? Is that how it happened? By God, it must have come as one hell of a shock to find you had framed your lover instead of your mother!"

There was a cry of dismay. It was Sophie. She reached out to her daughter, touching her shoulder. Irene wrenched away from her.

Persons put a hand on Irene's arm. "Book her," he said to Burns. "Murder One."

Outside, they could hear the crunching sound of a garbage truck. Dade looked at his watch. It was five in the morning. Red-eyed, Persons led Dade and Ellen down a hall. "It's back here," he said, opening the door that led to the squad room and to his own office in the back. "The FBI has a courier flying out from Washington. A couple of their agents have taken charge of it."

Upstairs, Dade had spoken privately for a few moments with Manuel. Dade said, "He didn't know anything. It was all so simple. He didn't even know the charges against him had been dropped. When he met Irene, she told him her mother had killed Paul. Irene said to Manuel, 'We have to help Mother. Take this to Tinka Kanavarioti at the airport. It's what Mother killed him for. Mrs. Kanavarioti will sell it. Without money, she won't be able to afford a lawyer. Manuel mentioned me. Irene said, 'Him? He hates Mother!' Manuel started to go. Irene said, 'You can't go in those clothes. The police are out looking for you.' He knew about the APB on him, because of the killing of Slaughter. I think she had another reason for making him go in her clothes. I think she suspected the police were following her. She was afraid of being caught with the diadem. If he was caught with it, she figured she was safe. And so was he—since he'd never laid eyes on it—never even heard of it. Safe, yes. But to make real sure, she made him take a gun along with him. 'To protect you. I'll meet you at the airport,' she said to him. 'We'll run away together.' They almost did. He didn't know the truth. He didn't want to know it. He still doesn't want to."

"He's free now, isn't he?" Ellen asked.

"Yes," said Persons. "He's free."

Voices came from a dark room. The door was open. Luisa was there, standing in front of Manuel. She went close to him. Then she slapped him across the mouth with all her strength. "*¡Puerco!*" she said.

"*Lo siento, Mama,*" he mumbled.

She slapped him again. "*¡Vamos!*" she shouted. "*¡Puerco! ¡Puerco!*"

Persons led Dade and Ellen down the corridor. Persons' face was pinched with fatigue. He said, "Would you two like some coffee? I mean, I need some. I think there's fresh in my office." They followed him to the coffee machine on a stand next to his desk. He poured out three mugs of strong black coffee.

"Tell him about your 'Hm,' about how you knew," Ellen said to Dade.

"As I said, the coincidence of the two of them showing up just at the moment Paul was killed still said, Frame. Since neither of them had any motive to frame the other, that meant someone else knew. Yes. I was sure that two others knew. Slaughter and Vincent. And then tonight, I found out a third knew: Tinka. When Slaughter was murdered, I saw that he must have been killed to silence him. It couldn't have been Vincent. Who kills a man and steals fifteen million dollars' worth of treasure and then borrows thirty-five thousand to save his neck? That meant Slaughter had told someone what he knew. Why? To get his hands on the diadem. 'You get hold of it and we'll split the proceeds.' That makes sense. Well, who was that someone? There were only two possibilities: Tinka—and Irene. But until I had Manuel's testimony, I had no proof. Once Irene killed Paul, she had to wait, hoping I could get Manuel off. She could, of course, have hidden the diadem with Sophie's things, making sure we found it. Then Manuel would be freed and Sophie would be arrested, but that would have cost her fifteen million dollars. But once we took

Sophie into custody and dropped the charges against Manuel, Irene felt safe. Then she made her move. Incidentally, Manuel told me and I believe him—he never touched the battery cable of Sophie's car. That she was delayed was sheer coincidence."

"And you said you didn't believe in coincidence."

"I believe in this one," Dade said. "As things stand, they'll try for the death penalty, won't they?" Persons nodded. Ellen winced, averting her face. Dade said, "Me, I like the old Greek way, when all is said and done."

Persons said, "What's that?"

"They gave the condemned man a chance to fight for his life."

"What are you talking about? Like with gladiators?"

"No, with the executioner, who had nothing but a knife. It was sort of kinder, and by the time the condemned man was hauled off to the place of execution, he'd generally lost so much blood, he no longer gave much of a damn."

Ellen put a hand on his sleeve. "Dade," she said.

"Yes, honey?"

"Shut up."

They had finished their coffee. Leading the way, Persons took them to a door where a burly man in a dark suit sat in a chair tipped back against the wall, an open can of Coke on the floor beside him. Seeing them come toward him, the man straightened up his chair and then got to his feet.

Persons knocked. "Charlie," he said. They heard an oiled clicking as the door was unlocked. It was opened by a balding man with bluish jowls and bags under his eyes. He was in his shirtsleeves and wore a shoulder holster in which there was a forty-five. "Okay, Charlie," said Persons.

They entered, closing the door behind them. The agent took his coat from the back of a chair and put it on. The room contained nothing but a desk with a kind of drafting table lamp clamped to it and a couple of chairs. Paraphernalia on the desk, an illuminated magnifying lens on a stand and brushes showed that this was the office of someone who worked on fingerprints.

On the floor, there was a safe. Charlie took a scrap of paper from his pocket with numbers on it. Consulting it, he squatted on the floor and began turning the dial delicately, listening. Depressing the lever, he swung the heavy door open. In the safe's dark interior, Dade saw the blue-and-white leather case. Charlie picked it up gingerly and carried it over to the desk. Setting it down, he opened the lid of the case and then lifted out something covered with tissue paper and set it on the table. It looked like the kind of stand on which hats are displayed in department stores. Layers of tissue paper were cinched in around the neck.

Charlie said, "From what I hear at the bureau, the thing is invaluable."

"Invaluable: precious, worthless!" Dade said.

"What?" Charlie said.

"It's all right." Having scribbled the word, Dade put away the notebook he had pulled out of his pocket.

Charlie said, "I kind of messed up the tissue paper when I put the thing back in the case. Shall I open it up?"

Persons nodded. Slowly Charlie peeled off the layers of tissue paper and smoothed them out with a meaty hand on the desk top. Charlie went over to the door and flicked off the wall switch so that the harsh overhead fluorescent lights were extinguished. Now, only the lamplight streamed over the gilded head. Charlie said, reaching out for the stand, as if about to lift it up, "You want to touch it, lady?"

"No," Ellen said.

"Go ahead."

"No. Thank you."

"A lot of work went into that thing," Charlie said. "Look at all the pieces."

"Something over sixteen thousand," Dade told him.

Patting the bulge of his shoulder holster under his jacket, as if unconsciously reassuring himself, Charlie angled the lamp up so that it shone horizontally. Then, lifting the stand, he held it aloft and turned it around slowly so they could all see it as the light bounced off the diadem and made it look like a golden helmet. "The lady, she ought to try it on," Charlie said to her.

Ellen backed away. "I really don't think we should touch it."

"It's not going to hurt it, lady."

"I think we'd better lock it up again," Dade said.

"Looks real good, doesn't it?" Charlie asked, showing it to them again and turning the front of it away from them so that it now looked like molten gold. The countless miniature idols of the goddess Athena trembled and flashed in the soft light. He set it down again. "I went to trouble," he said. He gestured at it.

"What are you talking about?" Dade said.

"Dirty, it was. Bits of this and that stuck in it. Hair, even. I cleaned it up."

Persons said, "You what?"

Charlie said, "Fix it up so's the lady can see it, is what you said to me, and you know you did." Persons turned away, making a low straining noise in his throat, like something broken.

"My God," Dade said.

Charlie looked at him. "Don't worry," he said. "I was very careful." He pointed at the desk. "This guy does fingerprints, so I took one of them camel hair brushes from his desk—"

Dade looked at Ellen. The two of them moved closer to the diadem and scrutinized it. Ellen said, dismay written all over her face, "I don't believe it."

"Clean as a whistle," Dade said, shaking his head.

"Thank you," said Charlie. He covered the diadem once again with the tissue paper and lifted the stand on which it rested back into the leather case. The top of the case had a deep, concave insert to protect the contents. Closing the case and fastening the latch, he carried it over and put it back in the safe.

Dade asked, "What did you do with the hair?"

"Threw it out." Dade looked in the wastebasket. It was empty. "Janitor come by. Garbage truck was due. Everything's back in order."

Dade and Ellen went into the corridor, Persons following them. The door closed behind them.

Persons said to Dade, "I guess there's nothing I can do. Except go home and blow my brains out."

Dade said, "You mention carbon-dating in your report?"

"I haven't written it yet."

"Persons, what do you know about carbon-dating?"

"Not a goddam thing."

"Then my advice is, keep it that way."

"What do I say, Mr. Cooley?"

"You say, Somebody stole some gold thing off you, here it is back, and here's my report on how we grabbed it."

They walked by the open door of Persons' office. Persons went on, tripping over his own feet. Dade took his arm. "This is your stop," he said. Dade steered him back into his office. Then he said, "Do me a favor."

"What?"

"Tinka figured Sophie could talk Paul into seeing it her way, so he could have both kudos and the money. Only one thing you can charge her with: receiving stolen goods, which she had in her possession about five seconds. No way you can even show she knew what she got."

"Okay, what do you want?"

"You don't want me down here defending her and screwing up your life more, do you, Persons?"

"What is this? We put on this goddamn dog and pony show at taxpayers' expense and I'm supposed to say it all never happened?"

"I talked to Tinka upstairs. Here's what happened. Tinka had called Sophie's house to check in with her and Irene answered the phone. She told Tinka Sophie had just been arrested, saying she had no idea why. Irene said she herself was at the house getting Sophie some clothes and the like to bring downtown to her. Then Irene burst into tears. She became hysterical. And with a stroke of what amounted to sheer genius, she cried out that she had found the missing costume jewelry, as she called it, hidden at the bottom of a hamper full of dirty laundry and was horrified, saying if the police found it, Sophie would go to prison or worse. She asked Tinka what to do. That was very cunning of her, since she knew Paul had sent Tinka to

Greece, ostensibly to visit their son, who is stationed at an American base there. When Slaughter told Irene what was going on, that made Irene suspect Tinka was the go-between.

"Tinka said, 'Listen to me.' She said that it wasn't junk at all and that she could sell it for them. She said they'd need money for Sophie's defense. Of course, at that moment, Tinka thought Sophie was guilty. She was desperate. She said Irene had to get it to her right away, that she herself would dispose of it for them. She knew a buyer. He was in New York and about to go away. Tinka said, 'Just get it for me.' Irene said that she'd have Manuel bring it to the airport as soon as she could get hold of him. Irene said, 'Because they're looking for him, my phone may be tapped. I'll call you and pretend it's a wrong number. That will mean he's ready to leave. You call back when you're ready to go. Call back from a pay phone and hang up when I answer.' Manuel, who was afraid he was next in line after Slaughter, ran off and hid. He was actually living in the library, using the washroom there and sleeping on the floor in the stacks. During the day, he went out for meals on campus and just disappeared in the crowd. Irene was afraid he'd be locked in for the night by the time she got there. Pretending she'd left her purse upstairs on a desk, she got a janitor to let her in. Now, they were set."

"So what do you want from me?" Persons said.

"Get the DA to plea-bargain. In exchange for what I just told you. Irene killed the father of Tinka's only child. Tinka will cooperate."

Persons nodded. He said, "You saved my ass."

"Bullshit."

Late that day, Dade and Ellen drove down to Ensenada for the weekend. She said, "Poor Paul. Poor Irene. Poor Sam Kellerman. Poor everybody."

"Poor Sam Kellerman?" Dade started to laugh. "Years ago, when I was staying at the Hassler in Rome, I ran into him."

"Did you really?"

"Are you making fun of me?"

"No. Please go on."

"He was standing in front of me in the elevator and I looked down at him—he was about a foot shorter than I am—and when I saw that fat, oily pimpled neck, well, I felt guilty for how I'd always disliked him, so I thought, What the hell? Why don't I try to be nice to him? So I clapped a hand on his shoulder and said, 'You old son of a bitch! Let me buy you a drink!' and when he turned around, it wasn't Sam at all, it was King Farouk!"

"You're not serious!"

"I am!"

"What on earth did he say?"

"'Yes!' is what he said."

"And what did His Majesty drink?"

"Everything. He reminded me of his late grandfather, who choked to death while trying to chug-a-lug a jeroboam of champagne. I'll say this for Farouk, he was very gracious. I remembered back to the days when I used to see magazine pictures of him when he was a slim young man at Oxford, very handsome, with aspirations of saving his country." He broke off, looking hard at her. "Haven't I ever told you that story?"

"Never."

"The perfect wife."

She gave him a kiss.

They sat in captains' chairs at a rough, round table in Cuevas de los Tigres in Ensenada and sipped margaritas from frosted bell glasses, the lip rubbed with lime, then dipped in salt. The room was dark and smoky. Ellen said, "Will she have anything left? I mean, with so much of Paul's insurance handed over to Vincent—?"

"She'll have more than enough."

"How do you know?"

"There was an enormous reward posted years ago by the museum for what they call 'the jewels of Helen.' They're paying it to Sophie," he said. Ellen raised her brows.

The voices of mariachis rose in minor thirds, floating over strumming guitars, a dozen men in ruffled white-shirts and a young boy singing together. The mariachis had formed a semicircle around them. At Dade's request, they sang "Rosita Alvirez." "She was lucky that night . . ." Dade repeated to himself, "Of the three shots fired at her, only one of them was mortal." "Rosita Alvirez!" the chorus sang with mock pathos. Dade sat back, thinking that when they went out the door after their lobster dinner, they would walk in the warm night along the deep rocky beach back to the long, low building of their hotel. The mariachis began to move away, forming a semicircle around a new table. Now, the voices were lifted, singing "La Luna Enamorada." The high piercing horn of a tenor soared over the soft strumming of the guitars. Then, as they finished dinner, the semicircle of musicians formed around newcomers being seated at a nearby table.

"Look!" said Ellen. Her jaw fell open. Dade followed the direction of her glance. The musicians were all looking with admiration at a the woman whose blond hair was worn in a long chignon. She sat with her back to Dade and Ellen. They could see her white forearm resting on the table, her fingers clasped by a strong brown hand. "Talk about coincidence!"

"Let's not. Ever."

Dade got to his feet, quickly calling the waiter over and paying the check. Taking Ellen's elbow, he steered her through the crowd. Ellen hung back. He tried to make her keep walking toward the door. She shook her head. "Dade, we have to," she said. They went back, pausing at Sophie's table. Sophie reacted with surprise, then lifted her chin and looked at them, beautiful, golden and motionless. Manuel leaped to his feet, starting to pull out a chair for Ellen.

"Would you get my wrap?" Sophie murmured to him. Manuel moved away. Sophie crossed her arms, placing her hands on her rounded bare shoulders. She nodded to herself. "We say, 'The truth is there from the beginning.'" She turned to Ellen. "I never knew she hated me that much." Ellen took her hand. "There. I've said it. I had to say it to someone." They could see Manuel crossing toward them. Abruptly, Sophie averted her face.

Coming up to Dade, Manuel said, "She going to get out sometime?"

"Sometime."

Manuel started to thank him. Dade patted his shoulder and walked away.

Dade took Ellen's arm and together they went outside. They

walked out to the dark strand. The stars over the sea were very bright. To the east, Dade pointed at Gemini, the constellation of the Heavenly Twins, Castor and Pollux. "Helen's brothers," he said. "Yes siree, Helen's brothers were stars." Above, Dade caught sight of the Pleiades rising.

"The Pleiades," Ellen said. Dade nodded, remembering that one of them had been lost, extinguished since the last days of Troy.

GENE THOMPSON, a native of San Francisco, graduated from the University of California at Berkeley where he majored in Classics, after which he studied and worked in Europe for some years. Subsequently, he and his wife, the writer Sylvia Vaughn Thompson, moved to a village in the mountains above Palm Springs. They have four children and two grandchildren.

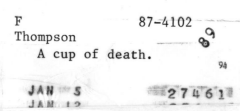